RALEIGH TWO
A TABOO MENAGE ROMANCE

DAISY JANE

Copyright © 2023 by Daisy Jane

All rights reserved.

No part of this book may be reproduced in any form or by any electronic or mechanical means, including information storage and retrieval systems, without written permission from the author, except for the use of brief quotations in a book review.

Cover design: Daisy Jane

Proofreading | Geeky Girl Author Services, LLC.

Alpha Reading | Laura Davies @thefantasybookaddict

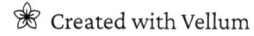

❋ Created with Vellum

CONTENT WARNING

While content warnings and advisories can be found on my website Reading Guide, I'd like you to know that **this book contains sensitive content not safe for every reader.** Please proceed with caution if you have sensitivities to the following: domestic violence, sexual assault, rape, drug use and/or drug addiction, unexpected pregnancy from a difficult relationship and/or sexual encounter and finally on-page childbirth.

Please keep your heart & mind safe while reading.

Fate rules the affairs of mankind with no recognizable order.

-Lucius Annaeus Seneca

PROLOGUE

RYKER

THREE YEARS AGO

My thumbs fly across the screen, chin tucked to chest, all my focus on my phone.

> Answer your damn phone Rhett!

> Fuck off Dad.

> Just, stay right there.

Though I'm only texting, the words erupt from my gut, angry and hot, and I swear to God, if anyone can make me volcanically angry, it's him.

Dots ripple, and his message appears.

> I can't wait for you; that's what you don't get. My ride is fucking coming. I can't just stop the fare on a ride share because of you!

I can almost hear his maniacal laugh, the one he hands me when he's spinning out of control. I read the message again and it takes all the strength I possess not to roll my eyes. I get he's hurting. He's allowed to hurt.

He also needs to realize he's a young and wealthy man who's been afforded every luxury and benefit since birth. Fuck, since his inception. And this current emotional turmoil which has been, more or less, self-inflicted, does not win him the right to be a little fucking prick.

And yet, as he's threatening to leave the state for good, he knows he's got me. He can go if he wants, but I am not a stupid man–that's part of the fucking problem; I've always been too aware of how my son liked to live his life, and my cognizance has always irked him. I can't make him stay if he wants to go, but I am also sadly, deeply, and acutely aware each time we part that it could be the last time I see him alive.

I look up to see the bank near, and quicken my pace before returning my focus to my phone.

> Let me say goodbye

Stomping through a mobbed downtown sidewalk just a few feet from my destination, I then type the one thing that could hold him in place, the one piece of information that could potentially keep him there, waiting for me. He doesn't need it because I've set him up too well, but addicts never turn down more money.

> I'm on my way to the bank; let me bring you a traveling gift, at least.

The rush of cars near the curb fills the air, and my heart stammers as I stand idle in a sea of people, a step away from the bank's entrance.

I see no dots, so I type again, heart clenched in my throat.

> Wait, please, son.

More whooshing of cars and voices around me.

> Ten minutes and I'm gone.

Even though he's agreed, it doesn't feel like a victory. Instead, I stand amidst downtown lunch-hour chaos, willing the whirring in my brain to slow, but the storm inside me rages.

"Watch out, motherfucker!" *Slam.*

My shoulder jolts forward as two men steady themselves at opposite ends of a large box, moving it with tentative steps.

"Sir." A woman in a navy suit with a chestnut chignon and a string of cheap pearls smiles at me as she dips her head, greeting me with all the enthusiasm of *a bank greeter.*

I slide my phone into my pocket next to the other one and reach for the ornate gold handle on the bank entrance.

No sooner has the door closed behind me when I'm engulfed in the eerily calm silence of the lobby.

"Hi," I nod, annoyed by her greeting distracting me from my racing thoughts. But my face hides my annoyance, and I manage a curt smile.

I remember playing cards with my friends when I was thirteen and them saying, "Ryker's got a poker face." The truth was, I didn't know what that meant until I asked my dad afterward. He told me a poker face is one of the most valuable tools a man can own.

Wearing the same inscrutable expression as I wear in the boardroom and bedroom, I survey the large lobby, complete with Carrara marble floors, and look for the shortest line. At one window, there are several people, all clutching pink slips and shifting their weight from foot to foot, passively alerting the teller they're tired of waiting.

Not that line.

My gaze sweeps over the rest and stops on a window with just two women in the queue. Quickly, I step in line, glancing back up at the large metal clock hanging from the center of the wall. It's already been two fucking minutes. There's no way I'll make it across town in ten.

Fishing my phone from my pocket, I send him a very short text asking him to please wait.

> In line at the bank. Give me an extra ten. Please. Just let me see you off.

I don't know if it should make me feel bad or good that he reads the message right away, his read receipt is on. Turning it off would require a moment of sobriety wherein he could understand *how* to use his phone and its settings.

I've never done it for him because knowing if he's seen my messages or not is often the only way I know he's alive.

He doesn't respond. I shove my phone away as I catch the woman in front of me twisting backward, squinting at the clock on the wall.

"Ten after," I say, recognizing the narrowed eyes and tilted head.

Her features soften as her gaze drops from the far-off clock down to my face, right in front of her. Her eyes are wide and blue, set perfectly apart. I've never seen hues of blue so intoxicating; cornflower blue with pops of cerulean near the pupil. They're breathtaking.

"Thanks," she says, snapping me free of my intense focus. I don't spend a lot of time searching people's eyes for truth and validity. In business, the tells are easier to spot in the mannerisms. Touching your hair when you talk, looking away during fastidious details, using stall tactics–those are the heavy hitters I keep an eye out for. I have never needed to resort to an old-time stare down.

But I have to force myself to look away because in the city, hovering behind a beautiful young woman while staring at her is grounds for getting maced. After a nod of acknowledgment, I force my attention on the teller, watching her explain god only knows what to the woman at her counter.

"I would have figured it out, but it would have taken a minute," the blue-eyed woman comments, bringing my focus back to her. Since she's talking to me, I'm allowed to really look at her and smile as I take in her beauty.

She looks young, young enough to be my fucking child. Early twenties, likely. Her hair is a natural goldenrod. The way some strands are more washed of color than others tells me she likely spends time in the sun when she can. She tucks a piece behind her ear as she shoots me a wide grin, the rest falling in loose waves down her back. "Okay, maybe I *wouldn't have* been able to make it out."

I push back my suit jacket, exposing my wrist, and tap the screen of my watch. "Not sure if you've heard of this invention, but it's a clock for your wrist in case you have bad eyes." I wink, and her pale cheeks flood with color and that little blushed grin she gives sends a flood of energy to my groin.

"Wow," she teases, her smile toothy and wide. Her full ruby lips do nothing for my nasty wandering mind, and I stifle a chuckle at the moment; *my son moments away from storming off in a drug-induced tantrum, the urgency to get to him biting at my heels, a multi-million dollar deal at noon* and here I am, thinking about this little blonde's red lips wrapped around my cock. I bet she whimpers like a needy thing when she sucks dick, too.

"When did you upgrade?" she asks, a playful lilt twitching her lips.

"Upgrade?" I ask quizzically, a small smile playing on my lips.

"From the pocket watch your dad got you as a kid." She taps her chin as she pretends to ponder. "Or was it an abacus?"

Fuck, I like this girl.

I'm not a man who's afraid to accept he's aging. First of all, because I know forty-one isn't old, and secondly, because I've done it all. Age is only a thing when you aren't living. Shit passing you by is a concept only for people afraid to live. And that's never been me. Plus, when you're twenty-something like I'm assuming this woman is, everyone feels old in comparison.

I wink at her. "An abacus is for counting, not telling time. Nice try."

She hooks her snapping hand through the air. "Dang. Well, I had to at least try to tease you, right?"

I nod. "I'd expect no less."

The noise of the bank falls away, and it's the first time I've felt like I was alone with one person when in a room with many. She rests her hand on her chest, fingers draped on her collarbone, tips playing with the silver heart necklace looping her neck. "I don't know why I always check the clock in line. It takes how long it takes. I can't leave until I've done my thing, so why does the time even matter?" she muses aloud, and while I usually steer clear of banter and small talk with strangers, I can't help but engage.

She rolls her ruby lips together, and my dick twitches. "It's hard not to be aware of time when you're waiting."

She nods, and then her eyes rove over my chest, down my legs to my dress shoes, before flicking back up. And I don't miss for one fucking second the way her mouth falls open for a few seconds *before* words come out. That breathless, quiet moment where she's digesting me the same way I'm devouring her.

"Yeah," she says, eyes on mine. I wonder if her heart is beating a little quicker right now, too. It's almost laughable getting a little flustered by a beautiful woman at the bank. Shit like that rarely happens to me anymore, not because there aren't gorgeous women everywhere with a keen eye for an expensive suit but because I'm just not open to the experience. I'm not looking to lock eyes; I'm not looking for belly flutters; I'm not looking. Period. Yet, she's all I can see. "I held the door open for like ten people." She shakes her head. "I like being nice, but honestly, had I known all those people would get in line in front of me, I may not have done it."

We share a smile. "Don't blame you."

The woman who has been hogging the teller for the last few minutes finally begins stuffing things into her purse, and the blonde in front of me watches for a moment before looking back at me. "Oh, looks like I'm next."

I smile again. "Looks that way."

And then, in a split second, before the blonde can get to the teller, before the woman at the window can walk away, before I can make my withdrawal and race back to my son, and before anyone in the building can even blink or exhale, everything changes.

Two shots ring out, vibrating in the space around us, causing a room full of strangers to unify in sudden terror. Spinning around to face the source of the ringing pops, I am actually stunned into silence for a moment.

Four men stand along the back doors, the woman with the cheap pearls and chestnut chignon a lifeless heap on the floor. Next to her, a crumpled security guard bearing a thick gash on his temple, dark red blood slowly oozing out, staining the white marble beneath. Wearing black with white Venetian masks to hide their identities, each bears a weapon. Between the four of them, they have two automatic assault rifles and two AK-47s. I know these weapons because I outfit my own security with them.

In fact, if Rhett hadn't put me into such a goddamn tailspin this morning, my security would be outside this building right now, probably detaining these fucking lunatics before any of this happened. My eyes go to the woman in the navy suit again, the one crumpled on the floor like a lone dirty sock with no pair. Cast aside as if she were nothing.

"Oh my god, oh my god," the blonde next to me chants, her voice rattling with fear. And it's not until I hear her panic do I realize exactly what's going on. "Oh my god, they're going to kill us. They're robbing this bank and they're going to kill us," she babbles in a panicked stream-of-consciousness, her eyes flitting between the armed robbers.

"Arms up," one of them shouts, though the room is nothing more than strained breaths and whimpers, so yelling isn't even necessary. But he does, and his voice booms so loudly it feels the entire building rattles a little. The fourth man, standing guard at the double doors, slides a dowel through the gold handles. The fact that they're robbing a bank and only securing the door with a piece of wood ripped out of someone's closet brings me some assurance that whatever this is, it should be fast. If they meant to hold us hostage or kill us, they'd likely protect the door much better.

Yet, my insides don't feel assured.

"Arms fucking up until we have your devices," he shouts, moving quickly through the room with another white-masked counterpart, nudging people with his rifle until they hand over their phone. With my arms raised, I look over at her. Wet eyes wide, she blinks up at me, and I nod for her to follow suit.

"Put your arms up. We'll be okay," I assure her. She nods and raises her hands into the air slowly, tears cascading down her cheek.

The men collecting phones finally make it to our line, and I calmly toss my phone into his pillowcase and watch as the woman next to me does the same. A moment later, we're being directed to get on our bellies on the ground and not say a fucking word.

"It's just about money. They won't hurt us," I whisper to her, our faces pressed against the floor, inches apart.

She nods, but her tears come more steadily with each passing moment. I'm not afraid of death, and I'm sure as hell not afraid of being eaten up by gunfire. I'm not done living, but I've lived, and if I go now, I go now.

"I haven't even done anything worthwhile yet," she whispers, her palm curling into the floor. I press my palms to the floor around me, too, and try to steady my racing mind.

I'll never get to him in time. Not now. And since I can't do anything about *that* situation, I force myself to focus on the here and now.

"I've never even traveled. My entire life, I've wanted to go to New York, but I've never been."

"You'll go," I assure her as more tears stream down her face, crossing the bridge of her nose and plunking against the floor near her hand. "There's plenty of time."

"I'm only twenty-three. This can't be it," she whispers as the soft clicking of a spinning combination lock fills the terrified silence around us. In the last line, we're nearest to the walk-in vault that corners the bank. Mere feet from it, actually.

"You hear that?" I whisper as quietly as possible. "That's the vault. They're opening it now. It's probably a time delay, but after it opens in fifteen minutes, we're free. Okay?"

Twenty-three. She *could* be my kid. Jesus Christ.

Even though she nods, her blonde hair tangling in her tears, she asks, "how do you know?"

"They just want money." I believe the words, so they come easily. "That's what everyone wants. Money."

"Then they'll let us go?" Her eyes are wide, searching mine the way a ship lost at sea desperately hunts for a beacon of light. I think of the navy-suited woman with the cheap pearls and how she lay lifeless on the floor.

"Yeah," I reassure her. "They'll let us go. As soon as they get the money."

"No fucking talking!" A man across the room shouts, his white plastic mask jostling as he shoves the butt of his rifle between the shoulder blades of a man lying sprawled across the floor. He groans in reaction, and the beating quiets us down.

Unable to soothe her with words, I inch my palm toward her palm until our pinkies touch. Wrapping mine over hers, I give her a slight nod, hoping to impart calm on her in any way possible.

Why do I care about calming a complete fucking stranger? A twenty-three-year-old stranger, no less. Is it because *before* we were held at gunpoint, I kept thinking about wrapping her honey hair around my knuckles and crashing her red lips to my dick, watching her suck me deep, wondering what she'd sound like eagerly swallowing down my cum? *Maybe.*

But some foreign hardly used place inside of me illuminates as she blinks eyefuls of tears at me, her wobbly lips attempting a small smile. Against the hard floor, my chest aches.

My mind starts to wander into territory I have no business being... like, what's her name? What does she do? Where is she from? In a whisper, I say, "rubber bullets."

Her brow cinches quizzically while she inches her palm closer to mine, our pinky and ring fingers intertwining.

"The guard and the greeter," I falsely reassure the because chances are, we *will* get out of here okay. "Those were probably rubber bullets. They'll be okay."

"They sounded real," she breathes.

"Rubber bullets sound like real bullets. And they can knock people out the same way."

"There was blood," she says.

"I know."

We just stare at one another, and I don't tell her that man got whipped with a gun or punched is okay because the truth is, I just don't know. I don't know if they're rubber bullets either, but if I can make her feel even slightly less terrified in this situation, it's worth the weight of every lie told.

"They'll be okay." I swallow hard as I serve up what could be the next healthy lie. "You'll be okay, too." The truth in that statement is that I *really* fucking hope she is.

"What's your name?" she asks, keeping her voice low.

"Ryker," I tell her, the name feeling foreign on my tongue. I'm not on a first-name basis with many people, and I'm usually being introduced as half of the Raleigh Two. But the intimacy of my first name feels right, given the situation. "What's yours?"

"Ember," she breathes, bottom lip wobbly. "Do you live here in the city?"

I know she's trying to distract herself. In the distance, the masked men argue. I can't make out what about, and it's not my business. Pay them focus and they'll pay it back. That much, I know. So, I reply to *Ember*.

And fuck, if that isn't a hot little name.

"Just visiting. Was on my way out, actually."

She bites her bottom lip and attempts to peer around, lifting her head from the floor just slightly.

"Don't," I say, sliding my palm up her neck, cupping the side of her throat and jaw. Resting my hand on her, I let my thumb stroke against her cheekbone. "Just stay put, okay?"

Turning her head a millimeter, her eyes flutter closed, seemingly calmed by my touch. "Thank you," she whispers. "Ryker." Her eyes pop open, and I slide my hand off and back to the floor, our pinkies finding each other again.

"It will be over soon, Ember." I study the freckles smattering her cheeks. The way her hair shines beneath the fluorescent lights. The ballerina pink of her fingernails. She is probably the most delicate, beautiful young woman I've ever seen. And despite being held at gunpoint together, I know I'd never forget those wide blue eyes and that electrifying smile.

"What will you do after this?" I ask.

She licks her lips, and even though I can tell she's trying really hard to be brave, I can feel the fear running through her as her hand trembles beneath mine. I grab it tight.

"Travel. I'm gonna travel," she murmurs. "And find love. Finally, I'm gonna fall in love."

The idea that this woman exists in this world without

love is a little mind-boggling to me. Then again, young men these days are a lot lazier than I was at her age. Or at least the *one* young man her age *I* have experience with is.

I want to chuckle to soften my words but can't afford the luxury of making any noise and attracting unwanted attention. "You can't rely on love." But looking at her, the way she clutches the ground so vulnerably, sharing her hopes with a stranger as she probably prays that my face isn't the last one she sees, I can't help but soften to her. Or, for her. "Love yourself. That's the best and most reliable love out there. Self-love."

"Spoken like a man who has a broken heart hanging in his chest," she whispers, her lips clinging together on the words. My mouth is dry now, too.

She's not wrong. *Astute little vixen.* And while I make that bone-deep fracture seem like nothing more than a splinter all of the time, today could be my last opportunity to be honest.

"It was broken once, that's true."

"And now?" she sucks her bottom lip in, rerouting a tear beyond her mouth, around the curve of her chin. I don't know if our talking is helping her stay calm or not, but on the chance she'd be freaking out if we weren't speaking, I answer her question.

"It's like any other break. Like if you broke your foot," I say, enchanted by the vibrant blue of her eyes and the glow radiating from her velvet skin. "Eventually, it heals and you stop limping. But every once in a while, it fucking hurts. And every so often, you remember what it felt like before the break. And you know that even though you *can* walk freely every day, you'll never walk quite the same."

Tears drip heavily from her eyes as she wipes discreetly under her nose, so as not to draw attention to us. "I'd rather never walk quite the same way than never feel that extreme pain. Because before that, somewhere, there was pleasure. And happiness." She licks a tear from her lip. I want to fix this beautiful stranger crying on the floor next to me, and I have no fucking clue why. I have enough on my hands with Rhett. "To feel that bad, you have to have felt really, really good."

I blink a few times, gathering my thoughts, careful not to sound like an old pessimist. Though I fear I already have.

"It was good for a little but bad for a lot." I smile a little just to see her return it. "Take care of you; that's your best investment, I'm telling you."

She sniffles, the wrinkle in her nose somehow a strange mix of adorable *and* sexy. "I don't look at love as an investment."

I would normally shrug at this point in the conversation because debating the realities of love and marriage with a twenty-something is pointless. They haven't experienced any real fucking pain. Nothing that could ever make them understand the all-consuming pain of loss and grief that stains your soul forever. The void that remains open and raw, no matter what.

"You'll never be alone. Someone will find you. You're too gorgeous to go unnoticed." Discreetly, I reach into my pocket and fish out my handkerchief. I'd debated handing it to her at the risk of seriously looking like an old man. But her tears are just too painful to experience. It's like watching a child get hurt; it's just plain fucking wrong.

She pats the handkerchief beneath her eyes, then slides

it beneath her cheek and stares at me. I don't know why we lie there on our bellies, sharing secrets. I mean, I know any onlooker would say it's being hostages in a bank robbery. And yeah, I guess that's what's driving Ember.

Fuck, that name. My cock thickens at the name of it. But why do I care? This bank robbery goes sideways, then fuck it. I'm done. I'm too tired to worry about anything anymore. I've been fucking biting my nails, racing around the United States, making phone calls to save my son for years, all while running a goddamn town. Not a business. Not multiple business endeavors, but owning essentially an entire town.

I'm fucking spent.

If this is it, so be it. I want Rhett to get better, take control of his life, and be the man I raised him to be.

But he can't move past his pain. And fucking hell, we all know I can't make him. I've pushed. I've pulled. I've smothered. I've withheld. I've done every goddamn thing. I've spent upwards of five hundred grand on therapies, doctors, prescriptions, treatments, and centers.

"You're very handsome," she says quietly, almost low enough to make me question if I heard it. She doesn't seem like the type of woman to compliment a man. She seems too... shy and docile.

"Thank you," I reply, my face sore and starting to grow numb against the cold, hard floor. Somewhere behind Ember, a hostage rises to his feet, and my heart leaps and lodges in my throat. Why anger people with automatic weapons? A moment later–

"Get the fuck down! Get up again and I'll fuckin' roast you."

Ember's knuckles grow white from gripping the floor so tightly. "Oh my god, oh my god," she whispers, her eyes filling again.

I place my palm on top of hers and flatten them. "No, no, no. Don't panic. He stood up. He caused that. You're not standing. We're right here." I move my thumb along her pinky. "You're going to be fine."

There's cursing near us, but I don't panic because followed closely behind is the metallic clinking of a safe door swinging open. Thank fuck.

"Where will you go in New York?" I ask her to keep her distracted and maybe because a part of me is enjoying this brief respite from my real life.

Being a hostage is a fucking vacation to Ryker Raleigh. That should tell you what you need to know.

"I don't know," she admits shyly, her eyes already darting away from me in the direction of the unseen safe just feet away. "A hostel, maybe. I've, um, always wanted to do that."

I'm about to tell her that a hostel isn't a great idea for a woman traveling alone, but then the masked men are shouting about throwing security footage in the microwave before they go. They curse and yell as they pull two bank employees off the ground, dragging them to the back office.

I never stop rubbing Ember's hand, and her eyes don't leave mine.

There's a terrible smell just a few quiet minutes later, followed by the sound of chirping smoke detectors singing loudly through the entire building, its piercing echo making everyone clutch their ears.

Suddenly, out of nowhere, there's a billowing cloud of

heavy smoke engulfing us. There's smoke fucking everywhere. And then her hand is ripped from mine. Then there's a man wearing a vest, his face covered by a visored black helmet, pressing his chest to my back, yanking me to my feet like I'm an *invalid*.

"Let me go!" I shout as the smoke somehow thickens. A cough worms through my chest, and I can't hold it back. Lungs burning, hand on my stomach, I cough and reluctantly let the man drag me in a direction that feels too far to be the front door. But once daylight and fresh air sting my eyes and kiss my cheeks, I know I am indeed out of the bank.

Immediately I turn around, searching for her. There are hoards of police and SWAT members, looky loos, and people genuinely disinterested in the spectacular movie playing out just feet away. But *people* are fucking *everywhere*.

And if she's around, I don't see her. And before I know it, I'm being pushed back into an open ambulance; a stethoscope shoved down my shirt, a band wrapping my arm.

"Are you hurt?" A medic hovers in front of me.

I shake my head. "No." Pushing the man away, I hop out of the rig. "Nothing fucking happened. We just laid on the floor." My eyes rove over the hoards of people, fearful cries belonging to no one specific ringing out in the air. Spotting a blonde woman, I run to her, not paying attention to her features. By the time I reach her, she's turned, and I can see from her profile it's not Ember.

"S-sorry," I mutter, heart racing, feet stumbling forward through the crowd. Sirens sound, but nothing is louder than the panic pounding in my ears. I have to fucking find her.

Grabbing the arm of a police officer, I grab his name from his badge. "Officer Stevens. I'm looking for a blonde woman, early twenties," I begin describing her but he's already lost interest edging away from me with his baton pulled.

"If you were inside and haven't been seen by medical, please, find a stretcher and have a seat," he advises, never once looking my way. Then he's gone, and I'm left pushing and clawing through a hoard of people.

After five minutes, I can't find her, and I don't want to give up, but I'm grabbed by another medic.

"Have you been triaged?" he asks, pulling a blood pressure cuff from his bag.

I attempt to shrug him off but he's surprisingly forceful. "Sorry, sir, you have to be triaged."

"Hurry up. I'm looking for someone who was inside."

The medic's face softens. "Don't worry, there were no fatalities." He adjusts the cuff and begins taking my blood pressure. Where did she go? My eyes never quit searching the crowd, never stop taking in details. As the medic takes my pulse, a police officer wanders up with a notepad, pages of details already written and pinned to the back of the pad.

"Were you in there?"

I nod. And I spend the next ten minutes answering questions, all the while, I never stop searching the crowd. But I never see her.

When my information is taken, I rise and mill through the remaining groups of people, desperate to find her.

But nothing. From my pocket, I hear my phone ringing. My actual phone, not the decoy I tossed in the bag. Unfortunately, owning a town entails security and decoy phones for situations just like these.

The screen surprises me.

"Rhett, I'm on my way," I say, racing toward the corner of the street where I can easily catch a cab. The only benefit of a crowded, shitty city.

He laughs, and I grit my teeth holding it all back. I've supported him in so many ways for so long, and part of me just wants to tell him to suck it the fuck up. Handle his pain like a man and get some fucking therapy. And take it seriously. Do the work.

But he's an addict, and I cannot tell him to suck up his woes because of his *disease*. He has a disease, and I cannot let my frustrations take hold of what I know to be true. He *needs* help.

"I'm already gone. Thanks for showing up for me, *Dad*."

He ends the call before I can argue, but the truth?

I'm all argued out. I've fought for him for so long. I've loved him when it felt impossible, and I always will.

But maybe the thing he needs right now more than anything is to go.

Maybe that's what we *both* need.

CHAPTER ONE

EMBER

PRESENT DAY

I've seen that show *Snapped*. The one where women get completely fed up with everything and finally collide head-first with their breaking point. I always wondered how they got to that place and allowed themselves to pacify or tolerate their existence so long that they were no longer rational or human. That was before Rhett.

I moved across the country for adventure. I came here to be courageous, find love and live my life. I do not fit the bill of a woman who took a reckless chance on someone who can't be trusted with her heart. Someone who would be pushed past her limits. Someone who snaps.

I'm not someone who gets stuck in a lose-lose situation.

Yet here I am, staring at the gold letter opener lying

across my desk, the one my mother had engraved for my college graduation. And all I can think is: is it sharp enough to puncture skin? Can it sever an artery? Hurt a man who attacks me? Help me defend myself against my own husband?

Because rage, fatigue, and disappointment do not discriminate. They don't pass me by just because I went to college and buy makeup from Sephora. Nothing means a damn thing when married to an addict.

You're stripped down to base feelings and questions, every other extravagance and luxury around you becoming instantly trivial. You just want to know why? And when?

Why is this happening and when will it end?

"Look at me, Ember," he begs, his rollercoaster of emotions further exhausting me. One moment my body is tense, locked in a state of self-defense, jerking back from his booming voice and clenched fists, and in the next, I'm allowed to relax all while my insides stir with fear and unease. It's... truly exhausting.

My eyes leave the letter opener. I better understand the women who snap. I do. And while I'm still clinging tightly to the thread of sanity I have left, I will never judge those poor, exhausted women *ever* again.

"Please stand in the doorway, please," I beg, my voice wobbly. With my sleeve pulled over my palm, I push tears from my cheek and nod. "The doorway, please." When he's high and spiraling, I make him keep his distance. Initially, it was for my safety, and now I'm not so sure who I'm keeping safe.

He stumbles backward a few steps, reaching for the doorframe before he's there. A few missteps and he's toppled over, a heap of distress and drugs struggling against himself on the floor. I watch as he manages to get to his feet, taking out two bottles of Chanel Number Five and an entire tray of earrings with him as he clutches my dresser for dear life.

Once he's relatively steady, he shoves his hands through the sides of his hair, smoothing back the sweat and grease. Who knows how long it's been since he's had a shower. I haven't seen him in three days, and he showed up here to pack a bag because he's going on a "work trip."

I don't know why I argue. I don't know why I care. I don't know why I'm fighting so hard to save this thing between us because the truth is, he was always a mistake. A choice made from heightened emotion and hormones. I knew it the morning after. But I've always been someone who sticks to things. Doesn't quit, doesn't throw in the towel, and never gives up.

Looking down at the ring glittering on my finger, I can't believe it's been three years. Three years of wedded hell. And I'm just about at the end of my rope.

I let him lie about a work trip. It's got to be a lie. I don't even know if he still has a job anymore. I'm sure he doesn't. But at this point, getting him out of here for another few days will give me time to pack and get the fuck out.

Finally.

After all, *it's time I put myself first.* Love myself first. Because the beautiful man from the floor in the bank three years ago was right. I thought he was jaded, but as it turns out, he was right: the best investment is loving yourself.

And it's time to get serious about my personal fund.

"When you get home, I'm not going to be here. I want a divorce."

Those four words. Alone, they're powerless, but when you string them together, they bear the weight of an anvil. He deflates as he processes, and then, the anvil settles. Dropping to his knees, he pulls the ends of his hair; eyes squeezed shut.

"Don't do this, Em. Don't." His eyes plead, but I refuse. I refuse to believe he wants anything more than to make himself feel good. "When I get back, I'll get help." He licks his lips, kneeing toward me on the floor. "I'll get better."

I shake my head. I don't know if I ever loved him or just really wanted to be in love. Even without the long-lasting and bone-deep love, I still don't want to see him this way. I do want him to get better.

"Go, please, just go." My eyes fill and my throat burns. "Please."

The sadness in his eyes evaporates, darkness grabbing hold. Pinching his gaze on me, he unsteadily gets to his feet, gripping the edge of my dresser as he does. "I'll go," he breathes, stalking toward the bed where my back is pressed to the headboard, knees pulled to my chest.

"No," I start, knowing the exact look burning behind his eyes. "No, please, please, just go," I beg, but it's too late. That shadowy monster inside of him has taken the reins, and I know there is nothing I can say or do to stop him now.

His hands are on my ankles; my back drags against the comforter as the covers ball up beneath me. Then I'm at the edge of the bed, the familiar metal clink of his belt sending my brain to a faraway place. I focus on the light on the ceiling as he forces my legs open and shoves himself inside me, rough and dry, causing tears to spill down my face.

The mattress, crooked atop the box springs, slides around as he uses me, sending it jolting into the night table. My phone slides off the surface, crashing to the floor, along with a paperback book and a lamp. I hear the crisp shatter of the bulb. My head turned away from his sour breath and dark eyes, I watch as a small shard of glass rocks against the floor before settling in the grooves of the hardwood.

I've fought before. Many times. And it only made it hurt worse, scarred me more profoundly, and never changed a fucking thing. So I don't fight. I lie there while he takes what he wants, chipping away another piece of me, as I force my mind elsewhere.

I watch the light flicker as the neighbor in the apartment next to us starts their vacuum. The light always flickers when they vacuum. I imagine the clean lines she must be leaving in her wake and how I always love fresh vacuum lines.

Everything is achy and painful, and my throat burns as acid rushes up in response to his sweat splattering against my skin, on my face and chest. And I just watch the light and think about the sixty-three-year-old woman next door vacuuming... until he's done.

He crushes his mouth to mine for a moment before peeling himself off. "I'll be back, Em. Okay?"

How he could think that after raping me, I would give a fuck *what* he's doing or *when* he's coming back, I'm not sure. It's partly his sickness as an addict, but it's partly him, too.

My husband is *not* a good man.

He's hardly a *man* at all.

The door rattles the entire apartment as he leaves, and it's not until I have the deadbolt on do I feel able to breathe. Then I finally do what I've threatened to do many, many times. I open my suitcase and toss clothes inside, watching as the last three years of my life get condensed to three cubic feet. I'd rather have three cubic feet and a clean slate than everything while being tied to a void.

Tidying up the apartment, making sure I grab any important documents, I add a bottle of Tylenol last, then zip it up. In an effort to get the feeling of his skin writhing against mine washed away, I take a shower and scrub myself twice. With wet hair and in pajamas, I pour myself a glass of wine and drink it all in three swallows. When I've found the bottom of the bottle, I go back to bed, my alarm set for early the next day.

But my alarm doesn't get the opportunity to sound, and instead, I wake to a call in the middle of the night.

CHAPTER TWO

RYKER

"And now we'd like to get into the globalization aspects. You good with that, Mr. Raleigh?"

I nod my head. We aren't taking any small town start-ups global, and these efforts are all in vain. Most of us know it. Still, letting this team present to me gives me time to mentally check out.

"...increasing our cooperation on a global level and how that's achievable in the short-term," the man goes on, clicking as a slide flies across the screen, utilizing calming blue hues and a large black font.

He rattles on, and with my knuckles curled under my chin and finger resting against my lips, I take in the room of people I employ. Men in tailored suits, women wearing thousand-dollar heels, white teeth, botoxed skin– everyone has everything they've ever dreamed of. They probably all drove here in luxury cars. Fuck, *I* drove here in a luxury car.

And I wonder, are they as fucking miserable as I am? It's been three years since Rhett left. The years of cleaning up after him were bad, but years without him have been worse. Life has a way of kicking you in the nuts like that. One day you think you're as miserable as you can be, and the next, you're worse off. Then, when you think you can't possibly be dealt another shit hand, boom. You get sucker punched by a tiny little vixen who vanishes as quickly as she appeared.

My eyes connect with a young blonde woman wearing a Chanel suit, her sleek bob resting on the tops of her shoulders. Her lashes are long and her eyes are blue, and for a fleeting second, my heart beats a little quicker. My poor, confused fucking heart. She smiles, and I look away as soon as my brain realizes her blue isn't *the* blue. The blues I've been seeing in my dreams for years.

"I'd like to open it up for questions now if anyone has any," he says, sliding his hands in his slack pockets as he rocks back and forth on dress shoes shinier than the fucking sun.

Just then, the glass door whooshes open, and a nervous-looking mousy secretary clutches the metal handle anxiously. She lifts a partially curled finger in the world's weakest attempt to interrupt; thankfully, her eyes lock on mine.

"Mr. Raleigh," she whispers. "You have a call. It… is an emergency."

An emergency? I cast a glance to my right-hand across from me, Guy. He scrolls quickly through the full calendar displayed on the iPad in front of him, returning his gaze to mine a moment later. "I don't know," he says with a shrug.

No new equipment installs at the canning factory. No new kitchen appliances are being delivered to the diner or burger joint. No deals are being inked, and no street repairs are scheduled. In theory, there shouldn't be a Monday morning emergency. And even then, they wouldn't contact me about it.

Most of my emergencies are related to my schedule. Something's going wrong in town and by glancing at the calendar, Guy can usually pinpoint what it is. But today, we're looking at a virtually meeting-less week.

This appears to be an organic emergency, and I haven't had one of those in over three years. The woman at the door clears her throat, grabbing my attention. "It really sounds urgent."

I cock a brow. "Who is it?"

"Mr. Raleigh." She looks around the room before her eyes come back to me. A shiver slithers down my spine like a snake on its way to fill me full of venom. My body goes hot and cold all at once, an immediate and unforeseen fight-or-flight grabbing hold. I'm not easily flustered, but the way this woman is looking at me, the fact that *he's* on the phone... I'm consumed with the urgency to answer.

The chair slams against the glass wall, leaving a resounding rattle echoing in my wake as I pad toward my office down the hall. I lift an arm in the air as I yank the door open. "Connect him."

My ass isn't even in the leather when I grab the handset and shove my knuckle into the button resting next to the blinking red light.

"This is Ryker," I answer, my voice unsteady and husky.

My torso aches with the burning breath I'm holding as I stroke my sternum, starved for a response.

She said it was Mr. Raleigh. Could it be?

"Ryk," finally, there's a voice on the other end of the line, but it's not the Mr. Raleigh I'd hoped it was.

I sink into my chair, sighing out a partially relieved breath. "River, Jesus, I thought..."

My brother's voice is both rough and understanding. "I know, I know what you thought, and I'm sorry."

Clasping my hand to my forehead, I spin in my chair to face the window overlooking the town. This building wasn't here years ago when our great-great-grandfather scooped this town up, but as soon as River and I took control, we built it as the Raleigh Two headquarters. Perfectly tucked into the corner of downtown, the fourth story where I'm perched offers a luxury view of the quaint town of our namesake.

"Lucy wouldn't let me talk to you. She said you were in a meeting."

"So you lied?" I ask, remembering just now that the secretary's name is indeed Lucy. It's why River and I work so well as a team. I remember the high-level shit, take care of the finances, and the big decisions, and River is the day-to-day details guy, the one walking the shops downtown, who knows the people and works with them day in and out. We offer the best of both worlds.

He clears his throat, and it throws a clog in mine. The hair on my neck rises in concern at his moment of silence. "Well, I didn't lie."

"What's the emergency?" I ask, wishing right now that

my brother has suddenly developed a sick sense of humor and is about to play a fucked up practical joke on me.

"Riv," I say, leaning forward in my chair, a deep ache in my chest.

"I got a visitor a few minutes ago here at the house." We may be forty-four, but my brother and I live together. Always have. Even when Rhett was young and my wife was still around. At the end of each day, my twin brother is the only person who is always there for me, no matter what. He can proudly say the same of me.

The brandy I'd slipped into my morning coffee suddenly goes sour, and my gut spasms. Cold sweat sweeps my temples. "*What*, Riv?"

"There's someone here to see you."

"At the house?" Why is my body on high alert? Why isn't my brother saying anything despite the fact that he's talking? "What's going on, Riv?"

"Come home. There's someone here to see you. She's got news about Rhett." He lowers his voice but not for privacy. More like he can't bear to force strength for a second longer. "Get home."

My body jolts forward of its own accord. Just hearing his name puts heat behind my eyes. I haven't heard from him in three years. Not even for money. And I've monitored his accounts. A week after he left, he drained them, and that's the last I heard.

We could have had him followed. Fuck; I could've even paid to have him forcibly brought to Raleigh. But he was miserable here with us, and helicoptering over his entire life became too tiring.

Now every single goddamn fiber of my being aches for not having him followed. Because this phone call doesn't have the same energy as the other years ago. The *"he's in jail and needs bail"* calls from random girlfriends or buddies, the *"he got fucked up and needs help"* I'd get from strangers who'd find him bloodied and broken on a street somewhere, or the calls from him where'd he just hold the phone to his ear and sob unintelligible complaints until it crushed me and I'd go find him.

This call gives nothing away, and the subtext of the unspoken is what has my brain rattling as I speed back to our home, fifteen miles outside of town.

I'm racing toward the news I've been trying to avoid for years; I feel it burning through my veins, the pain already eating me from the inside out.

He didn't want to tell me over the phone, or maybe she, whoever the fuck that is, wanted to tell me in person. Maybe she needs to qualify or explain. She's probably some fucking junkie, just like Rhett. Maybe a girlfriend, but likely a user. Users gravitate toward and run with other users.

It doesn't matter who she is. All that matters is that she says the words. That I hear the words. Riv, too. The words that will break us both jointly. Loving Rhett has been so hard. I've only wanted the best for him. River, too.

But as I get stuck at a train, the warning arms lowering seemingly more slowly than usual, I silently pray that I'm not actually driving to find out that my son is dead.

I hold onto that sliver of hope for the rest of the drive.

CHAPTER THREE

EMBER

It's strange how unprepared I feel for an event I'd been almost certain was going to take place every day for the better part of two years. In my first year of marriage to Rhett, I was convinced we were living in wedded bliss. I couldn't admit to myself that marrying a man I'd only known for a handful of hours was a complete and utter mistake born from trauma and residual adrenaline.

The worst lies are the ones you tell yourself.

I stopped with the denial and refusal bullshit around the start of year two when my mom's wedding ring went missing and my *beloved husband* came home soaring in a drug-induced bliss; that was it. The moment when I admitted my mistake.

The last two years, I fought. For him, mostly, because while I realized I wasn't in love with him, it didn't change the fact that I did *love* him. I loved his gentle soul and, in a fucked up way, maybe his pain, too. I wanted better for him, more for him. I also wanted to leave knowing that he wouldn't OD the moment I was gone.

But the night before he died, the night he took my body without permission yet again, that's when I snapped. And in that break, I realized that chalking up the last three years to a mistake was far less gut-wrenching than living in a mistake 'til death do us part.

My bag was packed. I planned to leave early the next morning. To finally, after seven hundred thirty days, put myself first. Love myself before him.

Maybe I'll finally get to do that. But right now, exactly four days after that life-changing phone call, I'm cleaning up his last mess.

His death.

The way the doorbell chime echoes throughout the house tells me it's large. But I didn't need the ping-ponging ding of the video doorbell to tell me that. When I pulled up out front, my jaw fell to my lap.

Rhett told me his father, who'd he lost contact with shortly before we married, was "filthy rich." And a part deep inside me always wondered if that was a lie or not. I think I always knew somewhere inside I'd meet him. That as soon as I got pregnant, he'd be itching to make up with his own father as he was on the cusp of becoming one.

The idea of us having a child together now only makes me hate my delusional hope from three years back. We were never going to have a child. We were never going to make it. *He* was never going to make it.

Guilt consumes me as I wait on the impressive porch,

which appears to wrap the house. Rhett may not have lied about his father and it changes nothing about how he treated me, but I still feel like a disgusting human being for making assumptions about a man who was so clearly struggling for his life.

The door clicks, yanking my attention from the purple wildflowers growing along the porch's edge. The man standing on the other side of the door seizes the breath straight from my lungs and dries my tongue, making my mouth sticky and hot.

He's so tall and broad, with shoulders that look like they were built from carrying lumber and lifting weights. Rugged, from his shape to his clothes—dirt-laden jeans, brown work boots caked in Earth, a flannel with the chest pocket torn at the corner, he pushes a large hand through his dark hair. The movement sends a rush of his scent past the threshold. It feels like I've been shot with a bullet made of arousal as I greedily inhale him.

Studying his face a moment, my belly flutters with subtle recognition. The little flip my heart does has me feeling like I know this man. But the way he stares my way blankly I know I don't know him.

I look down at the name typed into my notes on my phone. Is this him? I look up at the handsome older man in the doorway, who is still staring at me blankly.

"Uh, I'm looking for Mr. Raleigh."

He drags a hand along the side of his jaw before pinching his beard-covered chin a moment. The color of coffee, his beard is full and rich, and I've never wanted to rub my hands through one until now. God, what the fuck is wrong with me? I swallow, willing away the filthy thoughts taking place in my brain. Why in the world am I thinking about that at a time like this?

"Which one?" he asks finally, almost like he was waiting for me to mentally regroup. I look at the note again.

R. Raleigh
8908 Columbia Circle
Raleigh, California

My head snaps up to him, eyes wide. I step back and survey the house, my brain exploding at an alarming rate as I realize *why* this house is so big.

"Are you like, *Raleigh,* as in, this *town?*"

He rolls his lips together while stuffing his hands into his pockets, and as much as I liked watching him stroke his beard, I'm glad he's not. I'm here to deliver terrible news, not *feel* something for anyone.

"Which Raleigh are you looking for?" he asks again, this time softer.

"R," I say with a reassuring glance at my phone. Then I lock the screen and stow it away. I'm clearly in the right place.

He laughs a rich but light noise that makes the bottom of my belly tingle like someone's pouring it full of hot sand. "That's not very helpful." He takes one hand from his pocket and motions to the black iron numbers drilled into the exterior near the door. "Both men that live here are R Raleigh."

For a long moment, we stand there. I'm trying to understand why, if this was his life, was my husband so supremely fucked up? The handsome construction worker speaks. "And yes, we are the namesake of this town."

Jesus Christ. Who knew? Clearly not me because I swear I have to force myself through a few dry swallows to get my brain back together. I can't believe he had *all of this*. I can't believe Rhett wasn't part of this. Whatever happened had to be pretty fucking bad if he walked away from this.

"I'm, uh, I'm not sure which Raleigh I'm here to see. But," I say, pressing my hand to my collarbone as heat blurs my vision, the words getting stuck in my throat a little. I struggle around them. "I'm Rhett's wife. And I'm here to speak with his father."

River, who introduces himself as such, disappears somewhere in the home after telling me he'd be right back. He's left me sitting on a couch that feels like velvet wrapped around a cloud, the fire in front of me painting my bootied feet in an orange glow. The entire flight to California, I'd thought about this moment. What I'd say to him.

How do you tell someone their son has died? All I ever knew was that they had a falling out. Rhett really honestly never mentioned him. Not to me, at least. Somewhere in that second year, I realized that Rhett had a lot of friends, and I wasn't one of them, as much as I should have been his *best*. But he wasn't mine either.

Now that I'm here, I don't know what to say. I don't know how to explain who I am or what Rhett meant to me. I don't even have those answers.

The thunk of his work boots against the marble floors

has my spine lifting from the couch, straightening as he enters the room. Sitting on the edge of a large Morris chair, his knees spread wide, elbows resting on the wooden arms, he dips his head at me.

"I called Rhett's dad."

"Okay," I croak, my voice broken and hoarse with foreboding.

"He oughta be here in fifteen to twenty minutes. Maybe a few more." He rises again, and as the flames dance in the hearth, they highlight the edges of his body, making him appear almost godly before me. "Can I get you a drink?"

I nod. "Anything." I'd even drink bourbon at this point. I need something. Maybe the reason I'm being completely inappropriate and getting... kind of turned on by this man is my way of coping. Some people turn to food, and I know better than most that some people turn to drugs in the face of trauma. But maybe my thing is, like, inappropriate crushes. Maybe I'm just subconsciously coping.

I smooth my hands down my thighs, exhaling a harsh stream to steady myself. That's all it is. A weird-ass coping mechanism.

He returns, and I ignore the flutter between my legs as he lowers an amber-colored liquid in a fancy snifter to the table in front of me. "Brandy," he clarifies.

Leaning forward, I take a quick sip and feel it burn as it slides down. The static buzz of the first drink wiggles through me as I return the glass to the table.

"I'm Rhett's uncle." He takes a drink from his glass as he returns to the chair's edge. Before I can ask his brother's name—so I can know Rhett's father's name—he sets his glass down and jumps in. "And you *married* Rhett."

I nod, rolling my lips together to calm my racing nerves. His eyes are so gorgeous that even in the dim space, they captivate me. He scratches his cheek, awaiting my response.

"I did. Three years ago."

"Three years ago," he repeats. "When precisely?"

Knowing Rhett lost contact with his dad right before we met, I think I know what River is getting at. I twine my fingers together, resting them in my lap. This might be hard, but this is not nearly as bad as it's going to get. Rhett's father isn't even home yet.

"I married him right after he... ran away, I guess." My pulse hammers in my throat and my jaw burns from how tightly I'm holding it closed.

River drags the blunt tips of his thick fingers slowly along his chin down the length of his throat. Every single rough hair in his beard rustles as he does, rousing my lower half.

"Ran away is right," he adds after a moment. "He hasn't spoken to his father in years," he says again, his neck flexing as he grapples with anger.

"I know." I lift a hand and wiggle my ring finger. "I was married to him. I'm fully aware he has no family." I don't know why I'm feeling so defensive of Rhett. He was not good to me. Maybe I feel defensive of him because I want people to know that he *tried*. We *both* did. We didn't want to fail. As fucked up as he was in his head, he couldn't have wanted to die.

"He *always* has family, but he's chosen to ignore them," River corrects angrily until his face stills. His angry free falls, leaving him with a blank slate when he asks, "did you say *was* married?" The lump that moves down his throat is thick. "You aren't divorced, are you?"

I shake my head, the warmth spilling over, down my cheeks, to my lap. "No," I croak. "He died four days ago."

The admission breaks the dam, and I crumble. Before I can blink, River is on the couch next to me, pressing me to his chest, his thick fingers stroking through my hair. At one point, he swipes through my tears with his handkerchief before he eventually stuffs it into one of my fists, both of which end up curled into his shirt.

He doesn't say anything but holds me as I sob. Ugly, deep, loud, wet. I cry against him until my belly aches and my shoulders hurt. I cry for what feels like an hour but can only be fifteen minutes because River pulls away from me as the home security system announces the garage door has opened.

He rises to his feet, outstretching a hand to me. "My brother's home."

CHAPTER FOUR

RYKER

A thousand times wouldn't accurately estimate the number of times I've thought of her since that day.

In the days following the bank robbery, I probably thought about her hundreds of times an hour. She wasn't just beautiful. She was breathtaking, and in her vulnerable honesty, I felt a connection between us radiating through. It's an inside-out thing with her, and I'd be willing to bet on that. I don't make bets I know won't be in my favor, either.

When I lost contact with Rhett, I thought about her even more. How simple her dreams were, even if I knew how truly complicated they could be to achieve. Go to New York. I wonder if she ever went. If she made it there. Many times I thought about flying out and walking the city streets, looking for her. But that was obviously fucking crazy so I didn't.

I didn't know her last name. I didn't know anything about her aside from her name, age, and dreams. And yet, not being able to find her again after we were pulled out felt a lot like being torn from my soulmate. I'd felt empty and restless for days, imagining her and where she went.

Maybe it was coping with Rhett's absence.

Or maybe it was just her.

Either way, I dreamed of her. I clutched my cock as I pictured her lips and those soft pink nails. I imagined her stroking me into her mouth, wrapping around me and smiling as I gave her a warm tongue full, my hands held steady in her silky, golden hair.

I dreamed of more, too, though.

Holding hands under the table in a crowded cafe. Guiding her through a filled museum with a palm on her lower back. Watching wind whip through her hair as ocean air kisses her velvety cheeks. I even imagined the noise her bare feet would make on the kitchen floor as she poured herself a cup of coffee and then joined us as we woke up together by the fire.

As a grown man, I wouldn't consider myself a dreamer. A dream is something you want but are too lazy to work for. A goal is something you want and have a plan to obtain or achieve. She was just a dream. Because I couldn't have her. There was no fucking way.

Three years later, I'd be lying if I said I no longer pictured her face when my eyes closed at night. If I said I didn't sometimes find her in my dreams and wipe her tears away all over again.

I'd accepted the fact that she was no more than an

apparition. Because she was gone, with finality, and that was an unavoidable fact.

But as I walk into my home and spot the visitor my brother called me home for, I nearly fucking choke. Gripping the wall, I stand there a moment in the privacy of the hallway shadows and listen to the soft murmuring between her and River.

I haven't seen her face.

I can't see her profile.

Fuck. I can't even *hear* her words. Or tone.

But I can *feel* them.

My entire body tingles with awareness as she lifts a delicate hand to her face, pushing golden locks of hair behind her ear.

It's her.

It's fucking her.

The woman from the bank.

How? How in the actual fuck? My other hand falls to my neck, where I loosen my tie and gasp for a breath, being much louder than I'd intended. As I struggle to calibrate that she's here, in my home, sharing a drink with my twin brother, they twist their gazes behind them.

River rises, and she does the same. Facing me now, I can't do anything but stare at her. Soak her in; every silky, beautiful fucking inch. She looks just as beautiful as she did that day, maybe even more so. Yet the tip of her nose is brushed with pink the same way it was at the bank, alerting me to the reason she's here.

Something is wrong.

I tear my gaze off her to look at my brother. Pain hides

beneath his stoic demeanor, and it tells me everything I need to know.

"Ryker, sit," he says, and I do. I take his spot on the sofa after loosening my tie completely. I can't stop looking at her as she sits down across from me, finishing the amber liquid she'd been drinking. Her shoulders shake a little as the drink scorches going down, and I only look at my brother because he speaks.

"Ryk, this is Ember."

Ember. The name rolls around in my mouth like butter on a hot skillet, smooth and rich. I love the way my chest vibrates as I draw out the name.

"Ember," I repeat, searching her eyes for recognition. Does she remember me from that day? Is it possible that she doesn't? I don't *just* remember her. I've paid mental and physical homage to her nearly daily since. And yet, her eyes are blank, mouth drooping as she tangles her fingers around the empty snifter.

"Ryker," she nods, "nice to meet you."

River clears his throat. "Now, tell us both what happened."

Her eyes flick between my brother and me, worry etching her forehead in long lines. "Should I–" she stops herself as she slides the glass onto the tabletop. The fire pops, grabbing all of our focus for a moment. "Should I tell him first?"

River takes a seat next to me, extending his arm and dropping his palm to my knee. With a squeeze, he keeps his eyes on Ember as he says, "talk us through it."

Rolling her lips together, I reach for my brother's drink and find the bottom after one long swallow. Shrugging out of my jacket, sweat begins to bubble along my hairline as the intensity of this moment grabs hold of my calm.

Something is very wrong. And yet, *she's* here.

My brother leaves, only to return a moment later with the bottle of Brandy. He refills his glass, takes a sip then passes it to me. I need it, but I don't want to overdo it, so between the two of us, if we go at this pace, we should be okay.

Though the way my gut flinches as she wipes away a stray tear before she's even begun talking makes me question if I want to be sober.

"Three years ago," she starts, her eyes focused on the rippling surface of her alcohol as she swirls it lazily in the glass. *Three years ago, what, baby?* I ask myself, wishing I could join her on the couch and pull her into my chest the way I never got to those years ago.

But I don't honestly think she remembers me, and that fucking stings a little. But not as much, I have a feeling, as what's to come.

"I moved to New York on a whim." Her glassy blue eyes come to mine, and everything beneath my ribs aches profusely. So much so that I pass the drink to Riv and rub my knuckles down my sternum. But I don't say a word.

"Anyway, on my first day there, I met someone. I think he had gotten there a few days before me. Anyway, we had some ticket drama at Grand Central, and... in the chaos of our sudden moves, we fell for each other." She doesn't meet my eyes, and I don't know if it's intentional or not, but it hurts all the same. "We got lost in each other a little those first few days, and when he suggested that we get married the next day..." she shakes her head, closing her eyes in a moment where my heart breaks for her to relive these moments for us. I don't want her to hurt. Opening her eyes, she smiles sadly as she looks between Riv and me. "It was foolish, I realize, but at the time, it was just... so incredibly romantic."

Riv rises, passing her a handkerchief just as she begins crying. Sobs wrack her shoulders, but he doesn't stay by her side to comfort her. Taking his spot next to me, we give her a moment to calm down as she drags the bandana beneath her eyes.

"Anyway, I found out pretty quickly that he had a drug problem." Her breath hitches as though she's reliving their shared past. "I'd say he tried to get better." She looks me square in the eye. "But we both know that would be a lie. He passed away Mr. Raleigh."

When Riv called me and said to come home; I knew it was because of Rhett. My heart broke on the drive over, anticipating, but *knowing* that it was true, *knowing* he was gone... My head falls to my hands, and I clutch it as the first, deeply therapeutic sob hollows me. Sliding over, Riv drops his arm along my shoulders, pulling me toward him. I go easily, and I don't know if he holds me or if we hold each other, but we both cry.

Rhett wasn't just my son. I wasn't the only one who loved him. I was never alone in my efforts to save him, either.

When I regain my composure, Riv takes my cheek in his hand and brings our foreheads together. His beard scratches my chin from proximity, and his bottom lip trembles as he struggles through his words. "We'll get through it. You know that?" His fingers curl into my neck as he holds my face to his. "We'll be okay. *You'll* be okay."

I let my eyes close for a second, trying to gain power and strength from this moment between us. I've been there for Riv, and lord knows he's been there for me. We rode through the desert and weathered every storm, him and me.

This won't be any different, even though breathing and existing suddenly feel so much more strenuous. The weight of Rhett's death presses against my throat and my heart, smothering and dulling all of my senses.

Somehow, we're back in our seats, Riv's hand still gripping the back of my neck. If he weren't doing it, I might float away.

I remember just then that *Ember* is here.

Ember.

I blink up at her through my foggy eyes and see that she, too, has been sobbing right along with us. And then it occurs to me that everyone that loved Rhett is currently in a room together. He should be here, too.

"How?"

She swallows hard, and I know it's difficult to talk about. I'm sure it is. But I have to fucking know what finally did it. Was it bad drugs laced with something? Or was it finally just too much? Was he alone? Fucking hell, if he was alone, I'll never forgive myself for not fighting harder that day. I let him go. Why did I fucking let him go?

"He overdosed." Her bottom lip trembles, and she doesn't wipe the tears that fall. "Heroine."

"Was he," I start, losing my voice to despair before I can finish the simple question. I clear my throat as Riv's grasp feeds me comfort, soothing the back of my neck. "Was he alone?"

Turning her gaze to her hands, still clutching Riv's handkerchief, she sniffles a few times. "He wasn't with me, but no, he wasn't alone." The wounded and grief-stricken expression she's wearing when her head lifts to face us again tells me that Rhett wasn't at a drug house, either.

"Where was he?" I ask, wanting more than anything this one last respect for my son. For him to have not lost his life to his disease and be a fucking adulterer on top of everything else. But I've worn the look she's got on. Riv has, too. So even though I'm asking, what I'm really doing is dreaming, projecting hope onto someone who I know can't give it. And that's foolish shit.

"With a friend," she breathes, using the tear-stained fabric again, brushing away fresh tears. That's what my son gave her. Three years of tears, of that I have no doubt. My stomach burns, acid and alcohol, pain and regret.

"Which friend?" I ask, not that I'd know because when he left for what I now know is New York, I didn't know any of his friends. And we hadn't spoken since, so it's likely that Ember knows that.

She raises her chin, answering with a controlled strength that makes me proud of the respectful woman she is. She may not know that Riv and I are well aware of who Rhett really was, but she's not trying to paint that picture to us. And that's admirable. "Her name was Billie. She called me right after it happened."

I pinch the bridge of my nose, trying to imagine a woman named Billie, a needle hanging from her vein as she struggles to dial three numbers. I look up at the beautiful blonde sitting in front of the fire. I have to remind myself, using my every fucking strength, that Rhett was sick with a disease, and he didn't choose Billie and needles; *the disease did.*

"He was very sick for a long time. He didn't choose her over you, Ember," I hear myself saying, wondering if it's for her as much as it's for me. I need to hear it. I have to remember. Rhett was my beautiful son, and he was broken and complicated, but he wasn't a deliberately cruel person.

She nods. "I know that." Our eyes idle together in the room, hot from the fire and the adrenaline of this unforgettable day. Riv is still gripping my neck when she adds, "I really do know that."

Then I ask two things I've never wanted to have to say.

"When did he die?"

She looks over at Riv and then back to me slowly. "Four days ago."

"Where's his body?"

"It's going to be here in Raleigh in two days. This was the only address I could find, and you had the same last name so I called the funeral home and just... flew out here." She smooths her hands along her thighs nervously. "I realize that if this was a bad or old address, this would have been extremely stupid and wasteful."

Riv takes his hand away and gives my back a single stroke before lacing his fingers together between his knees. "But you went for it," he says.

Her gaze simmers me, those blue eyes more intoxicating and addictive than I remembered them being. "I had a feeling I'd find you," she says, only this time, she's only looking at me.

CHAPTER FIVE

EMBER

Ryker. As soon as I saw him, I looked back at River and all his familiarities locked into place. He didn't just remind me of Ryker because I've been dreaming about him for three years—which I absolutely have been. But the reason why is... unbelievable.

Even after telling River and Ryker exactly what happened to Rhett, I'm still struggling to process. In the kitchen, around the counter, the three of us sit as we listen to the slow drip of coffee brewing, the hum of percolation creating a comfortable background noise to our stoic silence.

"What's next?" River finally asks. I look up at him, and I can't deny the rush of desire that comes over me when our eyes lock. Dragging my gaze over to his brother, I stare at Ryker. Handsomer than I remember, his clean-shaven jaw is a stark contrast to his brother's full beard. He feeds a hand through his hair, his natural coif falling easily back into place as he drops his palm to the counter with a thud.

I can't believe it's *him*. And my expression, due to years of schooling my emotions as a defense mechanism, remains impassive. I may be in a state of disbelief, but they'd never know it.

And even though his cheeks are stained with tears, and his entire world is falling apart around him, my insides still come alive. My confused body thrums for him the way it did back then. The way it does... *for his brother.*

In a way it *never* did for Rhett.

Rhett. My mind doesn't cease its relentless spinning as I remember *my husband*. My fractured, broken, addicted husband. Ryker is his father. The man who held my hand and wiped my tears when our lives were in God's hands has been my father-in-law all along.

The word fate rolls through me, and I clutch a palm to my stomach, trying to temper the wave of nausea that follows. Rhett hurt me because he was broken inside. I chose to stay, knowing he was unwell. Does his disease forgive how he treated me? No. But I didn't leave.

I wondered, on the flight here, why, after being held hostage and finally deciding to live my life, would the universe lead me to Rhett? Of the millions of souls to connect with in the wake of trauma, why in the fuck did I have to meet Rhett?

River pours coffee into three identical mugs as Ryker, who stands by his side, drops a consoling hand on his shoulder.

"Thank you," he says roughly, and I watch them share a

private look that speaks volumes about their relationship. They're close. They held each other. They both cried. Rhett was clearly deeply loved, and they very clearly deeply love each other. Why, then was Rhett like he was? What happened?

I know I can't ask. Not yet, at least.

"Well, the body comes in two days, and it's going to..." Ryker faces me, waiting for me to finish the thought.

"West Side Memorial," I add. "That's the only place I saw here in Raleigh. The only funeral home."

He swipes a hand through his hair, his broad shoulders deflated with his sigh. "Right. That... makes sense."

"Breathe," River rasps. The same way Ryker did for me on the floor of the bank, River drops his palm over the top of his brother's hand. Ryker's eyes fall shut as he summons the deepest breath from his lungs. Opening them, he lifts his mug to his lips and takes a small sip.

"Okay, so we make arrangements for the next two days. We'll call West Side and see if they can send someone here. I don't want to go into town right now."

River nods, adding, "let's just focus on that for now. Okay?" He turns to me, taking a drink of his coffee as I just stare at my own. "Where are you staying?"

I smile awkwardly. "I hadn't gotten that far."

"Stay *here*," River replies on the heels of my admission. "You'll have your own floor, but if we're planning Rhett's end-of-life service, you need to be here."

Ryker meets my gaze. "*You need to be with us.*"

Those six words resonate, echoing inside me, leaving me feeling weak and exhausted. I grab the counter, and around me, the world darkens a little, and the last thing I remember is four hands grabbing me before I meet the floor.

CHAPTER SIX

RYKER

"See if she's got anything in her car, and I'll get her settled in on the third floor," I tell my brother as we lift Ember's body together, getting her upright on a barstool. Her weight pressed against my chest feels awfully good for how *awful* this day has gone.

River nods. "Will do."

Slipping an arm beneath her thighs and one behind her back, I cradle her to my chest and head through the house toward the winding staircase off the main living room. I don't let myself look down at her in my arms as I climb the stairs two by two, ascending to the third floor. A master on every floor of the house, I lower her to the California King-sized bed that dominates the space.

Then I let myself look at her as the noise of my brother's boots climbing the stairs fills the space behind me. She is every bit as beautiful as I remember, and though years have passed, I want her all the same.

That's not true.

I want her *more*.

River drops her bag next to the bed. "We should talk. Let her rest."

I steal one last look before dragging a cashmere blanket partially up her svelte legs, turn on my heel, and leave the room. River closes the door quietly behind him, and then I pull him into a hug, long and deep.

"He was your son, too," I whisper, soaking in the way our hearts beat together, the unified cadence bringing me solace amidst this painful darkness.

Rhett's mother lost her life when she had him. She may not have perished during childbirth, but the crippling postpartum anxiety and depression took her, despite our greatest efforts to get her help. Riv and I tried it all, but it wasn't enough.

The same way we failed his mother, we failed Rhett, too. But I don't say that just yet because though I know it's true, saying it aloud right now would cut too deep. I can't grasp that sharp-edged reality. Not yet.

"Let's go downstairs and talk," my brother says as we part in the hall. Once we're back in the kitchen, Riv stands along the counter with me sitting across. He's standing, his arms stacked over his chest.

He may come off as intimidating to an onlooker, but I know him. He's waiting.

"What?" I ask. I'm so empty inside that I don't know if I can scrape together enough of myself to formulate more conversation, even for him.

"What's going on?" His face is impassive and cool as he stands motionless, staring at me across the dimly lit kitchen. Whatever attempts the sun made today, it's thrown in the towel as evening washes up against the side of the house, engulfing it like a wild wave. Riv's face is outlined in shadows, but his eyes are bright and clear and full of intention. He wants an answer, but I don't know what the question is.

"What do you mean?" I slide the untied necktie off, tossing it across the counter.

"When you saw her here, you knew he was–"

"I knew when you called, Riv. I felt it in my gut. When she showed up here, didn't you know?"

He shakes his head solemnly. "I didn't know for sure. But... I suspected."

"Right," I nod. "That's—"

"Not the point of this conversation," Riv finishes, lowering his curled fists to the counter where he seemingly braces himself for impact. "Tell me why you looked at her like she was the walking cure to all your problems." His eyes narrow, poking me.

I didn't think I'd ever see her again.

I meet my brother's gaze, the one that mirrors my own and collect my thoughts for a second. He waits patiently as I try to find words to explain the unlikely situation we're in.

"Three years ago," I say, keeping my voice low. "Rhett called me. He was high and..." I pull at the ends of my hair as I toe into the memory. I've revisited it many times in the privacy of my mind, but I've never spoken it aloud. "He was threatening to leave. He didn't say where he was going to go, but he said he was going to leave."

Riv nods, fully understanding Rhett's antics. He dealt with him the same as I did.

"This was back in San Francisco. I was in town for that meeting—"

"I remember," he nods.

"I was on my way out, had one last stop, but he called. I ran to the bank thinking a cash incentive might persuade him to wait."

"More money was always something that could motivate him."

"Right," I nod, "that was my strategy. I told him ten minutes and I'd be there to see him off. In my heart, I knew it could be the last time. I begged him to wait for me."

"He left anyway?"

Gripping my forehead in my palm, I shake my head. "The bank was robbed."

I lift my troubled gaze to see Riv's face littered with confusion. "What does that have to do with Rhett?"

I unbutton the top few buttons on my dress shirt. "I went to the bank to get him money, and while I was inside, it was robbed." I motion to my face. "Masked men. We were told to get down; it was very short-lived. Maybe fifteen minutes before the SWAT team smoke-bombed us and pulled everyone out."

"Was anyone hurt?"

I scratch the back of my neck as I recall the news articles I'd read about the event the next morning. "Actually, no. They used rubber bullets so the shots they fired broke some bones but weren't lethal." The woman in the navy suit with cheap pearls was okay, after all.

He nods. "Good, good."

Then our gazes clash again as Riv realizes he still has no answers as to why I'd been looking at Ember that way.

"She was in line in front of me. I told her the time. Then we were on the floor together, and I was keeping her calm. It was only fifteen minutes. But..." I think of her tears sliding down her cheek, plunking into the marble as our fingers locked. "I've thought about her every day since."

We stand there, Riv processing my story and me trying to wrap my mind around how unlikely it all is. "And then," I add, almost just to make myself believe it, "she moved to New York, met my son, and married him. And now she's here." I shake my head, and when I say it, I don't even look at him. I stare at my hand lying atop the counter, specifically at my pinky, remembering the way it locked with hers. "And she's Rhett's wife."

"Why didn't you tell me all this back then?" Riv asks, confusion and concern knitting his brows. "You said he just left, how am I only finding out about this woman *now*? Actually, scrap that. How am I only finding out now you were held at gunpoint, Ryker?"

I look down feeling every bit of the shame I felt that day. "Because I failed. I didn't get to him. I couldn't stop him walking out on us." As tears form, Riv hauls me into his arms and I'm comforted by the love that's never left me. "I'm sorry," I say, crumbling against my brother. We share tears, because he feels how deep my shame cuts.

"It's okay, I understand, it's okay," he reassures me, and I need it, because nothing feels okay at all.

Rhett's gone. She was his, and he's gone, and as fucked up as it is, I *still* want her.

No, I want her *more* than I did before.

Only now, it feels less possible than when she was a complete stranger on a bank floor.

CHAPTER SEVEN

EMBER

Waking up fully clothed in a bedroom I don't remember entering is jarring, but when I roll onto my back and take a few seconds to breathe and think, reality finds me.

Rhett is gone.

Rhett's father is Ryker, the handsome man from the bank those years back.

My head spins, and I know with all certainty that the dull ache swirling inside my head isn't from the brandy but from the jarring *truth* that my one time savior was my destroyer's father.

Swinging my legs over the edge of the bed, my feet collide with my bag. I run my toe along the grooved teeth of the zipper, remembering the state I was in when I'd packed.

Rhett having forced himself on me. Walking out to chase his next high and leaving me, broken.

Sadly, while this time I had declared I was leaving him, the rest was a standard exchange for us. Yet it was the last time I ever saw him. The bag at my feet once represented freedom and a new life, and maybe one day, it will again mean those things. But now, as I trace the edge of the bag, all I see is finality and darkness.

Across from me, a door is cracked; inside, a beautiful bathroom waits. After digging around my bag for some fresh clothes, I cross the spacious room, pushing into the bathroom. Lights come on as soon as I enter. The room is large with white subway tiles lining the walls and black and white subway tiles on the floor. White towels hang from a bar, lush and unused, with freshly wrapped soaps tied with twine in large glass hurricanes on the counter. The mirror is accentuated with three pendant lights and in the back of the room is a large clawfoot tub as well as a huge open-air shower. The tub looks inviting, but a relaxing soak amidst this moment feels self-indulgent and wrong.

Instead, I twist the complicated set of knobs in the shower until water rains over the back of my head. Immediately I hop out of the space and peel off my clothes, stepping under the warm rain as quickly as I can.

As much as it ever does, the shower temporarily soothes me for a few blessed minutes until the truth tiptoes into the stall with me.

The man who kept me calm during a robbery is my late husband's father. I am in his home, showering, and more than that, I'm still attracted to him.

I squirt a healthy dose of shampoo into my hand from the pump attached to the wall. Sudsing up, rosemary and mint flood my nostrils, and for a second, I lose myself in the energizing tingle running through my scalp. I may be washing it myself, but this feels like a salon experience or a hotel penthouse at that. I can't believe Rhett could have had all this, but... *didn't want it.*

Steering my thoughts back to him, I think of Ryker. The way his brother held them. How they whispered to one another and cried together. A voyeur of their private and painful moment, I sat watching and crying right along with them.

He didn't cry that day on the bank floor. He wasn't scared to die.

Guilt swamps me as I rinse the shampoo from my hair. I can't deny that I'm attracted to him and his brother, too. Identical in their eyes and build, Ryker and River dress like polar opposites.

River greeted me in work boots, dirty jeans, and a button-up flannel. His hands are stained from what appears to be a laborious life, and his dark beard covers the sharp jaw his brother has. But it's under there; I know it is.

Like the day I first met him, Ryker donned a suit and had his hair styled, hands clean, and shoes shining. He made my belly flip, even in the middle of this devastation. I feel bad about that, too, but I can't control it. My heart hurts. My brain is tired. My body needs rest. But the part of me that pays no mind to the rest, *she* likes Ryker. And she won't be silenced.

Same goes for River. *She* likes him, too.

Only, I realize this is a supremely fucked up time to *finally* be attracted to a man again. Or, I guess I should say, *men.*

I haven't really wanted a man since the first week I met

Rhett. I wanted him then. He'd done a great job of winning me over with swoony lines and delicate touches. He was everything I thought I was missing. He made love to me the first night we met, and it felt just like that–making love. Finally, I thought, finally here is my white knight.

I fled that bank robbery promising myself I'd live. Go to New York and find love. I just didn't know that I'd do both on the same day and they'd both be an epic mistake.

I haven't wanted to be touched since that first week. My body hasn't yearned for the rough fingers of a man to skate along my soft skin, teasing me, making promises that he fully intends to make good on. For a man to spread my legs and press his mouth to my pussy, to lick me in ways that make me call to god, to fuck me so good and hard that I can't even speak.

I stopped having those urges when I discovered the truth about Rhett and his *hobbies*.

As soon as I saw River, I felt all of those things. As poorly timed as it was, I can't deny that it felt good. After all those long, hard years, to feel like a woman in some minor way felt *like living*.

I turn the shower off after quickly conditioning my hair and washing my body.

Packing while in an emotional deficit is really not the best idea. Looking at the counter where I set my clothes, I realize I'll be wearing black yoga leggings and an oversized Nirvana t-shirt I've had since high school. I could rummage through my bag to find something less busy, but the truth is, what I wear shouldn't matter.

This is about Rhett and making things as right for him as I can now.

After getting dressed, I comb my hair while sitting on the edge of the bed, scrolling through messages from my mom.

> I see you arrived safely. I'd love a phone call, Em. I need to know you're okay.
>
> Thank god your location is on. I see you made it there safely. Let me know you're okay, Em. Please. Love you.

Quickly, I type out a text.

> Yes, I'm here. I'll call you shortly.

After I hit send, I notice the timestamp. 6:43 am. AM. Holy shit. I got here in the afternoon yesterday and slept until morning? I never planned on staying, though now that I think of it, I vaguely remember River telling me I'd stay with them. I guess it makes sense, since the three of us will do all the planning.

I'm planning a funeral for my husband. The man who wiped my tears on the bank floor that day is planning his son's funeral. We're in the same house.

I can't fucking handle the reality of it, and my phone slips from my hand, hitting the floor with a loud crash. The screen shatters, and I don't even care. I really don't. I pick it up and carry it out of the room with me, anxious to find one of the men living here to apologize for passing out. Then I can get some coffee, we can plan, and I can go far, far away from here.

It doesn't matter that I'm extremely attracted to them. They're part of my *before* story. They have to be—they belong to Rhett, *not me*. Once I'm happily living in my after, hopefully very fucking soon, they'll be nothing but a crazy story to tell at Christmas parties that no one believes because it's so unlikely.

That's all; I just need to get there.

I wander into the long, dark hallway and walk until my feet kiss the edge of the stairs, then I take them down. My hand skims the wood banister as I go, my legs feeling weak as I take each step. Finally, I'm at the bottom, where I recognize the hallway. It's where Ryker emerged from yesterday when he got home.

I retrace my steps and bring myself into the kitchen. My stomach flips delightedly at the sight of them. River is standing near the coffee pot, the cover of a book pinned behind it as he reads. Dark glasses rest on the bridge of his nose, chest bare, and black running pants ride low on his defined hips. I swallow as I memorize the sight of him. Biceps like canons, broad chest defined by masses of muscle, and a smattering of dark hair... everywhere, narrowing as it dips below his waist.

The happiest trail of hair I've ever seen.

He doesn't notice me right away, which gives me a moment to turn my gaze to the counter, where Ryker is stretched across, resting on his elbows. A black-and-white publication is spread before him, his hand holding his chin as he reads. Also shirtless, Ryker is wearing gray sweats, and while I can't quite see his full torso from here, I can see he shares the same defined shoulders as his bearded brother.

They are... spit pools beneath my tongue and in my bottom lip. I swallow, and the noise of my hungry, desperate gulp calls to them, and they both adjust their gazes from their reading to face me.

River pushes off the counter and sets his book down while Ryker stands, gripping the edge.

"We didn't hear you come down," River states as he reaches for a wadded-up shirt on the counter, tossing it across the room to his brother. With one hand, Ryker catches it, and I watch as they both tug on worn t-shirts, taking their glistening, gorgeous bodies from my sight. Removing my temptation.

Good. Wear shirts. I don't need to be thinking about what it would feel like to be sandwiched between the two of them anyway.

Just as I'm beginning to hate myself for even thinking these things, given the timing, Ryker clears his throat.

"Aida is coming at nine. She's the funeral home director." My head snaps to his brother as he taps the collection of papers on the counter in front of him.

"These are some ideas we put together last night, but, as his wife," River stops on the word, and I swear all three of us wince a little like the title doesn't quite fit. They're not wrong. Being Rhett's wife never felt right. I wished it had, but like my mom so eloquently says, *wish in one hand and shit in the other and see which one fills up first.* "You should have a look. Give us your feedback."

I slide onto a barstool, a perfect distance between them, and reach for the papers. The kitchen smells like coffee, aftershave, men's perspiration, and sadness; all *of it* is overwhelming and stifling. "Can I get a glass of water, please?" I ask, turning my gaze to Ryker.

"Absolutely." He's on his feet and filling a glass with

water from the refrigerator in a split second. My body tenses when he returns, handing me the glass while taking a seat right next to me.

The scent of them intensifies, and I take a long drink of cold water in an effort to eradicate the flutter between my legs. The core of my body is tied up in this sadness, but the rest of me is seemingly unaware, and as much as I know I shouldn't bring my legs together to satisfy the pulsing, I do. And I finish the water.

"Coffee?" River asks, already filling a mug. He slides it to me, and that's when I notice they're drinking it too. I look at the pot across the kitchen and see I've taken the last cup.

"How long have you guys been up?"

Ryker nods toward the sliding door that opens to the vast green yard. "We run at 4:30 every morning."

I cock an eyebrow. "That's dedication."

"You have to be dedicated to what you care about. Some days it will be hard to care, and that's when your dedication takes over and allows you to do the things you've convinced yourself you can't."

I don't know if we're talking about running or Rhett, but the intensity of his eyes hovering against mine makes the water in my stomach grow uneasy. Still eyeing me, he bumps a fist against the papers.

"Let us know what you think."

"We need to shower before Aida gets here," River says across the room to his brother. Ryker nods, then turns to me, sending another wave of sensory excitement my way. I know it's wrong, but I pull my legs together again and enjoy the fluttering in my clit. He's more handsome than I remember with a few extra lines in the corner of his eyes and a little more fatigue in his gaze. But still, he's a gorgeous specimen, and dead husband or not; I can't deny it.

"I'll fix us something to eat after I shower. It will likely take all day to get the plans finished. You can stay here again tonight, too." He drags a hand down the lower half of his face, staring thoughtfully at me. "Do you need anything? Or... would you rather stay somewhere else?"

"No." My answer is immediate, despite the fact that I probably *should* steal a minute to think this through. Should I stay here? Can I control this ridiculous feeling I have for these men? That's what I *should* be taking the time to think about.

I look over at River, who is rolling his neck, hands massaging stiff muscles. Giving Ryker a pacifying smile, I add, "staying here would just make it easier. I'm already here and... I'm honestly really beat."

"You slept a long time," Ryker says softly, his eyes etched with concern. He drops his hand to the top of mine, lightly pinning it to the counter. I think of the bank and remember how soothing his hand felt on top of mine then. It has the same effect now. The day feels a bit more possible around him. Which is irrational and insane, I know. But it doesn't change the fact that it's true.

"It had been a difficult few days before it happened, and I wasn't sleeping much. Once I got here, I just... finally crashed."

"I know," River says, wading over to our side of the kitchen and taking the spot opposite his brother. "We caught you right before you *actually* crashed."

"I'm sorry." I look over at Ryker. "He was your son, and here I am, fainting and needing to be carried upstairs." I shake my head, embarrassed by what clearly transpired last night.

"Don't be." Our eyes lock, and I search them as quickly as I can, desperate to find recognition, desperate to see that he remembers me from back then. That I wasn't the only one holding onto those few minutes *for years*.

But he looks away and takes his hand with him. "We'll be back down shortly. You get through those." And then they're heading up the stairs.

I look down at the papers, lifting the first sheet to read.

"To live in hearts we leave behind is not to die." –Thomas Campbell

Use the checklist below, and bring the following to the meeting with your West Side Memorial professional:

1. *Clothing, including undergarments (these items will be used to dress your loved one for viewing)*
2. *Eyeglasses and jewelry (these items may be removed and returned after the service if you so wish)*
3. *A recent photograph (for cosmetic purposes, for viewings only)*

I stop reading there, overwhelmed by the choices, and yet, none have really even been made yet. Clothing? What do I want Rhett to be buried in? I can't think of him in any other way than the last day I saw him—sweaty, wearing a ratty old hoodie, dirty jeans, and brand-new sneakers. He was emotional and high, his personality swinging up and down. He was a wreck, and so was I.

Pushing the papers aside, I get out my phone, glancing up the stairs once to make sure River and Ryker are actually out of earshot. Dialing, I chew the inside of my cheek as I anxiously await a response.

"Em? Oh, thank god," mom gushes, relief heavy in her sigh. "Thank you for calling. I'm not trying to overwhelm you; I just want to know you're okay."

"I'm okay," I say, hit by a sudden and unexpected wave of tears. "And I'm here. I'm at Rhett's dad's house. He and his uncle live together."

"How did they take the news?" She pauses. "I still don't understand why the hospital didn't call him."

"Rhett didn't have him listed." I knew this because I'd taken Rhett to the hospital at least five times over the course of our marriage. I was there the night he forcibly made the nurse remove his dad from the screen under the heading, *who to call in case of emergency*. "But both of them were aware Rhett was sick."

She hums a sad noise, meant more for Ryker than me. "I'm sorry it had to be you to tell him."

"Me too," I whisper. I use the end of my Nirvana t-shirt to swipe stray tears from my cheeks. "I'm staying with them again tonight. We're planning all day today, and Thursday, Rhett will be here in Raleigh with his family."

"When will the service be? Surely they'll need a few days to... get him presentable."

"I don't know," I admit, my mind whirring with the idea of seeing Rhett coated in makeup, lying in a casket like a doll. "And I don't think I can do an open casket."

"Well," my mom says gently, "let me know when the service is, and I'll fly out."

I tell her that she doesn't need to do it. My instinct is to accept her offer; having her here will make it easier for me to walk away from the Raleigh men. Seeing my mother will ground me, and that's what I need. But she never even met Rhett. Eloping wasn't her favorite, and to someone I'd only just met? She never said it, but I knew she thought it was a mistake. And she'd have been right.

I don't reconsider, because I don't want her to see me so broken. I pull the funeral planning paperwork in front of me again. Time to be a big girl and just do it.

"I'll call you tomorrow. Today is going to be long and tiring."

"Okay, I love you."

"Love you, too," I add before ending the call, lowering my shattered phone to the counter. Then I dive head first into the stack of papers, penciling in my choices or opinions on all twelve line items on the first page.

When Ryker and River come down, I stay focused on why I'm here. Funeral planning.

At the kitchen island, we eat breakfast, lunch, and dinner, along with Aida, who showed up a bit before her scheduled time.

There are no wanton looks or electric touches.

There are tears. Ryker and River hug a few times. Ryker wanders off to take a few phone calls, and River answers the door a few times, accepting deliveries of food baskets and flowers.

Planning a funeral feels like running an emotional marathon, but finally, at nearly 8 o'clock, it's over. My hands are tired, there's a dull throb behind my eyes, and I'm fairly certain that despite all the water and coffee I've downed today, I'm dehydrated simply from the amount of tears I've cried.

A lot of the tears today were for Rhett. That he left *this* behind.

And then for them.

Ryker and River. Who clearly loved Rhett, who are clearly suffering from his loss.

We ate all of our meals in comfortable silence. None of us had the energy or drive to make small talk, so instead, we provided each other with a much-needed break from words. We spoke only when we planned things, and it's exactly the way it needed to be.

As Aida slips paperwork into her briefcase, River grabs her coat from the back of a chair in the other room. Ryker rises, and he hugs her.

"We'll take care of him," she says, her voice husky. They pull apart, and Ryker's eyes are shining. "We'll take care of all of it, okay, Ryk?"

He nods, then River guides Aida to the front door with a hand at the small of her back. When it's just the three of us, I glance at my phone, seeing it's nearly eight-thirty.

"I'm going to go lie down."

Ryker nods as I stand. "Goodnight," he says as I make my way toward the stairs.

"Goodnight," I call back, to which River replies, "Night."

Back in the bedroom I'm staying in, I toss and turn in the Egyptian cotton sheets. No matter how high the thread count, how dark the room, how exhausted I'm feeling–I can't find rest. It's out there, but I can't quite get my hands on it, and after an hour of restlessness, I sit up.

I don't think I'm restless because I'm tired. Yeah, today has been taxing and grueling, but I think I'm restless because I've been dreaming of him for three years, and now *we're under the same roof together.*

I'll probably be leaving soon, as soon as the service is over. That only gives me a few days, and then I'll likely never see him again.

With my feet on the floor, I head to the hall, hoping they didn't retire to bed, too.

The chemistry we shared at the bank was clearly one-sided, and he just lost his son. River just lost his nephew. There's no room under this roof for anything but *grief*.

This, I know.

Logical me is *fully aware.*

But I can't stop myself.

At the bottom of the stairs, I see them sitting at the kitchen island we were at all day. Ryker's casual clothes that he wore post-shower have been swapped for another pair of gray sweats, and it's the second time today I'm seeing him shirtless. River is also shirtless, wearing pajama pants that are barely hanging on his trim hips. They're across from one another, silent but drinking, and the lights are low.

Stepping off the bottom stair onto the floor, nerves roaring through my veins, I ask, "room for another?"

Ryker lifts his eyebrows in surprise. River nods.

And even though I shouldn't and I know this is a mistake, I can't stop myself from going to them.

It just *feels* right.

CHAPTER EIGHT

RYKER

I don't like to generalize peoples' behavior. It's degrading and cheap. And I especially don't make that mistake with women, who are averse to being mentally boxed in by men. They deal with that shit their whole lives.

But the look Ember is wearing, standing at the bottom of the stairs, asking if she can join my brother and me for a drink... I *know* what it means.

Because it doesn't matter your age, gender, level of sobriety, or education—her eyes practically scream *I want to devour you*. It's universal, spanning all languages, like *taxi*.

She may not recognise me, but a part of her burns for me. Maybe for us.

In the few seconds it takes her to walk from the stairs to the kitchen island, I remind myself of one crucial fact: her husband just died. And while I'd easily bet my fortune that the son I loved so much was likely a shitty partner, still, I respect her pain.

And while I *know* that disarming look she's volleying between Riv and me, I know it's born from *pain*. I know what it's like to hurt so bad that all you want is numbness.

Maybe that's what she sees in us. A way to get numb.

She sidles up to me, the smell of my shampoo and soap on her making my skin hot and my cock throb. Having her here makes me wonder what else in this house is better suited to her besides bath products. I'm suddenly imagining everything I can give her.

"Whatever you're having," she says, dipping her head toward my barren glass. Across the kitchen, River grabs another, pouring out two fingers of Scotch.

She takes it, wrapping both of her slender hands around the crystal. Her fingers don't meet and my disordered brain imagines her hands around my cock.

Then I'm slamming the rest of my drink in an effort to punish myself for thinking of my dead son's wife that way. But God, it's the first time I've allowed myself to *really* look at her today. We'd been so deep in plans and so consumed with the sorrow that we kept our heads down. All three of us.

Now, though, she's all I see. Blonde wavy hair, down around her shoulders, eyes puffy from our shared distress, full lips clinging to the glass as she takes her first few sips. When I first met her, I knew she was beautiful. Only after time had passed did I realize just how beautiful because no one I saw ever came close. No other woman held a candle to her.

Sharing these intense emotions and connection to my

son–all of it only adds to the overwhelming and fast-growing obsession with her.

"How is it?" Riv asks as she winces through her swallow.

She presses a hand to her mouth, letting a cough reverberate. "Strong."

Riv winks at her. "The occasion spoke to a stiff drink."

She lowers the glass and looks at me. "I agree."

The question is there, on the tip of my tongue–*do you really not remember me?* But she's here for numbness, and while I don't want to use her as an avoidance to grief, I can't deny that if she wants to use me—if she wants to *use us*—we wouldn't refuse her.

I *couldn't* refuse her.

Another reason I'm a shitty fucking father. I'm sitting here silently planning my response to my son's wife hitting on me. But those eyes are possessively roaming over my body again... I'm only fucking human.

I pass River a look.

People say twins are connected, and I don't know how it works, but it's true. In a single glance, he knows that I want him to pull information from her. He knows that now is the time to figure out what she and Rhett really were. He knows as well as I do that those eyes aren't *just* for me. She wants us. But as my best friend, brother, and business partner, he also knows that I can't act on how much I want her until I know what things with her and Rhett were like.

"What was it like with Rhett?" Riv hedges, and a moment later, he's on the other side of her, and the three of us are sitting in a row. I like having my brother close, and more than that, I like knowing he's on the other side of her. To know that she's protected by us at all costs– feels irrationally good though in truth, she's not ours to protect. Not facing each other also makes it easier to talk. To say what we need to.

She takes another drink, and her shoulders wobble as she swallows. "Well," she says, wiping her mouth with the back of her hand, eyes focused on the almost empty glass. "He was in the right place at the right time, which led to a rash decision to get married."

"How long had you known him?" Riv asks, tipping the bottle of Scotch to refill all three of our glasses. A refill we need if we're going to have this talk.

"A week." She smiles as she looks at me and then back to Riv. "Sounds crazy, right?"

The way his face softens, how his eyes drop to her mouth a moment before meeting her gaze–I don't need to see her face to know the expression she wears. I can see my brother's face, and in it, I have the answers I need.

"Why?" he asks.

"Why did you do it if it was crazy?" I clarify, despite the fact that both Riv and I likely know what drove her to make such an impulsive choice.

She twists to face me, giving her entire back to Riv. "I wanted to *live,* and I thought that meant being impulsive. I thought I would fall in love with him and it would make our story so incredibly... *romantic.*"

River asks a question that makes her twist back to him. "Did you? Fall in love with him?"

The amount of time that passes between when he asks and she answers feels like an eternity, and I don't know if it's because she actually takes time or if it's because I want her to take time. I want so fucking badly for my son to have been loved, but the disgusting truth I bear is that I don't want *her* to have been in love with him because then *we* can't have her.

"I loved him," she says finally. "But I was never *in love* with him. I was in love with the idea of love."

Finishing the second drink in one go, she rests the glass on the counter and blows out a breath.

"I don't want to talk about the love I never found and the love I lost." Her grip on the glass tightens; I can see the color drain from her knuckles as it does. The massive kitchen seems to shrink, and the air becomes dense and difficult to breathe. "I just wanna feel good. You know?"

Riv and I share a glance because what she wants—is something the two of us could give her.

In fact, Riv and I have been here *many* times before.

Actually, this is how we live. It's been that way since we were eighteen, and both loved the same girl. Since then, we realized that sharing a relationship is how we thrive.

We're so good at sharing without greed and envy that every woman we've ever been with became obsessed with the idea of permanency with us. The idea of having us both seems strange at first simply because it's not mainstream, but it quickly becomes erotic, intoxicating, and romantic when they realize they get *two* men catering to their every want and whim. *Two* men to protect them, fuck them senseless and love them hard—it's addicting.

She's vulnerable right now. If we do anything with her, she'll never want to leave us. It's almost a guarantee. Not arrogance but absolute confidence that my brother and I know how to take care of, please, and fully commit to a woman. And that's all everyone wants, female or male.

But can I do that? Can I ask her to subconsciously go through a commitment to us as she's just recovering from her loss? Riv and I have always been able to love through adversity, to find pleasure when there's also pain. But we have *years* of life on Ember. She may not be able to balance it all, and it would be unfair to put her up to that if she's not ready.

"I don't think you know what you want," I say, trying, despite my thickening cock and racing pulse, to do right by her. To treat the tearful blonde from the marble floor all those years back with the respect she deserves.

"I do," she says quickly, turning and placing her hand on my thigh and sliding her palm up my leg, her pinky connecting with my shaft. She swallows, eyes locked on mine, not acknowledging that she's just touched my extremely hard cock. My cock tells a different story than my words.

"You want to get lost tonight," Riv says, making her face him. "You're sure?"

She nods, the overhead light making her golden hair glow. Hair that's probably been through my son's fingers. I look at her lap; thighs held together tightly as she faces my brother. Those legs have been pushed open by my son, *my own fucking flesh and blood.*

"You were never *in* love with him?" I ask, voice more hoarse than I had intended.

"We need the truth," Riv adds because the answer to this question doesn't just matter to me. River is invested in her emotional well-being as *much* as I am, but more than that, neither of us can do that to *Rhett.*

She shakes her head, a single tear breaking through her lashes. "I *wanted* to fall for him so bad."

A stronger man would probably stay in his seat. A better father *definitely* would. The exhaustion of the last few years weighs so heavily in this kitchen tonight. When I look at Ember and see hope and desire flooding her eyes, I want to see more of that. And I want some for myself.

River also wears the same hungry expression as he gets to his feet. He grabs beneath her seat, spinning the barstool to put her back to the counter. Standing on either side of her, we hover over her like her depraved bodyguards. "And what do you want *now*?"

Her shy smile makes me groan. Riv reaches out, wrapping her hair around his fingers. "I already told you," she says to me with a glimmer of lust in her eye before looking back at him. "I want to feel...*good*."

I reach out, sliding my fingers around the lean column of her neck, finding her skin warm and damp, as if she's anxiously anticipating this. My breath seizes, and I'd be willing to bet money that Riv is doing the exact same thing.

"I can make you feel good," I husk, her eyes lingering on my mouth long after the words are out.

"I can make you feel good," Riv adds, voice equally husky. My excitement ramps knowing my brother and I are feeling the same thing for Ember: *insatiable hunger.*

"Together, we'll make you feel good. You'll be our good girl. A very *good* fucking girl. And every day after this, you'll tremble when you think about how we made you cum. You'll be obsessed with us, we'll fucking ruin you." I tell her. She doesn't realize it's a warning. She will never be the same after we do this. And I have a feeling, this time, *neither will we.*

"After tonight, one man will never be enough," River warns. I release her neck.

She nibbles her bottom lip, gaze swimming between the two of us. "I'll take my chances."

Without conversation, we each extend a hand to her, Riv finally releasing her hair. I don't blame him for grabbing it; the way it shines beneath the kitchen lights gives me ideas, too. It makes me imagine seeing it in my lap in the car, between my legs in bed, and so many other fantasies I have *no business* owning.

She slips her hands into ours, and the moment she's on her feet, we're on her like wild animals devouring prey.

River lifts her shirt over her head, and I drop to my knees, pulling down her yoga pants as I do, leaving her little leopard-skin panties intact. Less than a minute on her feet, she stands before us, hands now cupped to her bare breasts, ankles crossed, bottom lip under her teeth. She's twenty-six, and my cock knows it.

"Are you sure you want this, us? Prove it." Riv says, taking on the dominant role he so easily fills. It's quite the opposite of our normal dynamic, with me commanding board rooms and him shaking hands and exchanging smiles with Raleigh residents. But when we're with a woman, that changes.

He hooks a finger through hers, slowly pulling her hands from her chest, exposing her naked breasts.

Her nipples tighten to nubs, gooseflesh spreading across her chest like a match catching and running through tall grass.

"There, show us everything we get to feast on tonight," he growls, lowering his mouth to her neck. She sucks in a breath as his beard grates her delicate skin, and I take advantage of being on my knees. Tugging the fabric of her panties aside, I leave a soft kiss on her lips, rock hard from the fact that she isn't waxed bare. A small strip of trimmed fair hair rests on her pussy, and after I kiss it, I run a finger through it and look up at her. Her eyes rolled closed, my brother holding her neck on one side and devouring it on the other; I watch as she reaches down to find my head, sifting her fingers through my hair. Guiding me back to her, I press my mouth into her cunt with a smile, loving how badly she wants this.

We want this. We didn't need a ceremonious conversation or a plan to know we were on the same page–Riv and I always are. It's how we work.

The first sweep of my tongue through her lips makes me groan; she's sweet like vanilla and honey and hope, and the way her thighs tremble beneath my grip as I spread her apart fills me with a hunger so ravenous I'm afraid I can never have another meal after this.

The most beautiful noise fills the room, causing my brother and me to still our eager tongues. She moans, her fingers fanning through his hair, in my hair, our names floating through the kitchen in ways we've never heard before.

"Yes, *Ryker*, yes," she continues her soft, delicate praise as I nuzzle into her pussy, licking her with tender strokes that cause her legs to wobble. "River, *River*, yes," she adds, my brother's hand falling to her chest. His thumb strokes over her nipple with the same care I'm using to taste her.

This is the part where we're gentle, easing her into being with us with white gloves, showing her our slow and soft side. But as soon as she's coming around my tongue, the gloves come off, and we'll show her how Riv and I fuck our woman.

Our woman. It feels so right when I say it about Ember.

Ignoring the fact that despite how it feels, it's not true, I feed her pink pussy an inch of my finger as I suck her budding clit into my mouth.

She drags her nails through my hair, her palm coming to grip the side of my face. When I pull back, her hazy eyes drop to me, and a slow smile spreads across her lips. "I like seeing me on your face," she boldly comments, causing River to freeze. He releases her breast, and I get to my feet, her hand falling away.

"On her back, on the counter," Riv states. Hooking my hands under her arms, I easily lift her onto the counter, her bare ass smacking the surface when I set her down. Riv and I stand before her, each working the tie on our pants. Her gaze darts from me to him, him to me, and by the time we've shucked off our pants and are standing exposed and erect, she's practically fucking panting.

Before we've even had her, all of me knows that she is a very, *very* good girl.

"It's not going to be all about you tonight, Ember," Riv warns, and from the corner of my eye, I catch his considerable bicep flexing, torquing, tugging. He's *stroking*. "We're going to make you feel so good you won't be able to *feel* anything else," he says, tone thick with precious warning. "But you're going to make us feel good, too. Understand?"

She nods. She can't possibly understand everything she's agreeing to.

"Lie back and open yourself to us," I say, finding my cock slick and steely as I grab it. "Show us what's ours." Stroking, her eyes follow my hand as River walks around the island. He takes her shoulders, leaning her back until she's flush with the counter. She shivers from the chilly surface, and her nipples pebble.

Riv's hands go to her breasts, and she yelps at his firm grip.

"Ryker's going to fuck you with his mouth, and I'm gonna suck your tits."

If she responds, I don't hear it because I'm already burying my tongue inside her soft center, pumping my cock. With my thumb, I circle her clit with wet, soft strokes, my tongue plunging in and out of her as I do. She wiggles and writhes; she moans and pants. Precum beads at the head of my cock, and I use my palm to stroke it down my shaft, feeling closer to the edge than I'd like to be.

I'm not a fucking one-pump chump, and neither is River. But I've longed for her in my dreams. The heightened emotions surrounding how we reunited play into how strongly I feel. Riv is feeling my raw energy and matching it. It's intense. More intense than usual, and I wouldn't have it any other way.

The intensity of this experience eclipses any doubts.

Sucking her labia into my mouth, I take gentle nibbles and follow with soft licks, alternating between tortuous and soothing. My brother tongues her breasts, and though I don't take my attention from her altar, I hear her fingers move through the rough hair of his beard, I hear her flesh beneath his wet lips, and I *feel* her moans vibrating through her core, into my open mouth.

The intensity of sharing pleasure is stronger than any drug. Nothing could be more addicting than experiencing the highest of highs with the person you are most connected to. Add in the vixen you've been jerking off to for three years? This experience already trumps all others in our many years of sharing women.

She braces her bare feet against my shoulders, and the position pushes me closer to that crumbling edge that I'm clinging to so tightly. She will come first; then *we'll* cum together. That's how it goes. And yet, sweat slithers down my spine and pleasure fogs my senses, the pulsing desire to cum so goddamn overwhelming that I have to let go of my dick.

Digging into the soft flesh of her inner thighs with my thumbs, I use the tip of my tongue to make slow strokes through her, then around her clit. Riv's rough rasp, *"god these tits,"* tests my willpower, and then she tenses.

"Right there, right there, *righttherightthere!*"

I hold her legs apart and lean back, carefully petting her swollen bud with the pad of my thumb. I want to bury my face in her and feel her orgasm pound against my lips, fill my mouth, and swallow her.

But I *have* to watch the way her cunt drips for us. I can't look away as she succumbs to her orgasm.

Pink lips swollen, open, eager for our cocks; I watch her cunt seize closed and spread open, over and over as she cums in hypnotic surges. It's fucking sexy and beautiful and somehow, *knowing* I am treating this woman better than my son ever did makes me both strangely proud and uniquely sad.

"Atta girl," my brother praises, no longer sucking her breasts. I rise, stretching upward, thumb still stroking her. Her back is still arched off the counter, and my brother's hand is on her breast, fingers pinching her nipple. Her eyes are closed, cheeks and chest flush.

"Now get on your knees for us." He wraps an arm behind her, lifting her away from the surface in one movement, lowering her to the kitchen floor.

Holding my cock, I make my way around the island, my hip bumping Riv's as I stand next to him. With my left and his right, we hold our hard cocks, stroking slowly as we stare down at Ember.

"I can't believe this," she whispers, eyes still heady and hazy, intoxicated by desire.

"Fucking two men at once?" Riv asks a bit bluntly. He's never one to mince words.

She swallows, and the sound has my balls tingling, thinking about what *else* she's going to swallow tonight. "No," she says meekly, glancing away, "I just... finally feel so good."

"We haven't fucked you yet, Ember," he reminds her. I like that Riv says her name a little slower than I do.

With my hand not holding my cock, I cup her cheek, hooking my thumb in her bottom lip. "Do you want us to fuck you, Ember?"

She nods. "I do."

Riv takes over, cradling her jaw in his thumb and forefinger, turning her to face just him. "Not tonight." He releases her, the hard warmth of his hip nudging against mine.

Her eyes fall to our hands cradling our cocks. Taking us both by surprise a little, she swats us away, using hers as a replacement.

Looking enamored and excited, she strokes us in unison, and I can't help but steal a glance at how her hand looks around *him*.

Beneath the beard, Riv and I are identical twins, even still at forty-four. The last time I saw him without a beard a few years back, we could still fool people with how identical we were. I watch Em pump him, then look down to watch her stroking me. My chest tightens at the moment which, to most, would seem sinister or salacious; brothers enjoying this together. But for us, it's everything.

Our bodies were built for this pleasure. It's why we're all here—our sexual urges. If we don't honor those urges, what's the goddamn point?

I don't fuck with Riv, and he doesn't fuck with me, but we enjoy ourselves together, and we don't hide a single part of that pleasure. He catches my eyes as I glance back at him.

"Let's give our girl a mouthful, brother."

I nod, and when we look back down at Ember, she's eased nearer to us on her knees, mouth open. She brings the slick head of my cock to her mouth and sucks, pumping him as she does. I groan and let my head fall back.

I want to watch because it's Ember.

But I realize she may have had a point about wanting to get lost and go numb. The last three days wash over me as her moan writhes through my cock, making me choke on a groan.

My son is gone, and even though it felt like he was gone for a while, he's *actually* gone this time.

I keep my head back, my growls and groans growing louder to silence the chaos in my mind. She takes me out of her mouth with a wet pop, and when Riv groans loudly, I know she's taking him in her mouth. Maybe even down her throat.

Keeping my eyes closed, I focus on the beauty of this moment. I refuse to get lost in what it means, what's going on, or anything else. This moment is for the three of us to let go and feel good, and fuck if that's not exactly what I'm going to do.

Only, after a few minutes of her hot little mouth gargling my cock and then his, she stops.

Opening my eyes, I notice my brother holding her tight by the chin. She stares up at him with the adoration that comes in long-established relationships and wonder if maybe she's a little drunk. Because there's no way she can be that into us after just a few days.

The *I want to devour you* eyes have been replaced with *anything you say* eyes. I'm not jealous because she eyes me, still in his grip, with the same expression.

"My brother's gonna give you a hot mouthful, and you're gonna keep it on your pretty little tongue. You hear me?" It feels so good and strange to hear these things being said to her. "Then I'm gonna give you more."

She nods with glassy eyes, lids hooded, nipples hard, and skin flush. She edges toward me before he forces her to still, using his hand on her jaw to bring her focus back to him.

My brother reaches between his legs with the same hand that cupped her face and fills his palm with his swollen sac. "I'm gonna empty these, Ember; we'll know what a good fucking girl you are when you swallow."

There's *something* about blowing your load inside a woman when she's already warm and wet from another man. When that man is your flesh, blood, and life—that "something" becomes *everything*.

Without another word, she seals her lips around my cock, and I watch in awe as she feeds herself every single fucking inch.

Riv and I are big guys, at over six feet four. And I don't know what fucking adage there is about big, tall men but our cocks are no different. I'm a soft six and a hard nine, and so is my brother.

But the way Ember slides my cock into the depths of her throat, how her jaw must burn to accept the girth — "*Fuuck*, Em. That's..." I have no words as her lips kiss my groin, her watering eyes blinking up at me. Veins bulge in her neck as she begins to gag a little, but my brother's reassuring hand comes to the back of her head, weaving his fingers through her silky hair.

"Stay on it; you can do it. Push yourself," he growls, urging her to deepthroat me longer, to take her body further than it's ever gone.

She gags, thick threads of saliva hanging from her chin before I swipe them away. Riv grabs my hand, weaving our palms together for a quick second, then uses the spit from my hand to stroke his cock.

Em's eyes follow the movements, and the little whimper of pleasure that comes from her in response ripples through my shaft, making my balls ache.

"Fuck, Em, I'm close."

Riv, still holding her head, tugs her back. "Breathe now. Good girl."

She grins, spit coating her chin and lips. And before she can soak in the praise, I have my finger hooked in her mouth. "Open, and hold out your tongue." The command is huskier than my normal tone. Riv, knowing what it means, angles her head back just slightly.

He holds her at the perfect angle as I pump my fist down my length one more time, the first shot of my release streaking across her tongue and into the back of her throat.

"There he goes; take him, Ember. Take his cum," Riv growls, the raw desire in his voice making the hair on my neck rise. Another thick, hot ribbon of cum drops onto her tongue, and then my cock is pulsing wildly in my fist, a few more shots settling into the pool already there. When I've wrung out every drop, she holds my gaze.

Was she thinking about this three years ago? Does she even remember? Did my son ever do this with her? I don't allow the thoughts to settle and ruin the moment. Rather, Riv doesn't because as soon as my cockhead is no longer pressed to her open mouth, he's pulling her to him.

"You hold his cum right there; you understand?" He asks, gently slapping her cheek, making a drop my cum slip free. With his finger, he scoops it up and brings it to his mouth, licking it off.

With the same hand, he pumps his cock again. I grip Ember's head, a little gentler than Riv did, and angle her the same way. He strokes again before reaching out, gripping my shoulder tightly, dropping his head forward, then going still. With his fist curled around his crown, I watch his orgasm break free. He cums in thick, long ropes, adding to the mess on her tongue.

When his spine rolls and his shoulders shake, I know he's done. I let go of her hair, lean forward, and whisper, "hold it, baby, but close your mouth."

She does what I say, and I seal my lips to hers. She's salty and swollen, but no lips have ever felt so good against mine. I pull away, and River takes her mouth with his. When he steps back, I help her to her feet.

"Swallow it, Em," Riv advises. "Swallow all that cum. Show us what a good girl you are."

Her eyes are sparkling as her cheeks swell, then *gulp*. She juts out her tongue, pink and bare, and holy fuck, she did it. She gagged on me, sucked me, took him, then she fucking *swallowed* us both.

And now, she's smiling.

"I knew it," I say to my brother, alluding to the fact that my initial attraction to her three years ago was not off base.

I have a particular skill in spotting women who like to be shared, while Riv has been less lucky. Knowing what I'm referring to, he winks, then scoops our pants from the floor.

"Put your cock away, pervert," he says in response, earning a laugh from Ember and myself. Once the three of us have lazily put our clothes back on, I grab the bottle of Scotch and shake it.

"Nightcap?"

Riv nods. "Yep."

Ember yawns. "I don't want another drink, but I don't want to go up to bed and be alone." She twists her hair over one shoulder, looking between me and my brother. "Can you have your drinks by the fire? And I can just... curl up with you?"

Less than a minute later, Ember's head is in my lap, her feet are in Riv's, and she's sound asleep. We clink our glasses together above her tired body.

"To an unforeseen yet enlightening night," Riv toasts.

I clink my glass to his. An enlightening night indeed.

CHAPTER NINE

EMBER

Waking up in the room I'd slept in the night before, I'm overwhelmed with irrational disappointment. I didn't know I'd expected and hoped to wake up with one or both of them, but now as I analyze the peaks and valleys of the ceiling texture, I realize that I did.

I *wanted* to wake up with them. I yearn for them.

Turning onto my side, stuffing the pillow into a ball beneath me, I think about that. Waking up with... the man from the bank. Is that what makes my head spin, or is it that they're brothers who have no problem being sexual with a partner together? Or... is it that I'm completely okay with not just the idea of brothers sharing, but I *more than want* to be shared by them.

I think about Rhett as drops of rain spatter loudly against the window. The skies are gray, and I can't help but think it's symbolic of this house. Hovering in a colorless existence, waiting for light. Last night was meant as a distraction, but in the glow of morning, it felt a lot like light. Hope. Living.

I haven't felt like that in so long. If ever, really, if I'm being truthful about my life so far. Marrying Rhett was a blind attempt at spearing excitement and bringing it back to my life. Remembering the day I met him, my eyes fill.

He looked so much like Ryker. I remember thinking that the man from the bank must've really made a fucking impression on me if thousands of miles away, I'm seeing his features on a complete stranger's face.

Rhett's hair was lighter than Ryker's and River's but had that same silky, natural shove of the hand coif. His eyes were so green that my stomach fluttered when they locked onto me. I remember thinking, that's the same breathtaking emerald of the man who wiped my tears. And because thinking about a total stranger who I had known for less than twenty minutes felt crazy, I told him his eyes were the greenest I'd ever seen.

And then he asked me for coffee.

In hindsight, the way his knee bounced beneath the table at the coffee shop should've alerted me to his energy. And in taking in that energy, I should have contrasted it to how he slept for sixteen hours after we had sex. The travel, he'd said, had left him exhausted. And that made sense.

A soft knock at the door makes me wipe my eyes.

"Ember," Ryker's voice is thick and masculine, and bumps spread across my arms in response. Between my legs, there's a pulsing, and as fucked up as it is to want Rhett's dad, I can't help it. My body can't pretend the way my brain can.

And I'm tired of not having what I want. I'm tired of pretending to be content when I'm devoid of pleasure.

It's fate that brought me to Ryker. I'm choosing to believe that.

"You up?" he asks quietly.

Sitting up, I smooth my hands down my hair and rub the sleep from the corners of my eyes quickly before responding, "yeah, come in." Did he put me to bed last night? Or was it River?

The door opens, and Ryker strides through, taking a seat at the foot of the bed. Aftershave and rain waft over me, and my heart beats a little faster. The ends of his dark hair are wet, and his normally clean-shaven jaw is blanketed in light stubble. His gray shirt is damp, and the black athletic pants he's got on pull tight to his groin as he shifts to face me.

I look away quickly, not wanting to get caught checking out his crotch. When our eyes meet, there's a hint of a smile on his lips, but he doesn't call me out.

"Sleep well?"

I shrug. "I think so. I don't remember coming to bed."

"We brought you." So *they* both brought me up? A hot thrill runs up my spine at the image.

"Thank you," I say because I'm suddenly feeling warm, flushed, and achy. He reaches out, wrapping his vast palm around my foot. His squeeze radiates up my leg, sinking into my already wet center.

"Come down for breakfast before River takes off. He's gotta go into town today but don't worry," he says, his thumb stroking the arch of my foot. "I'm taking some time off."

"The perks of being the boss," I say with a measured smile.

He nods. "The perks of owning the town. But," he hedges, "Riv's gotta see about a downed light pole. Once he gets it squared away, he'll head home, too."

The idea of being with them here all day again makes me hot and breathless, but then it occurs to me that Rhett's body is arriving in town today. My stomach dips, and all the good things I was feeling suddenly fade to dark, black guilt.

Here I am excited to be here, but the only reason I'm here is that Rhett died.

Ryker wiggles my foot. "Have some coffee to go with all that thought." I blink, realizing he's noticed my demeanor shift. "The three of us should talk."

I nod, and then he leaves the room. I pull on a sweatshirt, feeling a subconscious need to cover my body around them. Heading down, I find River standing right where he was last night as he clutched his brother's shoulder with one hand and his cock with the other, unleashing his orgasm straight into my mouth. This morning, his cock is put away, and he's wearing work boots, a flannel, a beanie, and a Carhartt vest. He looks just as good now as he did last night.

"Morning, Ember," he says, passing a mug of coffee to me across the counter. I sit and sip, listening to Ryker and River exchange a few details about their work day. They're so... close and functional. I don't understand why Rhett hated them so much. I can't make sense of it.

"Why did he hate you?" I blurt out, wishing, based on

the wounded expression clouding both of their faces, that I had softened the question. "I mean, why did Rhett not want to be here, in his home, with his family?"

Ryker hangs his head as River extends his arm, gripping his brother's neck with a consoling grasp. "It's complicated," Riv answers.

Ryker's phone illuminates on the counter, and he lifts it quickly. River and I watch his eyes dart back and forth on the screen until he locks his phone and tucks it away.

"His body is here, in town." Ryker faces me; all color drained from his expression. "I don't want to talk about this right now."

River casts me a pointed look in which I feel scolded, then guilty. Why did I ask? Or, at the very least, why did I have to blurt it out that way?

But I *know* why.

Because I want to be here but need it to feel okay. I need to know that what we're doing isn't cruel.

Screwing the lid on a coffee tumbler, River comes around to where I'm seated, lowering his face to my ear. The tickle of his beard against my cheek makes me heady, but I focus on what he's saying as I stare into my mug.

"I'll be back in a few hours. Have a bath. Take it easy." When he walks away, his scent lingers. Pine, cedar, soap, desire. I sneak an inhale and let my eyes close for a moment of peace.

When I open them, River is gone, and Ryker is sitting next to me.

"Are you okay?" he asks.

I roll my lips together, staring into eyes that look more verdant this morning than last night. "I'm fine. How are you?" I place my hand on his upper arm, spreading my fingers over the disciplined muscle. He glances at my hand and then back up, the green in his iris' replaced with wanton darkness.

"I'm glad he's home," he responds, eyes idling with mine. "I wish it weren't this way, but I'm glad he's here anyway."

"I'm sorry about earlier," I say quickly, knowing it needs to be said. "I just, I'm confused because Rhett really didn't want to come home, and now that I'm here and have spent time with you and River... I don't know. I guess I just don't understand why he *wouldn't* want a life here."

Ryker sips his coffee, and I watch the steam disappear before my eyes. A lot like Rhett did.

"I understand why you want to know. I just... don't feel up for discussing it right now, that's all." He rests his temple against his curled fist, blinking at me from less than a foot away. The man who read me the time three years ago is now sharing his darkest, most private moment with me, and it still makes my head spin.

"Ryker," I say, lowering my voice despite the fact that River's gone.

"Ember," he says with a fatigued grin like he wants to give me his best energy but can't summon even an ounce. I want to replenish him, give this man something to cling to.

"I remember you. Three years ago, at the bank."

He leans back, and his hands slide off the counter into his lap, one of them grabbing mine immediately.

"I left for New York the next day. Thinking you're going to die makes you do things. I told you I wanted to travel, and I wanted love, so I went after it." I like that a proud smile tips his lips just a little, but I hate that his eyes don't move. "Your son," I start, but hearing his name might be more emotionally fulfilling. "Rhett," I try again, "was the first person I met. And the reason I was drawn to him is that he reminded me of *you*."

Ryker slips off the stool and stands right over me, grabbing my face in both of his palms. He crashes his mouth to mine, and I can taste his coffee and his pain, and I greedily open my mouth more to take it all.

Then he leads me upstairs, and I know I'm about to take more.

CHAPTER TEN

RYKER

"Are you sure?" she asks, voice teetering with hesitation.

Reaching behind, I yank my t-shirt off over my head by the neck. Hooking my thumbs in the waist of my pants, I shuck them off, too. My body is humming with anticipation, which temporarily brings my heart respite from the clawing pain, and I know it's her presence giving me that gift.

Having peeled off her sweatshirt, I can now see Ember remains in the leggings and shirt she wore last night. And for some reason, the knowledge slaps me across the face. We'd tried to numb her last night, give her a taste of what she was looking for. Now, as she stands before me with puffy eyes and the *same clothes as yesterday*, I wonder if that was wrong. In love or not, she's hurting too. We aren't the only ones.

"I'm not sure of anything right now," I admit, because as much as it's true, I *still* can't stop myself. I want her too much. I want this too much. For too long. "Anything but *you*."

"What about River?" she asks as she begins exposing herself to me in a slow, methodical disrobing. Her eyes hold mine so intently my pulse can't help but race.

This is different from last night when it happened so fast that we didn't give ourselves time to talk or even think. *This* is intentional and slow, and yet, my body thrums with the very same need it did last night.

"What do you mean?" I ask, kneeling to help ease her ankles out of her pants. Once we're in just our underwear, I guide her toward the ensuite master bathroom and turn all four knobs on the shower wall. Water cascades and I turn to find Ember taking *off* the leopard panties.

"You can have *me* without *him*?" She swallows, her fingers mindlessly tracing the edge of the counter.

Why doesn't she feel like a stranger? Why doesn't she feel foreign and uncomfortable? She should. It doesn't matter that we spent an adrenaline and fear-filled fifteen minutes together years back. I don't know anything about her. And yet I'm here, willing to betray my dead son so I can *finally* know what it's like to be inside her.

Would she whimper as I sank my fat cock inside her? Or would she be the kind to carve up my back as she moans my name while panting yes over and over? Would her cunt be warm and wet, or would I need to lick her first to get her ready?

I've wondered about those things for too fucking long.

I nod and take her hand, leading her inside the steamy

stall. "My brother and I have complete trust in each other" Reaching up, I detach one of the removable shower heads, bringing it to her shoulders. The warmth of the water makes her eyes flutter closed as she releases a soft sigh.

"Yeah?" she asks, popping one eye open.

I taste her lips as I continue moving the stream of water down her back, the metal hose dragging against my hip. I nod, rivulets of water running down my shoulders from behind. "Yes."

"Do you always share? Like, beyond sex? In *actual* relationships?"

Lifting the showerhead, I bring the spray over her hair, watching it morph from golden into a dark shade. "Yes. We share *actual* relationships."

Her nose wrinkles as I replace the showerhead, filling my palm with three pumps of rosemary and mint shampoo. "Turn around," I tell her, and I smile when she does it without question.

I sink my fingers into her scalp and massage gently, the soap getting sudsy after just a moment. "We share *because* we trust one another implicitly, and that's all there is to it."

She's silent for a moment. I realize it's a lot to take in. What we do isn't considered mainstream or normal because everyone else lives their life according to rules someone else wrote. People don't realize that in every system we have in place today, every law or rule or unspoken expectation was formed by a singular person who simply fucking *decided* it would be that way.

Fuck that.

I love women. My brother loves women. And it just so happens we take pleasure in sharing. For a long time, when we came back to Raleigh, we tried to make people understand. We tried to make them see that we love differently, but we bleed the same.

I stopped trying to make people understand the way I love when it began impeding my ability to *live*. I'd spent so much time trying to show people that different isn't the end all *fucking* be all. It was ruining me. It was ruining my brother, too.

Then we said fuck it and lived our lives the way that enriched us from the inside out. And slowly, people stopped caring. River showed up for them day in and day out. And when the time called for it, so did I in successful financial planning and execution.

And now we run this town and do it well, without the worry of harassment and bullshit.

I won't be judged by Ember. As much as I want her, I'm not going backward. This is how we live, and she can take it or leave it.

"He won't be mad?" she asks as I begin rinsing the shampoo from her hair. I love watching the soap bubble around her feet. She's got beautiful fucking feet, and it's not something that ever made me hard until her. My lifting dick is made flaccid by the thought that hits right after; did she ever shower with my son? I'm sure they did. What a fucking stupid question. I pump the conditioner into my palms and begin rubbing it into her ends.

"That's not how trust works."

"What about Rhett? If he knew I was here, with you and his uncle, would he be mad?" she asks, her voice hovering above a whisper. It's hard to hear her through the water, but I do.

I don't want to answer that question, not honestly, at least. Not to her. Not yet. And if she leaves in a day, not ever. But I can't lie.

I bring the showerhead off the wall to the ends of her hair and begin to rinse. "The only thing I want to talk about right now is you and that tight little pussy of yours." I spin her to face me and find her eyes wide with shock, blinking against the assault of water. "It is tight, isn't it? I felt it with my tongue. It's gonna strangle my cock, isn't it?"

She places her hands on my bare chest, fingers moving over lines of definition as she traces my pecs. Her eyes never leave mine. The water scalds my back, and I push dark hair off my face, never losing sight of her. "Won't it?" I ask again, growing more feral by the second.

She nods, but it isn't good enough.

I grip her chin and tip her face up with intention. "Speak."

Her bottom lip wobbles, and her hands begin to wander, sliding up my chest and coming to rest on my shoulders. "I'm tight," she whispers, and the admission earns her a bones-deep groan from me.

"I'm gonna wash every inch of you; then I'm gonna carry you to my bed and fuck you now the way I wanted to fuck you back then." I drop a hand between us and let my fingers stroke her until her clit blooms beneath my touch.

"How," she starts, taking a break to push hair off her face, rivulets of water trailing down her velvety skin. "How did you want to fuck me? Back then?"

I grab the soap and roll it between my palms, thick lather flowing through my fingers. Kneeling, I begin washing her legs, my cock rising to my belly from the sleek discovery of her wet skin. She drops her hands to my head, sifting her fingers through my tousled hair, and the subtle gesture knocks free a tightly protected piece of me. Warmth floods my eyes and chest, and I grip her ankles as I rest my forehead against her groin. I should be washing her. But with the tender way she strokes my head, I haven't felt so cared for by a woman since my mother.

That gentle caress is my undoing.

The warmth turns to water and tears spill down my cheeks. A moment ago, I was going to fuck her, and now I'm, what? Crying on my knees before her? I shake her hands off my head, needing to escape the tender touch. Thank fuck we're in the shower because she can't distinguish my tears. Rising, I spin her to face the wall and finish washing her body.

We trade positions, and she rinses while I wash, and our eyes never leave one another. I see the girl from three years ago. But I see pain in her that wasn't there back then. And it hurts me because I know my son did that. I don't know their story yet. I know how they met, and I can guess what he needed from her. But their real story, their day-to-day, it's still a mystery at this point. And right now, I don't need to wonder.

I need to fuck and get lost. And I am fairly certain we need the same thing.

I wrap her up in a plush towel and carry her to the bed. My towel drops off my hips as I lean down, and her eyes go straight to my rigid cock.

I grip myself at the base and snatch a condom out of the drawer. The gold foil sails to the floor as I tear it open with my mouth. She watches as I roll it on, and as much as I want to fuck her bare, I know that's too far. Getting on the bed, I position myself over her. She reaches up, wrapping her fingers around my wrist, holding me tight. With one hand on my cock and the other braced against the mattress, I look at where she's holding me.

She didn't reach down and grab my cock. Instead, she grabbed my wrist. She's holding onto me in a way that screams *don't leave me*, and I hate that I'm not sure if we're on the same page.

I've wanted her and I've wanted this, but I know we can't promise her anything. We can't give her the future she likely wants because River and I vowed we'd never do this again. Not after last time.

"Open your legs, Ember."

She does, and when I feel her heels dig into my lower back, I close my eyes and savor the moment.

"Ryker," she whispers, but I don't open my eyes. "We don't have to if—"

With the head of my cock pressed to her warm, full lips, I roll my hips forward and impale her in one deep stroke.

She hisses as I fill her, her palms coming down along my shoulders with a smack. "Ryk!"

The way she shortens my name, how her warm body closes around my cock, the smell of my soap on her skin. I haven't moved yet, and I've only been inside her for a few moments, yet this is already the best sex I've ever had. I know it, I feel it on a level I've never experienced before.

Once I place my other hand near her head, all I see is her. Hovering over her face as I work my hips back and forward, fucking her in slow strokes, reaching places inside of her that no man ever has. She tells me as much, and I enjoy the wave of pride it sends washing over me.

"*Ohmygod*, that's it, that's it, holy shit," she breathes, lifting her chin to the ceiling, eyes fluttering closed. "I've never felt it so deep," she adds, heels pulling me into her as my hips pull back, hollowing her.

"Fuck me slow and deep, Ryk," she whispers, opening her eyes to gaze into mine. I'd been watching her and seeing her recognize the deeper connection we have, that does something to me. Her cheeks flush, and it's not because I'm making love to her. I think it's because we both feel that thing we aren't talking about.

That unspoken, insane, illogical, and deep-rooted connection.

I hate that I feel it with her, but I do. And when she lifts off the pillow, straining up to sink her lips into mine, I know she feels it, too. She fills my mouth with moans of pleasure and words of need and tightens around me as I give her the slow, deep fucking she craves.

"You're going to make me cum like this," she warns on a exhale, her warm, sweet breath enveloping my senses. Fucking slow isn't something I often do, nor is it something I've wanted to do. When Riv and I share a woman, we fuck senselessly and drag our partner over the edge with us.

Instead, I'm on top of her and inside her, she's got all the control. I know for sure she does when she cups her hand to my face, her cunt seizing around my cock in a heavenly rhythm, and tells me not to cum.

When I push inside of her again, the bed knicks the wall, sending a pillow topping over onto the night table. Bottles clink, one crashes against the floor, and Ember's body goes completely rigid, her eyes suddenly wide. Her fingers hold me tighter, but she's motionless, and immediately, I know she's frightened.

I put my hand on her hairline, and stare down into her eyes. "You're safe with me, Ember. I'll never hurt you." I swallow hard, finding unexpected emotion thick in my throat. I am so caught up in this woman. "We will never hurt you."

With soft kisses, I seal my promise to her lips and pull back, finding her eyes wet, but soft at the edges, no longer frozen in fear. "Are you okay?"

She nods.

"Speak, Ember. I need to know you're okay. I need to know you know I won't hurt you. We won't. Not ever."

"I believe you," she says, looking down to see where we connect. "Now... don't stop." She watches my cock disappear into her body, and I watch her, and the whole thing has me dying to blow. "Yes," she purrs, a quiver rolling through her shoulders, "yes, Ryker, yes." And then, without a shove, she falls.

Her eyes roll back as her body clenches around my length, pulling me into her so deep that not cumming becomes my sole focus. I want to watch her expression morph between seasons of pleasure; I want to look down and see myself inside of her the way she did. But all I can do is hold my cock deep inside her tight pussy and hope I don't chip a fucking tooth from how intensely I'm clenching my jaw.

When her legs soften their grip around my waist; and her feet slide away from my ass, I look down to find her in a euphoric haze, hooded eyes star-struck and a little lost, swollen lips curled to reveal the most beautiful smile.

"Now take off the condom and put your dick in my mouth," she whispers, and while I should probably ask if she's sure, find out why she wants this instead of sharing an orgasm at the same time, I do what she wants.

Jerking back, my cock slides out of her; the condom streaked with her orgasm. I run my finger across the ribbed rubber, then slide it into my mouth. I went down on her last night, and tasting her felt like a drink of water after existing without. She smiles as she watches me. I want to know what she's thinking, but right now, I have to cum.

But she stops me as I begin unrolling. "Straddle my face and let me take it off with my mouth."

I motion between us, cock bobbing with anticipation. "Isn't it you who should sit on my face?" I ask, but inside, I like that she's got a dirty little edge to her. *All good girls do.*

Her laugh is soft. "Just do it before you get soft."

I stroke myself as I stalk my way over her body, letting my cock fall against her plump bottom lip. "I don't think that's possible with you in the room."

One more smile from her and then she's straining away from the pillow, swallowing my sheathed cock until her lips brush the barbed hair on my groin. She gags, and I feel the vibration of it in my balls. A moment later, she jerks her head to the side, spitting the wad of rubber onto the mattress.

I take her hand and place it on my shaft, but she moves both to my thighs, her nails lightly tickling as she smooths them up and down. "No hands," she says, sinking back down onto my cock. The headboard creaks as I grip it, and I look down, watching her deepthroat me with ease.

And she's right; no hands were needed because a second later, my dick swells in the warm canal of her throat, pulsing and aching as my orgasm barrels through me. My sweaty palms squeal against the polished wood I'm gripping as my hips jut forward, the first shot hitting the back of her throat.

She gags a little but swallows me as I cum, taking each thick burst like a drink of water, her throat making beautiful music. When I'm done, she palms my groin and gives me a gentle shove back. I fall onto my back next to her, panting.

"Are you okay?" I ask, twisting my gaze to catch her profile. She turns to face me, too.

"I've wanted to do that for a long time."

I quirk a single eyebrow. "Wanted to tear a condom off a man with your mouth, then swallow his load?"

Her smile intensifies. "You make it sound so dirty."

"Is it not?" I ask, curious to see where the bar of kink is for her.

Shying, color floods her cheeks. "I don't know. All I know is after last night, I needed to taste you again."

I push a piece of hair off her forehead, damp with sweat. "I thought the same about you," I admit, loving how she looks cushioned in the center of my bed.

"Have you ever done that before?" I ask, motioning to the abandoned condom with my head. She surveys it for a moment, then looks back at me, wearing another shy smile.

Her head wobbles in the pillows, an attempt to say no.

"Speak," I say again, though this time with a softer inflection. Same point, though; I crave her verbal cues. Maybe part of me is afraid she'll disappear and this will all be a dream unless I can hear her and prove it's not just a hurting man's wraith.

"No," she says bashfully. "I've given head," she rolls her eyes, "obviously. But never pulled a condom off a man during sex and *savored* his cum."

Savored his cum. Jesus. I thought she was going to say let him finish in my mouth, but I guess when I replay the pornographic movie of us in my mind, she did savor every drop. Every pump of hot cum I sent to her throat, she swallowed down. She swallowed like her entire existence hinged on taking my orgasm.

"You really wanted to taste it again that badly, huh?" I question, chomping at the bit to hear her admit again that she was craving my taste.

Before she can give me the answer I want, the alarm system on the house sounds, indicating a door downstairs has been unlocked with the code and opened.

"River's back," she says, expression tense. I place a kiss on her lips, sweeping my tongue along hers to savor any saltiness left behind. She moans as I do like she's never had a man kiss her after she's swallowed him. Or maybe… Riv and I are the first ones she's swallowed.

Immediately, my brain reverts back to Rhett.

This woman in my bed is Rhett's fucking widow. And here I am, prodding her to tell me how much she likes swallowing my load. Anger surges through me, but because it's a lot harder to be mad at yourself than someone else, I get to my feet just as River opens the door.

Ember, still nude, pushes up to her elbows, clutching the sheet to her breasts. Her attention volleys between the two of us until I let the anger simmer some and can finally speak.

I meet my brother's eyes, and even though I'm not even right with myself at this moment, he reads me the way he always does. Stepping inside, he closes the door behind him and tugs off his beanie, tossing it away. Raking a hand through his messy hair, he then unzips his vest and goes to work on the buttons centering his flannel.

"You're going to give him everything he wants right now, Ember because that's what it means to be our good girl. Do you understand?" Watching him feel good will help take the edge off my mood. It always does.

Sinking into the pillows, relief softens her tight expression as she nods. I can't believe she's so comfortable with our arrangement. Most women we hook up with need clearly defined parameters and limitations before they'll even unbutton their pants.

But Ember seems not just to accept it but... *like* the way we are.

"Speak," I rasp, glowering at her because I can't glower at myself. Why did I let the emotions take over? Why did I fuck her? Why are we fucking around with her? She's off fucking limits. We *know* this.

Still, I urge my brother on.

River's belt snaps in the air as he whips it free. He shucks off his pants and undershirt and, in a matter of seconds, stands completely naked, like me.

His eyes pin Ember to the mattress as he stalks to the side of the bed. "I want that pussy, Ember, so back it up to the edge of the bed and fuck me."

She scrambles to her hands and knees, doing exactly what he says. And I stay on my side of the bed, catching her eyes as she gets in position. We look at one another as my brother rolls on a condom, then eases his body inside hers.

Her eyes close, adjusting to the fullness he gives. Riv finds his handles at her hips, pulling her back on his cock.

She moans her approval, head falling forward, the ends of her hair tickling the mattress.

"Take the condom off and cum in her mouth," I tell my brother, earning me a grin from Em. "She likes cum. Tasting it, playing with it, drinking it," I growl, using her own little dirty words against her. She wants this, so I don't know why I feel like I'm trying to punish her. It's not her fault I want her and can't have her; it's not her fault we're intertwined in the worst way.

Still, I ache to punish her. Instead, I stand back in my bedroom and watch Em slam her body against my brother, fucking his dick fast and ruthlessly. He holds her hips so she doesn't lose momentum, but even his face is in a state of awe.

"Is that right?" he groans as she bounces on him again and again. "Did you get yourself a belly full of Ryk's cum before I got here?" he asks her, knowing full well with the way she's whining and moaning that she won't answer.

"She did," I answer for her, and I find that watching her with River helps my anger subside.

Maybe we're wrong for wanting her, but at least we're in it together.

"Good, good girl," he praises, earning more pleased moans from Ember. Without warning, her body seizes and she clutches the comforter in her hands, face falling slack.

"Oh," she breathes, then doesn't utter another word as she writhes against him, pushing her ass back. Her thighs tremble as Riv takes control of her hips, holding her down deep on his dick as she rides out her orgasm.

"She's done," my brother offers as he pushes her forward, his glistening cock popping free from her cunt. He reaches for her, filling his fist with her hair, and drags her to face him.

He tears off the condom and, without warning, sinks into her mouth with a hiss.

"*Fuck!*"

She bobs once. She bobs again. Riv stops, and all I can hear is Ember's throat working overtime as she drinks him down, too. Once his grip on her hair is released and he's sliding his shaft out of her mouth, my brother and I make eye contact.

"You okay?" he asks, reaching for his clothes on the floor. As he gets dressed, I speak to him freely, realizing Ember is there but not willing to sacrifice the therapeutic benefits of talking with my brother.

"I know this isn't like *before,* but... it feels wrong." From across the room, he throws me a shirt. I lift my hand and catch it, then do it again with sweats he's pulled from a drawer. I begin dressing and listen, feeling Ember's eyes on me the entire time.

"Let her decide," my brother says, now fully dressed and helping a weary Ember off my mattress. I help him dress her, each of us taking a turn tasting her mouth. My kiss is rough and bruising, the opposite of the way I slowly fucked her. River's kiss is slow and methodical as if to promise everything's going to be okay, a far cry from the way he made her bounce on his cock a minute ago.

I face her, and the way my body struggles to stay here

and have this talk tells me it's likely the right thing to do. The hardest things always are. Maybe if I had done more challenging things with Rhett, he'd still be here.

"You wanted to know why," I hedge, bile clawing up my throat. Or maybe that's just how the truth feels, like fire and acid twisting together, punishing me with the pain I very much deserve. "You asked why Rhett didn't want to be with us in Raleigh."

She nods, her faraway expression evolving into interest. "Yeah," she says, still bobbing her head.

A quick look at River, who gives me a single nod of assurance, and I take a seat next to Ember on the bed.

If she wanted to stay, she surely won't after this.

CHAPTER ELEVEN

EMBER

"Do you like your job?" River asks me, pulling me out of my thoughts. Ryker remains silent since he provided answers to my burning questions.

"Yeah," I reply, giving my conditioned response. Because teachers never admit they don't actually like what they do. They can't. The world gets horrified and offended at the idea that someone wouldn't want to listen to a classroom full of children for seven hours a day.

The truth is? I've begun to hate it because I'd hated all of life in general. But I get summers off, and in the last few years, I've been teaching remotely, only needing to boot up and be online a handful of hours a day. It's been nice. Equally, I didn't have to use personal time on these days because we're on a winter ski break. Whatever that means. Anything past two weeks, I'll have to tap into my very limited vacation time. I already used the one day the school so graciously gives you for a funeral. Even when it's your spouse, that's all you get.

And people wonder why teachers don't want to be teachers.

River's eyes narrow, poking me ruthlessly for answers as he slides me a plate. He's made us all sandwiches, and it wasn't until he started doing so did I realize how late it already was. Nearing two in the afternoon.

"*Yeah,* doesn't sound too enthusiastic." He scratches his jaw, the sound of his blunt trimmed nails grating the rough hair making bumps rise up along my arms and neck. "How about this, if you could do anything, what would you do?"

I snort. "Oh no, I played this game before. It landed me in New York, married to an addict." I shake my head, "no way." Realizing what I've just said, I immediately look up at Ryker, who I expect to find glaring my way for such a cool, insensitive comment. Instead, his eyes are soft as he comes to rest next on the bar stool next to mine and says, "I'm sorry you dealt with him alone for three years. We know what that's like, and it had to be very, very traumatic. I wish I could take that away for you."

He dusts his hand across my lower back, clinging tightly to my hip. He pulls me to him, and I nearly choke, unprepared for such tenderness. "I really wish I could take it away for you, Ember. I do."

Blinking, my words come broken from shock, but still, I force myself to tell him the truth. "I don't." I look up at River, who is closer than he was before, at the edge of the counter. He slides his hand to me, and I place it inside his. "I wouldn't have met you two."

Despite what I now know about Ryker and River and

why Rhett wanted nothing to do with them, I'm still glad I met them. Because I understand the situation from both sides.

Years back, when Rhett was just nineteen, he'd fallen in love with an older woman. She was only in her thirties which isn't even remotely close to old, but for a nineteen-year-old, she was much older. The problem was he didn't tell his dad and uncle who he was smitten with.

Perhaps due to losing his mom, which had been explained to them from their psychiatrist, River explained that Rhett had always been secretive, jealous, and protective of his romantic crushes. Rhett had a plethora of mommy issues, and I knew that first-hand. After lashing out at a dealer or coming home swearing that someone had ripped him off, he'd melt into bed next to me, cuddling up to me, seeking my validation and support.

I gave it because I wanted him to know love through his issues and not feel utterly alone. And I gave it because I foolishly believed I'd get it back one day. Seems very fucking stupid now because I would never have fallen in love with Rhett. It was wrong from the start. But in my mind then, it made sense. That's kind of what loving someone does. It alters you from the deepest, most private part of you all the way to the surface, leaving you a person you never believed you could be.

Rhett had grown up thoroughly confused about love. Ryker explained that when Rhett expressed he'd fallen in love for the first time, he and River were so happy to finally see him happy, they encouraged it. As men living a nontraditional romantic lifestyle, they didn't think the age difference mattered.

Rhett wouldn't bring her around. While he never told his dad and uncle why, as Ryker recounted that truth, the three of us shared a knowing look. Bringing a thirty-year-old woman around two single, gorgeous, rich as fuck, town owning men? Death warrant, then and there.

But that fear was his downfall because the woman left him anyway. They dated, according to River, who took over the story when Ryker swelled with emotion, for nearly a year when she suddenly called it quits. And that was when Rhett turned to drugs. Shortly after that, he moved a couple of hours away to, according to River, "hurt and do drugs in peace." He never came home again.

"It wasn't your fault," I'd begun to say to both River and Ryker as Riv told the story. But Ryker lifted a palm; his face stretched with a melancholic expression.

He finished the story.

He told me how not long after Rhett had moved away, Ryker met a woman in town. He'd been signing contracts on a business deal when the traveling notary caught his eye. They'd made playful and flirtatious small talk, and that's when he learned that though she traveled, she'd moved to Raleigh recently.

Ryker recounted that he used her for his next deal, simply wanting to see her again. Then she came back to the house for a drink. She met Riv. And, long story short, they became a throuple.

After half a year of dating, they'd decided to contact Rhett about having dinner together. They recounted the ways they enabled him in those first precarious years. They knew they were enabling him but, as Ryker said, "we didn't know what to do, so we gave him everything in hopes he'd one day come back." They were in regular contact, so scheduling a dinner was a normal thing.

Rhett showed up, albeit high, but he came. And that's when it all really went south.

Ryker and River had been essentially living with and fucking the same woman whom Rhett dated. The same one who broke his heart. The woman who was the catalyst, the final straw, the last development before he turned to drugs.

And, River said, "I knew as soon as I looked in his eyes that he was still in love with her. And when he looked at us, I could feel his heart breaking." He brought a palm to his chest, smoothing down his sternum thoughtfully, the memory haunting him. "I think mine did, too."

"We didn't know," Ryker had said to me a handful of times. And I knew they didn't know. I believed them. Because the pain in their eyes, both of them, was so poignant and real, it couldn't be faked. The woman, on the other hand, knew exactly who Ryker and River were. Why she wanted to hurt Rhett that way wasn't made clear to me, but River made sure to add, she knew, and when they learned that, they kicked her ass to the curb immediately.

Now, long after the story was told, we sit around the fire in moderate silence. River asks me questions about my life, and maybe a day ago, that would have been relevant. Maybe I would have wanted them to get to know me. And I don't blame them for what happened with Rhett. I believe they didn't know she used to be his.

But I want to learn from my impulsivity in the past.

Rhett was impulsive. New York was just as impulsive.

As much as it feels like a higher power holding me by the neck like a mama carrying her kitten leading me to Ryker, hell, leading me to River... I have to realize not everything is a sign.

Their last relationship was tied to Rhett, and look how it ended.

I'm not theirs. Meeting Ryk in the bank that day was just... *a coincidence.*

Not fate.

These questions about who I am and what my life is like no longer feel important. And despite so much of me wanting to stay here with them—because as irrational as it is, it feels good here–I know I have to go.

Rhett is here. The service is in a few days. After that, I'm gone.

Back to the conversation at hand, I split a smile between the two of them but get up. "I'm glad I met you both. I mean that." They rise, too, looking confused and a touch irritated.

"So you know the truth, and it's different now?" Ryker asks, harboring hurt in his expression.

I press my face to my hands, unwilling to argue about any of this. "No. I don't view either of you differently." I look to River, whose head is tipped sideways as he studies me. "I don't think you did anything wrong. I just... we're all stuck in bad patterns. You guys were involved with Rhett's ex, and look how that ended. Does getting involved with another of his ex's really seem smart? Can you ever get past it? Would you ever see me as yours or would I always be his in your eyes?" My eyes drop to the floor and in the faintest whisper I add, "It wouldn't be fair, I was never his."

None of us say the thing invisibly and cruelly tethered to that statement, which is the fact that a dead man controls and influences our future regardless of what any of us may want...

"And I need to stop being so impulsive. And this," I motion two fingers between each one of us. "We hardly know one another. We share pain and," I turn just to Ryker. "A fifteen-minute trauma three years ago. Outside of that, what are we *really* gonna do? Stay together forever?" I shake my head, the reality of everything almost too wild to comprehend. "I admit, it feels like I should stay. Like this is a sign." I meet River's eyes, and my stomach clenches when I find them sad. Looking at Ryker, I discover him the same way. "But I can't make this gamble. I lost too much last time. I think we're looking for things that aren't there."

Why does that feel like a lie as opposed to a mature decision?

"I'll stay until the service, and then, yeah, I'm going back to the city." I push off the barstool and shrug off the dizziness that comes with the emotional speech. But it had to be said, no matter what I feel–this is the *right* choice.

"We've had a good time," I say with a soft smile, desperate to lighten the mood. "But we're past tense. We *have* to be."

Then I leave them, head upstairs to bed, and stare at the wall. The sun sinks into the Earth, and the light painting the bedroom wall slowly fades to dark. I've stared at the wall all day, stomach in knots.

Why does the sensible choice feel like shit?

CHAPTER TWELVE

RYKER

The last few weeks have been an utter blur.

The service was beautiful. Simple but elegant, and I don't know if it's what Rhett would have wanted, but nonetheless, it was very nice. River delivered the eulogy because I couldn't bear to hear those words in my own voice. The irony is that I still did.

People from the town swarmed the funeral home, not because Rhett was an upstanding citizen whom they'd miss very much. I never projected or put pressure on my son, but I'd be lying if I said I didn't wish all of that were true.

I wish they came to support him and not the men who own their town and likely their business. Either way, on that day, all those faces there eased the pain a tiny bit. It felt like a way of disappearing a little without even having to move. And I needed that. On the day of my son's funeral, all I wanted was to exist without interruption.

Ember looked beautiful at the service. She had her hair in a braided bun at the base of her neck, a silver heart necklace around her throat. Her dress wasn't black but rather red. Because it was Rhett's favorite color. In fact, he died wearing his red Converse. She shook hands, whispered delicate thank you's, and overall, was as gracious and kind as any widow could be.

Then she kept true to her word, and she left.

"Morning," River says, making his way into the home gym we have in our extended garage. It's pouring rain, and we can't run. So indoor workout it is. He sips from his mug, hair a fucked up mess.

I point it out because brotherly picking doesn't stop at any age. "Nice hair."

He rakes his other hand through it but doesn't take the bait. Instead, he yawns and shares the truth. "Still sleeping like shit."

I nod my head as I slide a plate on the bar, getting ready to bench press. "Same." I pause and glare at my brother, who glares right back. We've already had this talk. The day she left, we agreed we'd talk it all out one time and leave it behind.

We both want her but agree we have to let her go. After all, she wanted to go. Since then, however, neither of us can get right with our decision. Because her not being with us feels wrong.

I guess I'd hoped after Rhett was at peace, we'd grow out of our interest. That time would peel us further from the idea that fate was the thing that brought us together. Unfortunate circumstances, weird luck, and strange coincidence are all that brought us together. Or at least, that's what we'd been trying to convince ourselves of.

But no amount of talking about it changes how we feel. Feelings are fucking assholes, aren't they? They just go ahead and do whatever the fuck they please without your permission. In a loving relationship with commitment and comfort? Boom, now you're thinking of someone else. Think you're past your issues? Fuck you, that's what. Here's a handful of new ones you can't escape.

Feelings get you by the short hairs and don't let go.

And no amount of money or clout can change that.

I lie back on the leather bench, twisting my grip on the bar above. "I'm afraid she was the one," I admit as I lift the bar off the rack and slowly bring it down to my chest.

I re-rack the bar at the top, sitting up to face my brother. "I know we're not talking about it, but fuck, it's been two months. I still feel..."

"Shitty," he supplies.

I agree with a nod. "But every time I think going after her makes sense, I think about my son." River lifts his chin, and we speak without words for a moment. "We owe him this. He wouldn't want us to be with her. Not again."

He nods because, of course, he agrees. We both know what's right.

We just hate it.

CHAPTER THIRTEEN

EMBER

"And you're sure you're okay? You still just sound so... blue," mom says, her voice thick with concern. Her concern clogs my throat, and I have to speak around the emotion stuck there.

"I'm a little down still, yeah, but overall... I'm fine," I lie.

I'm not fine. And with each day that passes, I seem to get less fine. The numbing throb in the center of my chest never ceases. I bring my fist to it, eager to knead away the pulsing ache, but then numbness hits, and I can't feel a fucking thing. And I can never reach the ache.

My lack of sleep is starting to screw up my brain, making me put my phone in the freezer and a cup of coffee in my purse. My stomach's a mess–if I can eat, I eat everything in sight. And the rest of the time, everything sounds repulsive and disgusting.

And I'm so fucking tired.

I won't lie. I'm crying a ton. Daily, usually. Out of confusion and pain, worry and stress—I cry about everything.

Mom's intuition that something is going on is spot on. That's why today, rather than remotely teach my 8th-grade students, I'm going to the doctor.

I've tried taking walks, using melatonin for sleep, journaling, baths, and therapy. I've tried it all, and I feel like utter shit. Now? I want drugs. Antidepressants, here I come.

"Are you sure?" she asks for the trillionth time.

"Mom," I growl, aggravated that she won't just drop it. I should praise her for knowing me with such attentiveness, but I just want to be left alone. I want to go get meds and move on from whatever this thing I've been calling my life has been for the last three years.

Time to be the Ember I thought I could be before that smoke bomb went off in the bank.

"Okay–well, call me later, okay?"

"I will," I sigh. "Bye, mom."

"Bye, Ember."

She calls me first thing in the morning nearly every day. She's like my alarm clock, in a way. And I'd love to be a stable, happy daughter like I used to be. And I believe I'll get there. That's what today is about.

After pulling on an oversized hoodie, some jeans, and sneakers and covering my greasy hair with a baseball cap, I get on the train. A woman on the train is reading a book called *He's Always Listening,* and the way she's nodding her head along with the text bugs me. Then again, everything bugs me. A stranger liking their bullshit self-help book shouldn't irk me, but thanks to my healthy dose of depression, I'm ready to tear the book out of her hands and scream, "*it's all fucking bullshit*" in her face.

But I don't, and that's mostly because I don't have the energy. I cling to the back of the chair, watching darkness sail past the windows until it's my stop. And then I trudge through the crowd, up the stairs, and pour myself onto the concrete in the daylight. Just blocks from the office, I walk as quickly as I can in my state. But it's hard because walking feels like scaling Kilimanjaro. A normal inhale feels like I'm breathing through a straw. And when my brain grows fatigued, and I can no longer hold the mental barriers up, and I think of them, it hurts so much I think I could die from the emotional pain of it all.

I wanted to stay. I also wanted to show them I had logic and respect for Rhett. But they let me go.

And we all know *if he wants to, he will.* So if *they* wanted to, *they* would have kept me there.

"Ember Whitlock to see Dr. Pasami."

The receptionist looks warily at how I'm spilled over the counter, arms crossed, head resting on them. "Okay, have a seat," she says, wearing a concerned smile.

I fall into the seat, feeling fevered and drained, my stomach sick. In the waiting room is usually the time I get my thoughts together. Run through everything I'm going to tell my doctor, and sometimes, if I'm really anxious, I even practice my responses. Only, I don't get the chance to perfect my "I want meds" speech because the nurse calls me back almost instantly.

After taking my weight and discovering that I've lost seven pounds in the last two months, getting my blood pressure and pulse checked, the nurse leaves me sitting atop a papered table like a child. I swing my feet while I wait.

My stomach grumbles, but the last thing I feel is hungry. Everything hurts. My spine aches, the nerves behind my eyes feel like someone's twining them together with their palms, and if it were physically possible for me to be a puddle, I think I would.

The door opens after the tell-tale wrist-flicking double knock, and Dr. Pasami strides through.

"Ember, good to see you again." My palms had been so sweaty waiting that I'm glad she doesn't go for a handshake.

"What brings you in?" She asks, straddling a black leather stool, locking her ankles together once she's settled. "Everything okay?"

I blink. I almost laugh. "Well, about two months ago, my husband passed away."

Her head sways to the side, tilted in that empathetic way people do. She brings a hand to her mouth and sucks in a sharp breath. "Oh no."

I nod. I've been crying for two months straight, and now, as someone is reacting to the news of my husband's passing, I'm bone dry. God, I must look like a fucking psychopath. I opt for the truth. "Honestly, I've been crying so much; I think right now I'm just so cried out." I lift my hands in the air and shrug. "I just want to feel good. And I want to be done crying so much."

Dr. Pasami nods. "I understand." She reaches out and strokes her thin fingers up my arm, but she's cold, and I wince. "I'm sorry," she says, pulling her hand back, giving me a partial smile. She measured that smile in her head and decided that this was just the right amount of happiness to serve up against my sadness. "Doctor's curse, cold hands," she smiles again, this time allowing her lips to curl a little more, deciding her anecdote is worth it. I don't fault her; I just don't want to be here.

"I want antidepressants. I'm not gonna beat around the bush. Give me whatever happy face sliding scale quiz I need. Ask me if I'm eating and sleeping–I'm not, I'm not. Do what you need to do. But please, please, just..." I shake my head, feeling the warmth behind my eyes now. "Please help me feel better."

She nods. "Okay, okay, Ember. I can do that. But you're right; there are some things we need to do first."

Dr. Pasami goes through a battery of tests she wants to do. Some, she says, can wait until a few weeks into treatment. Others, she says, have to come now to make sure I'm safe to take the medicine she's prescribing. Apparently, it's new and strong and comes with a candy bowl of warnings, so I'm getting blood work done.

I take the happy face quiz, followed by a bunch of questions about how I'm feeling and if I'm a threat to myself or others.

I go down to the lab and get the bloodwork done, and according to the Doctor, she'll call in the prescription once she sees I'm all good. I could have my medication in a week.

I cling to that promise for dear fucking life. The idea that help is close gets me through the next six days. Then Dr. Pasami called me, and everything changed.

CHAPTER FOURTEEN

RYKER

"And let me guess, you gave him another few days?" I smirk at my brother, who stands two feet away, uncorking a bottle of red wine. I jab the steak on the cast iron with a fork and flip it. The sizzle of the meat against the iron gives me a hard-on, nearly. My mouth waters.

It's good to feel happy about something. Even if it's just a fuckin' steak. It's been weeks since River or I have felt right. And now? We're making a conscious effort to move on.

We had a date tonight.

It was fucking awful, but now we're making steaks and having wine and about to discuss exactly why River is a complete and utter fucking pushover. The beard is to hide what a soft fucker he really is, I swear.

"He paid for his daughter's last round of IVF, you know that, right?"

I can't help but grin. "I don't have a problem with letting him not pay the fucking rent at all, Riv, but I want you to admit, you're a softie."

He thumps his chest with a curled fist, puffing it out. "I'm tough."

The cork releases with a pop, and I bring the bottle to my nose, then under his.

"Good?" he asks because I'm the wine guy, and he's the beer guy. We both like the hard stuff.

I nod. "Pretty good. It'll do. And it's not like we have Grade A ribeye over here." I slide the iron pan away from the flame and turn off the burner. "Grab the horseradish."

I begin pouring wine, and Riv is digging around in the fridge like he's never fucking looked for anything in a fridge before when the doorbell echoes throughout the kitchen.

Riv straightens, holding a jar of chipotle mayonnaise.

"That's mayonnaise, not horseradish."

He sets it down on the counter. "I'll get the door."

He disappears, and I grab the correct jar from the fridge, putting the chipotle mayonnaise away. I'm certain he does this shit just to piss me off, but I never acknowledge it because that's what brothers do. Out troll each other 'til death.

River steps back into the kitchen, and his demeanor has completely shifted, face slack, nostrils flared. I can't tell if he's shocked or angry or...

"Hi, Ryker," Ember says, stepping around the corner and pushing past my brother. I don't know why but I immediately pull her into an embrace, and she does the same. Looking over her shoulder, I see pinches and pulls in the cotton of River's shirt on either side of his chest.

He hugged her, too. And she clung to him.

She loops her arms around me, palms dusting up and down my back, and she holds tight. Like I'm her beacon of light in the storm. And I'd weather anything to be her savior.

"What are you doing here?" I ask as Riv comes to stand next to me. His elbow brushes mine, and the small gesture reminds me that I'm not alone in this. However she breaks my heart today, he's here, and his heart will be breaking, too.

Her eyes are wide, but the closer I look at her, the less I think it's excitement. Hell, I don't know that there's even happiness in her right now. She seems nothing but scared. And right as my stomach clenches, Riv presses his hand to his belly.

"What's going on, Ember?" Worry strangles his voice, so I speak up.

"Ember?" We lock gazes, and her eyes search mine. I want to be her beacon, but I need to know why she's here.

She didn't want to stay.

She left.

Then she clears her throat, looks to River, then to me. Her gaze volleys between us as she says, "I'm pregnant."

Sitting around the fire, Riv and I hip to hip with Ember across from us; we wait. She hasn't said a word since we came in here to sit down. The steak sits perfectly cooked and uneaten. I couldn't give less of a fuck.

Her lip wobbles as she begins. "It's not yours," she breathes, twisting her lean fingers together in front of her, so nervous. I hate that she was afraid to tell us. I thought she knew when she left here that we wanted her to stay. Doesn't that mean she'd know we're here for her? "It's not either of yours, which, well... you were there," she wobbles her head, raising her voice playfully to lighten the suddenly somber tone. "So you know it couldn't be yours. But, just to put it out there."

"Ember," Riv says. "Take a breath." The dominant side of him can't help to order her to help herself. He wants her to feel good.

Her eyes shine, and I know she's holding back tears.

"We didn't talk about this before. It felt... private, I didn't want to tell you. Also, the thought of making Rhett's death any harder for you... I just couldn't," she says, her face so serious and unmoving that a really terrible feeling starts in my gut. My mouth gets sticky from a lack of moisture, and my pulse picks up. I know what she's going to say. Why she froze up when we had sex. *Oh God, no.*

"The day he overdosed." She looks over to River, almost for reassurance that she has the strength to keep going. He must nod or give her some cue because she looks back at me, sure of herself. And while what she's about to tell me is going to hurt, I find a sliver of solace in knowing that she finds solace in him.

That's part of being in a multi-partner relationship. Being able to find contentment and peace with all partners.

She inhales unhurried, building strength. "He raped

me." Our eyes hold on one another, and I see nothing but truth and pain. "It wasn't the first time." My heart clenches. I want to wring his neck. I want to shake him and ask him why he would do such a fucking heinous thing? We tried so hard after his mother died. Rhett got good grades. He had friends. But he always resented me for never remarrying. He wanted a mother. We wanted to give him a mother.

But life is more complicated than that. We couldn't have just found someone to be a mother and join the two of us that easily after having been with who we felt was the love of our lives. But really, we were the love of her life because her life ended. We have to love again; that's how it works. And we just... never did. Not in time to give Rhett a mother.

"He raped me often," she continues, making my chest tighten, streaks of fire shooting through. Everything hurts, and my stomach swirls, my lips tingling. I want to get sick, but I force a dry swallow and hold her gaze with focus. She deserves focus, not a breakdown.

"I'm sorry you have to know that," she whispers, and I raise my palm to stop her from apologizing, but she continues. "The first time it happened I made excuses, I told myself he didn't really mean to grab my wrist so hard. He had no idea how much strength he possessed." She wipes beneath her eyes, and the gesture twists like a knife to the heart. My child caused her this pain, and I can't take it away. More so, she deserves to tell her story, so we need to listen.

"I truly made myself believe he didn't know it was rape. That maybe the drugs clouded his perception, maybe his mind was racing so quickly, his thoughts so scrambled, that he himself wasn't aware of his actions." More tears, more blotting, more twisting of the knife. "One time turned to many. I tried fighting. I tried pushing him off, crying out for help." She shakes her head, delicate tears dropping down to her chest, darkening the fabric of her sweatshirt. "It only ever made things worse. So I learned to focus on something, a noise, a color, an object. And just... try to disappear. Try to tune him out. Try to tell myself that tomorrow is the day. Tomorrow is the day I'd leave."

She tempers her gaze, her expression no longer intense but merely... sad. "Tomorrow always came, but I never left. He always convinced me that he needed me, that he couldn't survive without me. The worse his addiction got, the more true that was. I was ashamed and embarrassed to admit this to my mom. I hid it from my very few friends and..." She shakes her head, as if attempting to free herself from the dark memories. "The day I told him I wanted a divorce, was the day he passed." A sob wracks her chest as she says, "I'm sorry. I'm sorry you have to know this about him."

"Don't, Ember. Don't you fucking apologize for anything." River rests his palm on my knee. "We knew Rhett. Don't forget." He slides his palm an inch lower consolingly and gives my leg a pat. "We loved him, but we knew he was troubled." He takes his hand back, and I notice that Ember watches the exchange. "We didn't know this side of him. And I speak for us both when I say, I'm so fucking sorry."

"Are you okay?" I ask, not sure if she's just now understanding the true parameters of things. Riv and I are a package deal, and we share one goal: the same woman. Nothing more.

She licks her lips. "I'm okay. But I was worried you'd

be–" She stops and shakes her head as if she's scolding herself. "I mean, I don't know. I don't know what I thought. I don't know why I'm here. I got the news this morning and literally took a flight here. The first one. I didn't even bring anything." She lifts her arms as if to show us she comes with nothing. "I took a Wheel Get You here from the train station, which I took after another rideshare from the airport."

"Jesus," I curse, "I wish you would have called us. I would have gotten you. Riv would have gotten you. Fuck, I would've sent a goddamn car, even."

She shakes her head. "I wasn't... I didn't... I couldn't think."

I hate that I have to ask this, but after the way we parted, I feel I'm owed an answer. "Why are you here, Ember?" I dip my head toward River. "You didn't want this. You left us."

She rises, indignant and angry. "Why didn't you ask me to stay? You were supposed to ask me to stay!" She shakes her head, strands breaking free from the loose braid she wears over her shoulder. "*Both of you* should have asked me to stay." She stands straight, folding her arms over her chest. "Why do you *think* I'm here?"

I rise and enter her personal space, hovering just an inch from her lips. She smells like cinnamon and vanilla, and my dick thickens knowing she's back. *She's pregnant.* And she's here *for us.* "I think you were scared, and the first thing you thought of was us." I grab her chin and yank her lips to mine for a scorching kiss. "You knew you'd feel better if you came here, no matter what happened." I kiss her again, and River takes a mouthful of her neck. "You missed us."

Then we just embrace. Our kiss falls away and River loops his arms around her and me, too. She cries some but then just breathes us in, taking deep pulls and slow exhales. When she's steady, Riv and I sit around her on the couch.

"Let's take a bath and talk, okay?" I propose, knowing what warm water does for the soul.

She nods, and we're on our feet, Riv carrying Ember the entire way to his room.

CHAPTER FIFTEEN

EMBER

River's chest cradles me as I nestle against him with my back and legs outstretched. Across the tub is Ryker, who rubs my feet beneath the thick layer of bubbles suffocating the surface.

The phone call from Dr. Pasami notifying me that I couldn't take the antidepressants because I'm pregnant suddenly seems like the best thing ever.

I don't know how I'll raise the baby, but the news brought me back to them, and this is so strangely and beautifully just where I need to be.

"After the bank, I was more terrified than before," I begin, hoping to explain exactly where my head was at when I married Rhett. Because it takes two people to make a broken relationship, and while I may not have been an addict, I was still part of the problem.

Ryker kneads my foot, his large hands cradling and massaging me with ease. It's the comfort I need.

"I tried to tell myself that sizzle in my belly meant nothing. What I felt when you put your hand on mine that day... I swore it was meaningless, just the adrenaline. The moment. My hormones. It wasn't real." Riv's bearded chin drops to my shoulder as he wraps his arms around me, grabbing his wrist to lock me securely against him.

Ryker works on my ankle, smoothing his fingertips up my calves. His eyes stay on mine. In his brother's arms, him across from me, the crippling and exhaustive pain I felt when I woke up this morning is gone.

"I convinced myself you couldn't possibly have felt what I did. That even though I couldn't have it with you, *a stranger*, it had to exist out there. So I ran, I chased that feeling, I hunted." I shake my head, still frustrated by my own rationale at the time. "I needed to capture that raw burn I felt in my bones when you paid me attention. I needed to know that it existed beyond that bank floor."

Ryker switches to my other foot, and River releases his draped arm hug to scoop handfuls of warm, bubbly water, pouring it around my collarbone to keep me wet and warm.

"Then I met him. I met Rhett."

Ryker stops massaging my calf but holds onto my leg all the same.

"I had a mix-up at Grand Central, and I was... upset. Flustered. I dropped my wallet, everything scattered, and he was there, chasing down my credit cards with greasy strands of dark hair covering his face." I picture it in my mind, and I smile a little because even though it was a fractured dynamic, meeting him *did* feel so magical.

"His eyes captured me. And his lopsided smile felt... *familiar*. The sharp jaw... he reminded me of you. Which I now know is because... he was part of you."

We sit with that information for a long minute; the quiet bubbles seem to pop loudly in our new silence.

I earn their focus by speaking again. "But I was falling face first into him. There was no stopping me. He reminded me *of you just enough* while at the same time being a new chapter in my story. I went with it."

"When did you know?" River asks from over my shoulder, his voice a raspy rumble.

"Know he was wrong for me or that he had a drug problem?" I clarify, trying to sort out if the answers to those questions are even different. I don't think they are.

"A few days." I swallow, thickness forming at the base of my throat, making this next part all that much more difficult. But if the three of us are to have a functional relationship, I can't hold any of it in. "The second time we... had sex." Part of me wanted to say *made love,* but that wouldn't be true, and I've been truthful all along. Why stop now? We didn't make love, he fucked me. I took an orgasm from him, and he had an orgasm of his own. We smashed our bodies together to grab that high, the only one we're all slaves to, the ultimate drug of release through physical intimacy.

"I knew then, he was different, not present." I say. That memory may not be as unsavory as others I have of Rhett, but they don't need to know the details. Details that paint a picture that's been already emblazoned in both of their minds. "And I asked him."

"That was brave," Ryker states, tipping his head against

the rolled towel behind him. River wraps his arms around me again, pressing his palms to my thighs.

Sandwiched between them after being miserable for the last few months... I know I should have stabilized my mental health on my own. But I tried. And I was on my very last option seeing Dr. Pasami that morning.

It just so happens now that I'm here–even through the tough talks we have ahead–I already feel so much lighter. Their presence projects a bubble of weightlessness, and when I'm in it, I'm floating. High like Rhett used to be.

Or I'm like a moon caught in their orbit, their gravity stabilizing me. Maybe it's both.

I wish Rhett and I could have been what we each needed. We might have saved each other.

We were both starved for something, and neither of us knew what. And trying to find it together... led him to death and me to happiness. It's the cruel twist of fate.

"It doesn't feel brave now, and it really didn't feel brave then." I swirl bubbles with my finger and avoid Ryker's eyes. "I keep thinking that we found each other on purpose, so I could come back to you and meet you," I say softly, casting a glance up at River behind me. "But the truth is, I feel the same guilt that you two do. I keep thinking if I could have just loved him and if he could have just fallen in love with me, then maybe he'd have made it. Maybe love could've been his saving grace."

River's arms tighten, and his fingers delve into my thighs. His thoughtful rumble vibrates through my chest from behind. "That's a beautiful sentiment, Ember, but it's a fallacy. Love can save people, yes, but drug addiction is a disease. Love doesn't cure diseases. Don't romanticize the past to find a way to carry guilt. You have nothing to feel guilty about."

Ryker nods along with his brother's words, and I wonder if they always agree on everything.

"Do you two always see things the same way?"

Just then, River's hand slides inside my thigh, his thumb driving up my center, finding my clit. The pad of his thumb circles me as I keep my eyes on Ryker.

"Our hearts always align." His eyes lock with mine, preparing me for something more. "We shared Rhett's mother, in hearts, bodies, and minds."

I didn't know for sure, but figured as much, but hearing it reassures me. Tells me they know how to handle a woman, together, forever.

I swallow hard, my pulse hammering, and with River's finger softly strumming at my clit, making my body sing a beautiful song. I moan, spreading my legs, causing the water to slosh. Bubbles disperse, and Ryker reaches out, using two fingers to slowly enter me as his brother strokes.

"Thank you for telling us about Rhett. About the two of you," he says, curling his fingers inside me, making my legs go numb from pleasure. "Tonight, no more talking."

My throat is sticky and dry when I ask, "no?"

River grunts from behind me, his thumb continuing the sizzling pattern of rubbing me hard a few times, then circling me slowly. My orgasm is building, and a trail of heat climbs up my spine as it does.

"No," Ryker says. "You're thin, you look exhausted, and you just got life-changing news. Let us take care of you tonight."

"I didn't come here for that," I argue, though, in truth, I

don't know why I came here. I just knew here was where I had to be. "But I want it. I want you both," I say, my heart beat thundering at my bold admission.

I should feel like a whore, right? Pregnant with my dead husband's baby, in a bathtub with his father and uncle, getting finger fucked and played with. And maybe I am a whore. But right now, I'm their whore.

But I've never felt this sought after, this desired, this full of passion and promise.

"Turn your brain off, and give yourself to us tonight," River croons from over my shoulder.

Ryker's dark eyes hold mine, and in them, I see the simple answer. "Okay."

In a matter of seconds, he pulls away, sliding his fingers out of me to reach down and pull the white plug from the drain. River, who's almost stroked me to orgasm, takes his hand away, too. Hooking his hands under my armpits, he rises and brings me with him. Dizziness swims through my consciousness, and I don't know if it's the warmth of the water, the news, or the evening, but I'm appreciative of them as River holds me and Ryker dries me before wrapping me in a plush towel.

While River towels off, Ryker sits me on the edge of the tub, dragging a comb through my hair. Delicately, he works through tangles as River kneels before me, smoothing palmfuls of creamy lotion up my legs.

The brothers share hushed plans, but I'm unable to focus on anything but the stark contrast between this moment and another.

Dragging Rhett to bed after a four-day bender that first year of marriage. I'd run a wet rag through his hair–it was so thick with grease, I couldn't stand it. He'd laid in an unconscious stupor as I alternated smoothing a rag of fresh water over his head with pulling a comb through, trying to clean him up because he hadn't cared for himself in so long.

Riv, whose hair rests atop his shoulders, smooths oil in his palms before coating the ends of my damp hair. He winks. "Don't tell anyone I know about hair care; I'll deny it."

My lips curl into a smile as Ryker presents his upturned palm to me. I slide my hand into his, and he hoists me to his chest, my legs looping his waist naturally like we've done this so many times before.

When Ryker lowers me to his bed, shadows blanketing the three of us, I use the lack of light to my benefit, finding braveness in the anonymity of darkness. "How have you two been? The last two months?" I push my way up the bed, resting my back against the headboard, my eyes still struggling to adjust to the darkness. "I'm so selfish; I haven't even asked. It's been all about me."

The bed dips beside me and again on the other side. A moment later, four warm hands palm me everywhere. They're touching my breasts, palms sliding over my hips, pressing to my low belly, touching my pussy, discovering the curve of my neck.

As my eyes fall closed from the immediate pleasure and relief their touches bring, Ryker rasps an answer in my ear. "All we've done is breathe and miss *you*."

River's voice is quiet, contrasting my overwhelmed heart's loud and chaotic beat. "We've been fucking miserable without you."

Then River's mouth is on my breast, sucking my nipple

hard, his moans of pleasure seeping into me, making my veins buzz with life.

Ryker's hand falls across my belly as his lips skate over mine. "A part of us is growing in you," he says before stealing a passionate, near feral kiss from me. When he pulls away, I want his lips back immediately, but I can't move because River's mouth, suckling at my breast, has me rooted to the mattress.

"Let us take care of you," River says around a mouthful of my breast. I've never had my breasts played with like this. I've never been sucked as if I'm providing sustenance, but when they put their mouths on me, I feel like a fucking queen. I command their attention, earn their mouths, and own their hearts.

Do I?

I certainly feel, in the few hours I've been back, that I'm theirs. But I refuse to get lost in semantics while I'm being worshiped and cherished. I tip my head back, letting the down pillows swallow my thoughts, and succumb to their touches.

"Let us make you feel better," River says, opening his mouth to reveal my hard, wet nipple. His tongue slides up my chest, along the column of my throat, then traces my jaw before our mouths collide. As his tongue dances with mine, Ryker ducks beneath the sheet, reappearing between my legs.

"Prop her head up so she can watch," Ryker says to his brother, who uses one strong arm to shove a pillow beneath my head as I lift. Looking down to see my knees open, a corded back and a full head of luscious dark hair between my legs, the familiar tightness from low in my belly begins.

Riv keeps a hand over my abdomen as he sucks my earlobe into his mouth, filling my brain with sinful promises as I watch his brother eat me out.

"He's gonna suck your clit until your legs shake and your orgasm is all over his face, you know that, right? You know that's how we take care of good girls in this house. We make them cum, a lot, and always first."

A deep low humming parts my lips, and I realize I'm trembling now. Their hands are so big, their touch so erotic and comforting— they're my fix, my permanent addiction.

"There you go," Ryker nudges my clit with his nose as he strokes his tongue in and out of my wet warmth. "When it starts to feel really good, you let me have it, baby, okay?"

I don't know what he means. I don't understand words right now. All I can feel is the earth shattering pleasure in my cunt and the torturous graze of Riv's beard against my sweaty, soft skin. My knees feel wobbly, my back arches from the bed on its own, and my toes curl, dragging the sheet with them.

"Ryker," I breathe as the first wave of orgasm crashes down, disorienting me. Up is down, hot is cold, the room is silent, but my ears are pounding. Everything feels good and intense and warm and wet and– "*there,*" Ryker moans, pressing kisses to my hardened, swollen clit, now using two fingers inside of me. "You've been saving that for us, haven't you?"

River speaks again, grinding his thick cock against my hip. "Good girl, giving us your orgasms."

Looking down, I see Ryker rise to his knees, his swollen cock thick with excitement as he strokes. "Do you want me to put a condom on?"

I find his eyes in the haze. I don't want to ask this, not in the heat of the moment. But I am pregnant. I have another life to consider. I have to be responsible. "Are you... have you both been tested?"

"We're clean. We wouldn't do anything to put you or the baby at risk," River says as Ryker lifts his chin, his dark eyes holding me captive as he strokes.

The baby. *They're thinking of my baby.*

Rhett wouldn't have thought of me or put me first. He wasn't capable, and I don't hold that against him. But I also don't deny that this is the kind of relationship I've been searching for. A man who knows what holds me back, a partner who senses what I need.

"Then fuck me, already. Take me, make me yours."

Ryker growls, and River thrusts his cock against me. I reach down and find it, wrapping my fingers around the steel. At the same time, Ryker aligns the reddened crown of his cock at my entrance. "I'm gonna make you feel so good my little vixen; you're gonna cum on my cock, aren't you Em?" He sinks inside, the singular slow stroke making my toes curl. The way he fills me makes me burn, but deliciously so.

I nod.

River takes a bite of my shoulder. "Speak."

"Yes," I rasp, sounding desperate, realizing I *am* desperate. I want to be fucked hard, I want to cum again, I want to cum for *both* of them, and I want both of them to cum *for* me, too. Reality seems to drift away when I'm on my back for them, and I cling to that magical ability they have because it is such a fucking gift. "Make me cum," I moan, "make me cum. Please."

"Shh," Ryker soothes as he pulls out, only to sink his fat cock inside me again, this time even slower. He feeds me his erection an inch at a time as my legs shake and my cunt spasms, starved for the fullness he brings. "We're gonna make you cum. I'm gonna leave you wet and warm for Riv. That's how you like her, right, brother? Freshly fucked, swollen and full of cum."

Riv's teeth sink into my flesh again, only this time, I'm so wildly turned on that I have no idea if he's biting my shoulder, neck, or even my breast. My head swims with pleasure as Ryker fucks me, alternating between torturously slow and then quick strokes, overwhelming me in the best ways.

He drops a hand to his groin, touching himself where he's inside me. I've never had a man do that, and it feels like worship, like awe.

"I love the way I feel when I'm inside you, Ember," he purrs, our eyes holding each other's gaze in the moonlight. Then his thumb lands on my clit, and a sharp gasp leaves my lips. River's mouth returns to my nipple, and he squeezes my breast as he sucks me.

My clit blooms beneath his touch, and after a few more strokes, my spine curls, my breath seizes, and I cum. Ryker's cock swells, and my cunt pulses all around him, responding to his girth and length, cumming so hard my vision blurs. His cum floods my core in fiery streaks, his groans of sated bliss triggering a chain reaction of bumps along my flesh. The feeling of him finding his ultimate pleasure inside me spurs me to cum harder, and my body attempts to flail.

River keeps me from folding in half as the intense pleasure whips through me like an untethered kite kissing the wind. When he lets off my shoulders and steals his mouth from my flesh, there's rustling and the bed shifts, but I'm too busy floating to notice.

When Ryker's voice is in my ear, my eyes pop open, and I see River between my knees, draping my calves over his shoulders. I look down to spot the shining head of him, nearly purple with need, pressing into my center. He roars as he sinks inside, discovering the release his brother left inside me.

"I left you full," Ryk whispers, his tongue traversing my collarbone, before dipping down to explore the sweaty valley of flesh between my breasts. "That's how he likes it. Dripping," Ryker's voice melts against me, flanking me with comfort and warmth.

River fucks me rougher than Ryker, pumping his hips between my spread legs as the blood drains from his knuckles, his grip on my thighs painful and tight. But it's a good pain that embodies possession and need.

These men *want* me, and I know now with all certainty, as rivulets of cum slide down the split of my ass, Riv fucking me hard and grueling, that *I want them, too.*

Not just for tonight.

"*Fuuck*, Ember. You're holding my cum so good and taking my cock so well," Riv breathes as he slides his hands up to my knees, giving my thighs a break from his unyielding grip.

Ryker's mouth seals over my nipple, and when he gives the pebbled tip a soft bite, I cry out.

"*Ohmygod*, yes, please, more, more, more," I plea, begging both of them to give me everything.

"I'm gonna give you more," River warns, the slick of his

groin against mine making me clench my ass. It feels so fucking good; I feel so weightless.

"You want more, don't you? I can feel that little cunt *milking* me," River's dirty talk is doing *nothing* to stave off the third orgasm, which now barrels up my exhausted legs, swirling in my center.

Ryker pops off my nipple long enough to look up at me with love-sick eyes and swollen parted lips. *"Drain him,"* he says, and the two filthy words send me flying over the edge to orgasm.

As I cum, Rykers' hand moves to my clit and without mercy reignites my orgasm, refusing to allow it to fade. It's too much. It's not enough. It's like nothing I've ever experienced.

River slams into me, making the bedframe cry with fatigue as he howls like an animal, *"fuck, fuck, fuck!"* He ceases motion as explosions of light fire around my brain, my orgasm strangling my ability to breathe and think. I slap my palm into the mattress, moaning, River sucking my nipple with such delicate intensity that my breast throbs the same way my clit does.

I do milk River. I spasm around him in unpredictable bursts, loving the way his cum spears through me in urgent, hot streaks. Ryker's fingers are unrelenting and the spasms change, they evolve. Instead of the overwhelming urge to clench, to keep their cum in me, my pussy has other ideas. I cum harder than I've ever experienced. Warmth rushes from my body, between my legs, on River's cock. I blink, struggling to look down, trying to understand... "Fuck, that's right Em, gush for me. Gush all over my cock."

I'm still trembling from the intensity when River slowly

slides out of me, enthralled by our combined releases. He presses a towel between my legs to absorb what I can't. To absorb *us*.

The thought is so vulnerable and romantic. I can't make a baby with these men; I already have a life growing inside me. But the idea they can freely empty themselves into me, to be their vessel for release and life—it's an addictive high.

It's not drugs, but I do understand Rhett a little better. Because I'd do anything to feel this ethereal perfection again and again, I'd sell my soul for it, really.

Ryker stays by my side, carefully pushing hair off my face before pressing a soft kiss to my lips, taking his time to explore my tongue with his. "He'll get you cleaned up, we'll get you some clothes, and then you need to eat."

I press my hand to my belly, not ready to move, afraid I'll break the spell if I do. But River returns, cleaning me up with warm terry cloth and praise.

"You did good, but I'm not surprised," he says, wearing a crooked, sated grin. "You're a very good fucking girl, Ember."

Ryker groans his agreement into my ear, and then they lift me. Arms behind my back, I find myself sitting as they smooth my hair and swing my legs off the bed.

I swat Ryker away playfully. "I can get out of bed."

Though I'm teasing, they both still and share a glance. "You look like you've been suffering for the last two months," Ryker says, brow furrowed with frustration. "Taking care of you now that you're back is not a choice."

Ryker disappears, leaving River at my feet, pulling thick tube socks up my calves. He squeezes each foot after, smoothing his thick fingers up the remaining bare skin of my calves.

"We missed you," he offers softly, not in a secretive way but more so, as if he knows we're on the cusp of a big talk and doesn't want to spoil anything without his brother.

That's a loyalty I can get behind.

When Ryker returns, he's got a stack of silk in his palm, a washed-out lilac color, with department store tags hanging down.

"They're brand new." He outstretches a hand to me, and I stand, taking them with both hands. I don't think about how these were already here, that I've only been here twelve hours, and they did not have time to order or pick up anything specific.

Those were for someone else.

As bitter as that thought tastes, I smile and raise my arms. Ryker slips the silk over my head after taking it from my hands. River kneels again, and I balance a palm on his shoulder as I step into the pants.

The three of us walk slowly in a line down the stairs, Ryker behind me, keeping his fingertips out toward my back in the event I fall or become unsteady. It's just an extended hand—fingertips brushing my back—but the show of support floods me with a warm, fuzzy feeling.

They have me take a seat at the kitchen island, and they begin pulling items from the fridge and cupboards. At some point, they pulled on sweats—both wearing black. River wears a faded henley while Ryker remains shirtless. I watch them move around the kitchen, never colliding in the space, even when they're perpetually moving.

Ryker's body looks like it's chiseled from granite, and

while River is clothed, his is the same. They even groom their bodies the same, too. Physically, they're different in their styles. Ryker is a business professional sporting a normally clean-shaved jaw and shiny, coiffed hair. River is the man on the ground floor, donning a beard and flannels. They share the same pair of intoxicating dark green eyes.

They give me water and sexy smiles, then a mug of coffee comes from Ryker as River smooths a napkin across my nap. I hydrate and watch them cook, working in beautiful and unspoken synchronicity, making my heart swell. I hate that Rhett is gone from their lives, but it warms me to know they've nurtured their brotherly bond and have such a connection.

After they've prepared way too much food, they make me a few dishes and sit around me with their own bowls of food.

I lift the edge of one of the plates. "I can't eat all of this," I protest, staring at the medium-well-cooked rib eye, the baked potato, and the buttery string beans. River grins, and I long to drag my fingers through his mountain man beard.

"I'd be happy with a few bites. But you gotta eat. You're too thin."

From the other side of me, Ryker slides a bowl nearer to me. Inside are steel cut oats with fresh raspberries, granola, and maple drizzle. It looks amazing, and the maple smells even better.

"In case red meat didn't sound right," he says, sliding a spoon into the mixture. My eyes widen, and my stomach audibly roars.

River laughs, sliding the steak toward him. "I guess that solves it. She wants breakfast for dinner."

I look at the green clock glowing from the oven. It's nearly two in the morning. "Technically," I argue playfully, "it *is* breakfast. Just very early."

"Eat," Ryker advises as he reaches across me to swipe a bite of green beans from River.

"Get your belly full, then it's back to bed," River says.

"I thought we'd talk," I reply, thinking we were on the cusp of a serious "here's what we're going to do" talk. Disappointment weighs on me.

Ryker's smile is the reassurance I need. "We will. Once you're full of food and sleep. We want your mind right."

River scoops a bite of oats and fruit, bringing it to my mouth. "Now fill up."

Even though I'm still not hungry, I eat every bite and fall asleep easily when they guide me back to Ryker's bed. The idea of having a serious talk with them about our future is all the motivation I need.

CHAPTER SIXTEEN

RYKER

"We agreed we wouldn't do that again. We wouldn't go there again," I remind my brother, with less than half a heart. And he knows it.

"I realize that. But are we going to address all the ways this *isn't* the same?" River's voice wanders, and I know he isn't pointedly thinking *'because Rhett's dead now'* but I can't help but tense at his statement.

We did say we'd never get involved with anyone formerly involved with Rhett. It destroyed him before and we agreed we'd never do that again.

"We didn't know she was his, Ryk. Don't rewrite us as villains for no reason." He shoves his hands in his pockets, staring off into the foggy green pasture before us. We took our run outside this morning and decided staying out here for a talk was the best place. "We didn't know. He never brought her around."

"Same for Ember," I argue, even though I know what my brother is saying. The woman we dated whom Rhett had loved—we never even knew her name when she was his. It was a situation that came from spontaneity and coincidence, not malice. He never saw it that way, which hurt.

"Brother," River says, hanging onto the r, drawing it out so that he doesn't have to say, "*it's not the same and you know it.*" I know it's not the same. He doesn't need to say it.

"I know. I know it's not the same." I stare off into the foliage, noticing how even through the fog the green is vibrant and rich. A few days ago, after we ran, we stood in this very same place, and I made none of these observations. In fact, I believe I even had a moment where I cursed this property—why do two single middle-aged men need all of this if they aren't going to fill it with life? And now, all I can feel is the beautiful, expectant possibility this estate holds now that we have a future.

Do we?

I face my brother. "Is *it* there? The beginning of *it*?" He knows exactly what I'm asking. If *it* isn't there for one of us, we don't go forward with a relationship. We both need to feel it. The spark, the embers of love that need to be fucked and nurtured to bloom into tall, all-encompassing flames. If that feeling isn't there, we call it quits.

I know he feels it. I know he does because I watched him almost lose it a few times while he fucked her. River held tight to his control, only orgasming after her, but I saw the struggle. And that's always a sign for him. His heart is directly connected to his cock.

He faces me. "Yes."

With relief, I clap my hand down on his shoulder. "Me too."

Then we stare forward, huffing out white clouds of breath that linger in front of us.

"It's Rhett's baby she's carrying. And now that he's gone, I view that baby as *ours*. We're their only blood left, aside from Ember," I tell him, having worked all of this out as I lay awake this morning, waiting for the alarm to sound for our run.

"I agree," River says.

"I knew you would."

More silence as we think, because whatever we decide, there's no going back. You can't send away a pregnant woman and later change your mind. Likewise, you can't invite her to be part of your life only to change your mind down the road. That's not fair to anyone, especially the child she's going to be raising.

It's all in, or it's nothing, and that's why we're standing amidst the cool fog, sucking in the silence, churning out decisions. They need to be made, and emotions and lives are at stake; we need to make a choice and move forward.

"Does it bother you that I met her first and that we didn't meet her together?" I ask, and he knows I'll only ask this once, and because of it, I can trust his answer to be honest. We are always honest with each other.

"Not at all." He turns to face me again, this time yanking his hand out of his pocket, pulling it down his beard and pinching the coarse hair. "Is it strange to say she feels like she's already ours?"

My chest hollows as I exhale with relief. "No, I had the

same feeling. And I felt it before I knew she was carrying Rhett's child. I felt it at the bank that day. This sense that something monumental shifted. Like meeting her was going to change our lives. And it has."

"Rhett raped her," River says, his voice husky. "Are we going to talk about that?"

I close my eyes and let the cold nip my cheeks and nose. "We get her therapy. The best. Even if that means we gotta drive her into Oakcreek to see our guy. We do it."

River nods. "I agree. She needs professional healing from that trauma, and fuckin' her senseless and treating her like a queen isn't enough."

"I agree. But we do that, too, and we make all efforts to be the best we can for her."

River is quiet for a moment, and when he clears his throat, anticipation throttles my heart, making it beat like crazy. "She will want a legal commitment. For herself and the baby."

I palm my chest, everything nervous and achy. I'm falling for Ember, and I know my brother is, too. But what we're proposing is offering her a full life *before* we've officially swapped I love you's, before we've done the dating and the sleepovers. We're skipping the marathon to go straight to the finish line, but River's right; that's what she'll need because of her state.

Rhett took from her. It's our duty now to *give* her as much as we can.

"I would give it. Would you?" I ask.

"I would."

We face one another and shake hands. "We need to talk to her this morning. She looked like she lost weight. She looked unwell. I want her here with us as soon as possible."

River tugs the zipper on his vest up, covering the bottom of his beard. "If she needs to go back and get her stuff, I'll go with her."

I nod. "We need to talk to her. But before that, what do we offer her?"

As we discovered early on that we did best in a shared relationship, we laid ground rules. One of us would legally be a husband and the other would father the first child. Because of the copious amounts of shared and unprotected sex, only the first child would be a guarantee. After that, either of us could father a child, could breed our woman. As for the marriage, after five years, we could legally rotate. Or bind together in other ways.

River taps his chest. "I want to father a child."

I meet his gaze and find his eyes pinched with seriousness. "And I won't take that opportunity away from you again, but I'd like to experience it while my guys are still swimming."

I look down at my hand, outstretching my fingers to survey them. Ringless, all of them. "I'd love to wear the ring," I admit. River outstretches his hand to me again, and we shake.

"Now, the hard part. Convincing her to tie her ship to *two* buoys forever."

I roll out my neck as I turn around, seeing the house on the far horizon. River does the same and begins jogging, so I do too.

We head toward the house as he says, "Let's give her

some time. Convince her to stay here but not propose all this shit right away. She needs some time."

Panting, I agree with him. "Time," I say, "I'm on board."

I only hope she is, and based on the fact that River doesn't say another word on the jog home, he's hoping, too.

CHAPTER SEVENTEEN

EMBER

Smoothing lotion up my forearms, I get lost in my reflection.

My hair shines, my complexion is more akin to a sun goddess than a morning-sick pregnant widow, and the room surrounding me? *Massive.* No detail is left astray; linens complementing the wall color, drapes hang ceiling to floor, windows everywhere, crown molding, gold trim accenting the furniture, overstuffed decorative pillows— it's like a dream.

This was Rhett's reality to avoid. And now it's mine to have.

The night I came here after they put me to bed, I slept sixteen hours.

Sixteen.

And when I awoke, I felt like a new person. Even with so

many unanswered questions hanging above me, I felt so good.

That was a sign. And more good signs were to follow.

Ryker and River sat me down at a dining room table–a room of their house I'd yet to explore–and fed me while telling me it was my choice to leave but that they'd like me to stay.

And quit my job.

They'd said they would understand if I didn't want to, and they'd respect it. Or if I wanted to continue teaching, either remotely or in person, they'd arrange for me to do so in Raleigh. They preferred, however, that I spend the pregnancy taking care of myself, healing myself from all that had happened in the last three years.

Therapy was a must, they'd said while reassuring me that they, too, had been in therapy a handful of years as they dealt with Rhett's addiction. And treating myself to naps, walks, good foods, laughter, and essentially, anything and everything to make my mental health flourish.

Once when I'd been so fucking depressed I could hardly get out of bed, Rhett had advised me to get a drink with friends. That alcohol and loud music would cure me of my funk.

He was my funk, and anything short of admitting that was just a poorly executed band-aid.

To be offered everything I need and more now from the man who absurdly captured my heart on a bank floor and his identical fucking twin, no less–it feels like a dream.

I roll color onto my lips and rub them together. Finger-combing my waves, I turn sideways, analyzing my profile.

Below my waist, a small bump has emerged. I smooth my palms over it, and my chest tightens in response.

I never dreamed of being a mom because my sights were so set on love and exploration, discovering a slice of this vast world that I could call my own. Finding a man to love me with his whole heart. I never saw beyond those things.

Rhett's whole heart wasn't available, and if it was, I don't know that he would have given it to me anyway. I saw Ryker in him that day we met, and he saw hope in me. Hope for change, to forget... whatever it was; we found each other at the imperfectly perfect time.

Whether I asked for it or not, I am going to be a mother. And the security the Ryker and River have wrapped me in the last few weeks has gotten me excited. I finally feel like I'm where I belong, with not one man who wants me but *two*. And two who I'd give my whole self to in return.

The only thing I worry about now is... can I do this? Can I be in a relationship with two?

I don't care that they're brothers. Fuck, I find their relationship to be one of the things I like about them the most. Their undying loyalty and ultimate devotion—it's beautiful.

But in truth, what would I have thought about a situation like mine a few months ago? I probably would have thought it was weird, maybe even gross. I would have judged it, that I'm sure of.

I don't care what people think. I stopped caring the last time Rhett raped me, and I packed my bag. It was at that point I realized the only opinion I cared about was mine, and the longer I went without honoring my own feelings, the longer I'd be stuck in misery.

I don't care about the public judging me or us.

But my mom.

I drape my hand on my chest, the tips of my fingers connecting with the silver heart looping my neck. I always wear this necklace she gave me, and as I put it on this morning, I thought of her.

I don't need her approval, but I'd love her support. It would strengthen me in places that only a mother's love can provide.

Switching the lights off, I head downstairs, where Ryker and River are waiting for me. We're all in sweats—coming here with no clothes had me doing an Amazon order of essentials. When the packages came, Ryker grew frustrated that I'd paid for my own things. River explained that when they said they wanted me to get well and focus on me, that meant giving up all stresses, including financial ones.

So this afternoon, we're going shopping. As winter gains momentum, the limited items purchased from Amazon just aren't cutting it. I need boots for the snow, a coat, and honestly, so much more.

But before then, we're having a *talk*.

It's been two months since I showed up on their doorstep. They asked me to stay, and because I needed no convincing, I said yes.

Now, as my urges drive me to nest and make a home, I've initiated a more serious conversation, telling Ryk and Riv that after my morning shower, we need to have a meeting.

Antsy and nervous looking, I greet them each with a kiss on the cheek before taking what has become my usual spot between them.

"You look beautiful this morning," Ryker says, sliding

me the herbal tea we agreed I should drink. I miss coffee, but the desire to do everything right by this baby has overridden any bad habits I was hanging onto.

"Glowing," River adds, bringing me a piece of toast from the toaster.

I take a sip, too nervous to talk.

"Ember, did you want to shop for the baby today?" Ryker asks, smoothing his hand down my spine to bring me comfort. Since I've been here, they've paid such close attention to me–closer than I feel I deserve, in truth. But they've worked to read my emotions and understand me, and in return, I've bonded with them.

Now I'm afraid of what life would look like without them. What if my mom doesn't understand? Could I leave them because of her? Can I raise a child and explain at playdates and schools that the three of us are together instead of just two? Will our relationship impact my child?

My mind is spinning, and I don't know if it's extra hormones or just an overly complicated situation, but Ryker asking about shopping for the baby causes me to start crying.

"Yes," I sniffle, pressing a tissue to my nose that Ryker quickly handed me. "But we need to talk."

Through my tears, I notice they share a glance. "Is this about us? Because... we've wanted to talk about us, too. But you needed time." Ryker looks at River, who edges closer, resting a soothing hand on my forearm.

"Did Dr. Longo say you were ready for this talk?" he asks.

Ryk and Riv have lent me one of their vehicles, and I've been driving North an hour to see a psychiatrist in Oakcreek.

A kind, older man with infinite patience and wisdom named Dr. Longo.

I'd shared with Ryker and River after a handful of sessions that I wanted time before we had any serious talks. Working through some of Rhett's behaviors was my main focus—namely, finding healthy ways to cope with the trauma he'd inflicted.

I can't say after two months, I'm a solved riddle or a completed puzzle, but I'm getting there. And, in fact, Dr. Longo had advised me to have this talk with Ryker and River—to help put down some roots. Roots, he'd said, would give me security and that security would help my emotional and mental health flourish.

I nod. "He says I need roots to help me maintain the progress I've made. That I need to solidify my existence somewhere to nurture the strength I'm building."

"He's a smart man," Ryker says thoughtfully, stroking a hand down his clean-shaven chin. "And we're ready. We know what we want."

I swallow hard because I feel guilty for my truth this morning, but I know I have to share it. I take another sip of flavorless hot tea, missing my coffee so hard right now. With my palms flat to the surface, I blurt out the difficult thing that's been rolling around my gut like a boulder of doom, crushing my excitement and hope.

"I'm afraid my mom won't approve, and if she doesn't, I'm scared it will impact our relationship." After the words rush out, relief swarms me, alleviating all the invisible weight I'd been bearing. But then they're silent, and the nerves come back tenfold. "I know it sounds terrible," I ramble nervously. "But I love her so much that I would struggle if she didn't like this. And that's the truth."

"Do you have a solution to the problem you raise, or is the solution in the subtext?" Ryker asks. The question is a straight shot, and even though its directness is blunt, his tone never gives the slightest hint of condescension or annoyance. Neither of these men ever are. They're problem solvers, and as an anxious worrier, it's nice.

"Have her over. Have her meet us," River offers, wearing a lopsided smile that softens the wall of worry built up around me.

"Is it the age or the fact that we're brothers? Or is it just being with two men in general?" Ryker asks, not as convinced as his brother that their charm will win over my mom.

"D," I say with a soft smile. "All of the above, I think."

"Hmm," River hums thoughtfully. "Well, I don't like the idea of having her over here and pretending like we aren't together because that's what we've been doing these last few months, right? We've *been together*."

He's not wrong about that on *any* front.

I'm the lucky school teacher that captured the Raleigh Two, and those men have fucked me full of cum, licked me until I was a puddle, sucked me raw, and held me close afterward.

They've also listened to me work through hard memories with Rhett, which wasn't easy for either of them. In fact, Ryker began seeing Dr. Longo again, too. In true River spirit, River opted for more work and has begun construction on a large playground... not far from the Raleigh estate.

We've learned about one another's basic needs—I know

what they're allergic to and where they keep their passports. We've traded woes. Ryker shared the loss of Rhett's mom and how that affected everyone. River admitted that he'd never had a serious relationship without his brother because he didn't want it.

They also explained to me a little more about them.

And how they work.

And why.

Turns out, they'd seen lots of friends partner up and disappear. Each of them hated the idea of that happening, especially because they're brothers. Sharing and cohabitating allowed them to never lose their closeness, but it also provided them with a balance of responsibilities.

The more they've shared, the less strange it is and the more it makes sense. I didn't have the liquid courage I'd normally use to approach uncomfortable questions, but with a baby in my belly, I knew they needed to be asked.

"And there's never anything going on between you two?"

The look they gave me; I'll never forget it.

Frustration, fatigue, disappointment. Ryker huffed out a long breath, and River pinched the bridge of his nose. I put my hand on my belly and rubbed, making sure they understood that, as a mother, it needed to be asked. I said as much.

And it softened them. It took the edge off the question I felt compelled to ask. I'd asked it months back, but if we were going to be getting serious, I absolutely had to make sure. For my child.

"We share. That's what we're into. Not each other, but sharing." I can't remember which of them gave me the response, but I held onto that promise, knowing I'd have to say those same words to my mom when the time came.

And now... that time is coming. Because I'm pretty sure we're about to make a commitment to one another. It sounds crazy. It feels a little crazy, too. But I'm chasing happiness, and it just so happens that I've stopped here in Raleigh with Ryker and River. And staying here is where I'm happiest.

Deep down, I was slightly worried that my gut had led me astray once again. That three years back, that spark I'd felt for Ryk was just misunderstood adrenaline. And like Rhett, I'd been confused and hopeful but off base.

But as one day ran into the next, and we learned more and more about one another, I realized I was in love with Ryker and River. With them individually, but also both of them as brothers and as father figures.

I hadn't told them, though, because we mutually agreed to put off the big talk until I'd been in therapy for a few months. We're on the brink of the talk, and now I'm worried about my mom's reaction to us.

When I'd told her I was merely staying with Ryker and River, she'd acted a little funny. Not in disapproval but more so, she seemed underwhelmed by my choice. It's not her fault for wanting me to go back to the apartment I shared with Rhett—she wasn't privy to all the bad memories lurking there. And there's just no point in telling her now. She'd never sleep again.

"I don't want to pretend either; I'm just worried."

Ryker's cologne makes my pulse zoom as he leans in, dropping a kiss on my temple. "Let's talk about us, then circle back to your mom, okay? I don't like how tense you're getting." We leave the cold kitchen counter for the living room, where we can sit more comfortably.

I let Ryk and Riv weave our fingers together, and the three of us sit together in front of the large hearth in the main room. I drag my toes through the long, cool shag, loving the way it feels. The house smells like mint and eucalyptus, and the two burly arms brushing up against mine only add to the overwhelming feeling I'm getting.

This is home.

I just hope my mom sees it that way, too.

"I want to say I promise you everything, no matter what she says, but," I shrug, hormonal tears wetting my eyes again. "It was her and me for a lot of years. I respect her, and I love her."

"We respect and love you for that," River says, earning him a pointed look.

"What?" His brow dips, and Ryker clears his throat.

"We haven't exchanged those words yet," Ryker says.

Love. We treat one another with love, talk to one another with love, and coexist full of it, too. The fact that we haven't swapped those three words aloud should probably make me nervous. Maybe a prior version of me would have read into it and made the fact that we haven't said I love you to one another into something with deeper meaning. Like *they don't really want me, that's why they haven't said it.*

But the first week I came back, they both told me in no uncertain terms: we want to raise that child with you if you'll let us.

You don't offer those things if you don't have feelings for someone. I know that. And it's why I haven't pressed that we say it. Rhett said he loved me, but his touch, actions, and behaviors screamed the contrary. Words only have power if you let them, and three little words don't mean all that much to me these days.

Showing up for me does. It's everything.

But maybe they want the words. "I know we haven't, but I know you both do," I reply, bringing our linked hands to my belly. Ember, a few years back, wouldn't make an assumption like that. She wouldn't love two brothers at once, either.

But the Ember with a child inside her doesn't play games or waste time. I face Ryker first, his hand still linked with mine over my small bump. "I thought it was crazy to think I loved you back then. I talked myself out of it. Love at first sight is bullshit and all that." I shake my head, not concerned with catching the emotional tears that fall. "It doesn't matter, though. Because I am in love with you. I fall more and more in love with you every day. And I think I was meant to meet Rhett so that I could come back to you."

I seal the admission with a hot kiss, and though I could get lost in him, I turn away from Ryker to meet his brother's gaze.

"I didn't know I could give my heart to more than one person at a time. I didn't even think about what that would feel like or if it would be hard. It was never an option on the horizon for me." I smile, and he smiles back, making my cheeks grow warm. "But I love you, River. I love how you speak with kindness, touch with affection, and live with warmth inside you."

We kiss, and my body shivers in response to his beard scratching against my soft skin, reminding me of one of the many differences between the two men. I do love them both, madly, and I think, if I'm being honest, I truly believe I was fated to be theirs.

Ryker captures my attention when he appears on the ground, between my legs, eyes wide. He cups his palms to my knees, sliding his hands up my thighs. He tugs off my sweats, leaving my panties intact. "I love you, Ember. And I spent three years trying to forget you. But then, there you were."

River pushes my hair off my shoulder, giving him access to my neck. He plants kisses on my throat, saying, "I love you, too, Em. But you knew that already." His lips curl against my flesh as Ryker's mouth finds my panties. Over the fabric, he sucks my clit, the needy feeling between my legs blooming from their touches.

"How could I not know, you show me with every touch," I breathe, letting my head crush against the soft sofa cushion. "I just didn't know if we were the type of relationship that needed to *hear* it," I admit, one hand sifting through Ryker's hair, the other now gripping River's thigh as he nestles into me, sealing gentle bites with harsh kisses.

Ryker's lips are pink and swollen from friction as he lifts his head to look at me. "Everyone needs to hear it, baby. Now let us take away your stress."

I remember watching an old rerun of *Sex in the City* in college where Carrie said she needed to have sex to relieve her stress and that she'd gone so long without it she was getting edgy.

I rolled my eyes at that. *Yeah*, I thought, *sex is good, but it doesn't relieve stress. If anything, it's a short-term enjoyment that loads more stress on the back end. Messy clean up, pregnancy scares, STDs, all that.*

But being worshipped and fucked by Ryker and River? Carrie Bradshaw, *I see you.*

"Let's give her what she really loves," River rasps, repositioning himself on his knees on the sofa next to me. His groin aligns with my mouth, and his large hand clutches the top of my head, tipping my face up to his.

"And what do I really love?" I ask him, heart already pounding, pussy pulsing. I love being with them in every way, but we know what my favorite is. I just love hearing them say it.

Their husky voices and the low rumble in their filthy words destroys me. Makes me complete and utter putty for them.

Ryker hooks his fingers in the band of my panties, tugging them off easily. He groans as he studies my bare cunt, using the blunt tip of one finger to sample my wetness. "You want to get fucked in this sweet, tight pussy while my brother fucks your dirty little mouth, isn't that right?"

I nod; his stoic expression as he delivers my filthy dreams makes me that much hotter. The sight of River's sweats being lowered ignites a burning desire in my veins, and when I turn back to him, I'm face to face with his thick, hard cock.

He nudges the slick head against my lips, his thick fingers curled at the base, holding himself tightly. At the same time, Ryker grabs my ankles and pins them to the edge of the couch, knees up.

"Keep your legs open," he says as I slide a bit lower, shuffling my ass to the very edge of the sofa. He unties his pants before releasing his straining cock from the sweats. There was a time when pants being lowered would have sent me to a far away corner of my mind. But now, it sharpens my focus, it keeps me present as I sit and stare in awe of the men that worship me.

Once we're positioned the way we've previously enjoyed (several times), I smile up at River, then open my mouth. As he slides his cock onto my tongue with a resounding moan, Ryker's crown breaches me, and when his hands come down on my inner thighs with force, I moan around Riv's cock.

The feeling of being filled full and fucked while having a hard cock pulsing in my mouth is one of the most empowering feelings. Bringing two men to their proverbial knees has never made me feel sexier. And the way the three of us moan and grunt, curse and pant–our breathing and praise reaching a crescendo in our private space–only intensifies the dizzying orgasm blooming between my thighs.

I swallow down the salty precum flooding my tongue; River hisses as my throat spasms to swallow. "Fuck, Em, your warm little mouth feels so good."

From between my thighs, still pistoning into me in grueling, hard strokes, Ryker roars his approval. "What a good girl, giving up your mouth and pussy to us." He slams into me again, making River's cock spear further down my throat, earning him a hearty gag.

"Once you have that baby, Em, you'll be on your back again, getting bred because you're our vessel. Our goddess. You'll take our cum and give us more. We're going to fuck you so full; you'll be round with our babies for the next ten years."

River cups my face as Ryker's words sink in. He slides his shaft along my closed lips before nudging them apart, pushing inside my mouth again. "Our babies will feed off these tits," Riv grits, using the hand not holding the base of his cock to squeeze my nipple, rolling it roughly between his thumb and forefinger.

Ryker and River want to help me raise this baby. They've made it clear. We're going to be together. That's clear, too. But this is the first time I've heard they want more babies with me.

And I can't deny... I want that, too.

To be round with Ryk or Riv's baby—it's the ultimate aphrodisiac.

Ryker slaps my clit with his cock, the wet smack of it nudging me closer to release. Everything they do to me enflames me, I swear. "Yes," I moan in response to Ryk as Riv jerks back, holding the base of his dick so tightly his knuckles go white.

"Are you ready, brother?" Riv questions, his eyes pinned on mine. I want to reach up and drag my fingers through his beard, but my body is heavy, limbs weighty with pressure as my orgasm seizes control.

From where he's positioned between my spread legs, Ryker grunts, slamming back into me with urgent force. "Yes," he growls, "I'm fucking ready."

Riv's eyes roll closed as he fills my mouth with his warm flesh. Opening the back of my throat, I take him deep as his breathing grows ragged. Ryker's breaths are frantic and short, too, and I know... it's time.

In pulsing bursts, River cums, shooting a thick, abundant load into the back of my throat, triggering me to swallow. Glugging happily on his cock, sucking up and swallowing every drop of his orgasm, my own release hits.

As my cunt seizes, clenching around Ryker's meaty cock,

he holds himself to the hilt. He curses, and then his warmth fills my pussy, making me cum even harder.

He shoots, and I moan; he groans, and I keep swallowing, and after I've milked both of them for every drop and cum so hard I'm pretty sure I'll be sore tomorrow, we finally take a breath.

River slides his dick from my mouth, using his thumb to capture the spare drops of cum that slipped free. He licks it off his thumb as he smooths my hair back, giving me a sultry wink. Ryker hollows me, immediately crouching between my legs to seal his mouth to my pink, swollen pussy. Tracing me with his tongue, Ryker slowly laps at the traces of his cum leaking from me, taking his time to clean me up. When he's done, he rises to his knees and finds my mouth with his.

Our kiss is flavored with the three of us, and it is perfect.

Ryker slides my panties up my legs as River curses, struggling to get his partially hard cock back into his jeans. Once he does, he brings me water, and I watch as Ryker slips his beautiful dick into his slacks. When their zippers ascend, though I'm sated, I'm always a little disappointed.

"How do you feel now?" Ryker asks, sitting on the sofa and pulling me into his lap. River sits, taking my feet in his.

"Good," I admit. "So good."

"Good," Ryker says. "Now, we still want to talk."

CHAPTER EIGHTEEN

RYKER

"I believe that in order to make you ours forever you were destined to carry Rhett's child. That this Raleigh would bind us together irrevocably," I say, holding my chin high as I speak. I've never exuded as much confidence as I am now. I'm more sure about this than any deal I've ever done.

"We were fated to be together," River adds, stealing the word that has been making more and more appearances in my psyche lately.

"Your concerns with your mother's opinion reflect the deep respect and love you have for her," I continue, Ember's head ping-ponging between the two of us.

We've said the big words. But now that Ember is halfway through her pregnancy, our relationship needs to be defined in terms that the rest of the world can process. I understand how we work now. We're equals, together. But

Ember needs to be aware of the next step; she needs to understand the long-term relationship where there are three.

"Would marriage assuage your mother's concerns?" I ask, taking her hand between both of mine. My thumb rubs small circles over her bare ring finger. She got a ring from Rhett. He said he couldn't afford a nice one, but she found out that what he really meant was *I have more important expenses.* She put the ring in his pocket before his service.

I look over at River, then back to Ember; she's nearly holding their breath.

"How would that even work?" she asks, fingering the silver chain around her neck nervously.

"We want to move this forward, and if it would please your mother and you..." I begin, and... did I just propose? I'm probably using all the wrong words but we need to say them.

My brother's hand tightens around her thigh. "This is just a jumping-off point, but we thought maybe you could be married to Ryker to legally have our name. Nothing would change between the three of us," River says, pulling a large hand down his beard. "I'd like to father our next child, but we both want to have more children."

Ember turns to face me, seeking clarification. "You're okay with River knowing his child came from him, and the rest of our children's paternity being ambiguous?"

If that's the part she's hung up on, that's a good sign. Relief allows my shoulders to relax as I consider her question.

"Any child born of you is *our* child," I say, motioning between the three of us. "But River has yet to have a biological child of his own. It's a personal thing for him, but don't get confused: all the children born to you are *ours*." My expression is serious. "All of ours."

She looks at River, tipping her head to the side. She slides a hand under his, and he squeezes. "I would love to give you a child."

A low growl erupts from him, and he takes her mouth in a passionate kiss. There is no jealousy rearing its head–only happiness. Happy to see my brother in love with and loved by a decent, kind, beautiful, honorable woman. Finally. And to know that she wants us both, wants to mother our children and my *grandchild*—it truly is fate to find a piece that fits with us both so perfectly.

I wish Rhett's hand in our fate was better—that he'd been dealt something he could play with. Instead, he's not here. And I don't forget that, not ever. Every time I look at Ember, I think of him and what he's missing. I hurt for him daily, too, but I make a promise to him daily; I tell him we will take care of them both—her and the baby. That we will show her the love and give her the life that he didn't.

I am a man of my word.

When her focus is back on me, I squeeze her hand. "I won't let that be our proposal. A conversation midday is not the proposal you deserve. But I want you to think about it, okay? We marry, or whatever we decide, the three of us are in this forever. Raleigh is our town, but it's yours now, too."

"You would both give me that? Ownership, your last name, a home, an entire life?" she shakes her head, and it makes me angry that some part of her believes she isn't worthy of all of it and more. That my son made her feel that way.

"We will give you everything, Ember. But we expect your everything in return."

"Schedule a trip for your mom to come visit. Think about it until then."

"Yes," she shakes her head, panic seizing her expression. "This is what I want; I don't need more time."

"Don't," I say softly, smiling to make sure she knows I'm not angry with her. "Don't, not until you've thought about it and talked to your mom. We love you, Em, but until you can truly commit, don't say something you're not sure you mean."

A tear slips past her lashes, and I wipe it away quickly. River soothes her as he rubs her feet. "Okay," she finally says, sniffling. "I want to talk to my mom; I do. I've been putting it off, but I want to tell her. I'm *going* to tell her."

"We'll fly her out. We'll have a nice time getting to know one another, and we'll work on the nursery. How's that sound?" I offer.

She nods. "That sounds great. Thank you." Then she chews the corner of her mouth as her eyes lift to the fire, searching it for answers.

"What?" River asks, sensing her shifting mood.

"I just... I want to be able to say yes now; I hate leaving you both in limbo like this." She sniffles. She stares into the flames again, this time her face more solemn, as if she's deciding how she'll handle things *if* her mom doesn't approve. When her chin wobbles, I know I'm right. "No matter what, I'm here with you," she says, choking up a little. "But it will be hard if she doesn't support me."

River slides closer and plucks Ember from my lap, setting her on his. "Just focus on what a nice time we'll have being together, and don't worry too much about it yet, okay?"

She nods, and River and I exchange a knowing glance. We're not strangers to people frowning on us. Raleigh used to, but the more they saw us, spoke with us and got to know us, the more they realized we're good fucking humans who merely chose a different path with their relationship. They were there for us when Rhett's mother died. Saw what we went through. And while Rhett may not have been the town's favorite citizen, they turned up at his funeral as much to support us as to honor his memory.

We love differently, that's the only fucking difference.

I hope her mom can feel how much River and I are committed to her and the baby, and I hope she likes us, too. But the latter is just a nicety; the former is a must.

If anyone can easily demonstrate how far they'd go for Ember, River and I are up for the task.

CHAPTER NINETEEN

EMBER

It took me two full months to contact my mom. I'm not proud. And to say she was upset in learning that we'd spoken many, many times without me telling her that I'm pregnant would be an understatement.

She was *devastated*.

"Six months?" she gasped over and over as she desperately tried to calibrate.

"It was the last time Rhett and I were together. The last time we had sex, he died the same day."

She was silent upon that confession. I stayed quiet, too, just pacing the hallway on the third floor as I waited with bated breath for her to answer.

"That's why you've been staying with them for so long," she said on an exhale as if it all made logical sense now. I cringed a little at the way she'd felt she'd discovered a missing piece to understand me. I was with them because I love them, but she had a sliver of it correct: the pregnancy *is* what sent me to them.

"It's what brought me here, yes," I'd managed the strength to make the important clarification. "Would you please come out and visit? I'd like for you to meet Ryker and River."

The way she paused and said, "Rhett's father and uncle?" made my nerves spike yet again. She wasn't able to identify them as humans separate from Rhett and our trauma yet, but I hoped time here would change that. That she'd see them for who they are versus who they are related to.

"When?"

"Soon. Now. Whenever," I'd responded eagerly because I did deeply miss my mom. But selfishly, I just wanted to get this over with and deal with whatever the fallout would be.

She laughed a little but agreed. "Of course! I've been dying to see you. I wanted to come for Rhett's service—"

Mom never met Rhett. In the three years I'd gone home for holidays and special events, I never brought him. I was scared he'd get sick from withdrawal or bring his drugs into her home, or... that's not true.

I was *ashamed* of him and my choice to marry him. And I didn't want to soil my mom's house with those stressful realities.

When she wanted to come to his service, I'd said no. I said we'd keep it small. That was the plan. Turns out, the entire town came to support the Raleigh Two. It was that day I learned their nickname, too.

"Come now. Ryker and River want to pay for your travel fare. Please don't say no."

"I can't let them pay–"

"If you don't, they will find a way to pay for it. You'll get home and unzip your suitcase to find stacks of cash. Seriously. Let them pay."

She harrumphed but conceded. "Fine, fine. How's next week? I can take some time off of work then. How long do you want me?"

"A week?" I asked, pausing in front of the closed office door. There's an office on every floor, and Ryker has admitted to me that he was always eager to have face-to-face meetings. Now that there's someone at home, he works from home a lot over Zoom.

It's his choice, but the fact that both River and Ryker choose me every time they can, makes me know with all certainty that this is the deepest, realest love.

"Sure," my mom said, the pages of her day planner flipping in the background. "A week works. I won't be able to come out again until the baby is born... that is if you're still living there with them."

We ended the call shortly after, and her remark about me potentially not living with Ryker and River when the baby was born really struck me.

It made me realize that I need the words. I need the commitment. I need it all to quiet the tiny, insecure voice inside that doubts my worth. Dr. Longo says that voice will one day be extinguished and that I'm making great strides in handling my trauma. But until then, I have to work really hard to ignore her. "Put her on silent, or leave her on read, whatever the young people say," he'd said with a contagious smile.

After a week of nail-biting, pacing, and fretting... Raleigh

Security has picked her up from the airport and she's on her way to the house for her visit. She's finally going to meet the Ryker and River Raleigh.

The ends of my silk maxi dress drag against the hardwood as I walk up and back repeatedly.

River sits on a bench lining the foyer wall, and Ryker stands with his back to the wall near the front door, one knee up, arms folded over his chest.

"Em, it's gonna be okay. You're her daughter, and you're six months pregnant. She's going to be so excited and happy to see you. No question."

I stop in my tracks. "I know that. That's not what has me nervous."

"Oh, so this is nervous pacing, not excited pacing," Riv chimes in, smiling beneath his thick beard. He's grown it out even more in the last few months but went to the barber for a professional trim yesterday. On the other hand, Ryker is clean-shaven as always, looking handsome and suave. They opted for jeans and button-up shirts—and I wish they wouldn't look so good because it's truly distracting.

I'd love to sneak away to one of their rooms—for the last few weeks, as River rebuilds a master suitable for three and a bassinet, we've been alternating between Ryker and River's rooms. Having one of them behind me, one centered in front of me, masculine grunts and hard cocks all around–my mouth nearly waters at the fantasy.

I rub my belly, which has popped in size these last few weeks. I rocked a tiny bump–more of a bloat than a belly–for the first five months, but once month six hit, I ballooned. It actually looks like I swallowed a balloon or even a basketball. "I'm nervous about telling her about *us*."

River smiles.

"He knew that," Ryker says softly, and I look back at Riv, who's wearing a grin.

"She'll like us, and when we talk to her about our life plan, there won't be a lot of room for her complaint. Okay?" Ryker says, unfolding his arms to pull me to his chest, hugging me gently. He smells like amber and whiskey, fresh laundry, and high-end hair products. I've come to love that smell. Too much, maybe.

I push him off. "Okay, that's... you're..." I shake my head, "you're making me flustered."

They laugh as Riv gets to his feet. "Hey," he says, nodding to the panel on the wall. I glance at it, seeing thirty-six rectangles playing security camera footage. Immediately, I see what he sees.

The front gates at the end of the drive are opening. Mom's here.

"Relax," Riv draws out the word as my eyes widen, and I begin wringing my hands. I took care to curl beachy waves today, but with as much as I'm sweating, I'm sure the waves are replaced by frizz. Perspiration beads along my neck and temples, and I wipe it away.

"I'm so sweaty and gross right now," I admit, nerves churning in my belly just as the baby kicks. I press my hand to where the kick hit and rub. "He's kicking me like crazy."

"She, you mean," Ryk adds with a smile.

They've been coming to my appointments. A month or so ago, the doctor asked me if I wanted to know the baby's gender. I immediately squealed yes; the dream of nesting in pinks or blues coming to life.

But Ryk thought a surprise might be more special, and

Riv agreed. Then they shared with me the idea of a gender-neutral nursery, and after showing me actual blueprints of modifying an additional room in the house to make a bigger nursery, I agreed.

They've put more thought into our future, I think, than I have, but I blame the pregnancy for taking much of my focus.

"He or she," I smile, and then the doorbell rings. About to wipe my hands down my dress, River stops me, holding out the tail end of his black button-up.

"It'll show on your fancy dress. Wipe your sweat on me," he grins.

Ryker grabs the door handle, watching as I smear my hands against his brother's shirt, smiling. "It's going to be okay, alright? Trust the process."

"I think you say that about bold haircuts and house remodels, not meeting my mom," I say, wringing my hands together again as soon as they're dry. I take one slow, deep breath and give Ryker the nod.

He opens the door, and the three of us are greeted with a rush of Estée Lauder perfume, and immediately my eyes tingle with the emotion only brought by seeing your mom after a long time apart.

"Ember," she says, her tone full of warmth and love. She wraps her arms around me, and I bury my nose in her golden hair, the same hue I've borrowed from her. In her arms, I'm reminded of all the times she's soothed me and eased my pains, from skinned knees to failed tests, to broken hearts; she's always been there for me.

"Mom," I murmur, trying so hard not to be emotional, but I can't hold back. Tears stream down my cheeks as she grabs my shoulders, putting distance between us so she can eye my burgeoning belly.

"My baby is having a baby!" she gushes, her eyes wet. We hug again, and it's then I remember that Ryker and River are waiting, wearing grins from ear to ear. My happiness makes them happy, and that feels like a fucking hug.

"Mom," I say, feeding my hand into hers, taking a place at her side so she can fully see them. "This is Ryker Raleigh and River Raleigh."

She extends her hand, but halfway through, she slows down. "Raleigh," she says slowly. "That's so funny. Raleighs living in Raleigh."

Her hand slides easily into Ryker's, and he dips his head as he greets her. "Pamela, it's so wonderful to finally meet you. I'm Ryker. Ember has been looking forward to this visit for so long. Thank you so much for coming out."

She smiles at him and shakes River's hand.

"Pamela, I'm River, and we're so happy that you're here. Thank you for coming."

She looks between them for what feels like way too long, then peers at me, her eyes holding a message I can't decode. My stomach drops and clenches as my palms begin to sweat.

"Let's have a drink in the kitchen and then catch up, yeah?" I smile, knowing it's not reaching my eyes. *I just want her to be okay with this.*

Ryker leads the way as River takes mom's rolling suitcase from her, placing it in the foyer. At the long counter in the kitchen, I usher mom to a barstool and sit next to her. River presents her with a variety of drink options, but mom just smiles and says, "coffee is fine."

The twins have a brandy while they pour me a club soda, the quiet drip of the coffee percolating echoing around the too-quiet kitchen.

Ryker initiates conversation, sitting adjacent to mom. "Actually, Pamela, it's no coincidence we live here in Raleigh. We are the family that has owned the majority of this place for generations. It's named after our great-great-great grandfather."

She blinks, looking confused and surprised. "So... you own... the town?" She drapes her hand over her collarbone; her manicured nails playing with her silver necklace mindlessly. "I didn't know that. Ember didn't share that with me. That her husband was the *heir* to a town."

I wince because I'm not sure any of us were ready to talk about Rhett. Not yet. It makes admitting to her that the three of us are in a relationship more difficult.

Ryker's face falls a little, and my heart fractures watching him struggle to recover. I take his hand out of habit, and my mom's eyes don't miss the gesture.

"My relationship with Rhett was complicated. And unfortunately, we did not get to mend it before his untimely passing," he says, slow and intentional with his words as if he's rehearsed it. And I hope if he did, it wasn't to convince himself. He has to know he tried to help Rhett as much as he could. Some people are too far into the open waters to come back. That's a fact.

Mom studies him as River picks up the conversation. "Rhett lost his mom at a young age, and there was a lot of unhealthy coping with that loss that he developed as a teenager. We put him in programs, therapy; you name it, we tried it. My brother followed his son all around the country for a year, killing himself with fatigue and stress, until one day, Rhett just left. And after years of chasing him, we let him go. And we hoped he'd come back to us."

Eyes wide, mom looks at me. I hadn't planned on coming clean about everything, but... I guess stacking our lives on a lie isn't good. If she's going to know about us, she may as well know everything. "Rhett," she starts, working it out as she goes. "Rhett had a substance abuse problem?" Her inference skills have done some of the hard work, but there's so much more to unearth now.

I swallow, and River leans over the kitchen island to pat my hand, the one curled into his brother's. Mom doesn't miss that either. But we can't stop being us, not even for her. I'm learning at this moment that no matter how she feels, these men are my future. They have my whole heart.

"He did." My heart is beating so loudly my eardrums ache.

"You... you said he liked to party." She thinks for a second, eyes flicking up to River, then over to Ryker. "He partied a lot," she says again, trying desperately to make all this new information fit into the past.

"I didn't want you to worry," I start, but Ryker takes the lead.

"I loved my son very much, but I won't rewrite the past. He had problems, and he did not handle them or accept help. And while I'm glad he brought your daughter into our lives, I'm also just as sorry that he met her. Because he did not treat her the way she deserves to be treated."

Mom stammers a little. "How did he treat you?" Her eyes flame as she stares into mine before turning back to Ryker.

"And how... what are you saying? How does she deserve to be treated?"

"Ember, this is your story to tell, but we also don't want you to carry the physical stress of telling it. With your permission, I can explain to Pamela everything you've been through," River says, his voice thick and steady, an unwavering pillar of strength and support. My lower half pulses as my gaze moves between these two men. I should buy a lotto ticket; that's how lucky I feel.

"Please," I say quickly, trying desperately to hide the emotion straddling my uneasy tone. They'll think I'm teary over Rhett when in truth, I'm teary over my blessed reality.

Mom's focus pinches on River as he pushes off the counter, grabbing the now full carafe of coffee and filling mom's mug. He slides it to her, but she doesn't drink. She blinks at him, and he gives her a small, reassuring smile.

"Okay, first, I want you to prepare yourself. If you thought your daughter was strong before, you're going to look at her in a completely different light after this." His somber eyes find mine, and my veins fill with the overflowing love my heart pumps through my body.

"Rhett was addicted to heroin. He was able to hide that from Ember when they met, and unfortunately, they eloped before she realized. And she stayed with him. She stayed, and though there was no love romantically, she continued to give up three years of her life to take him to the doctor's, pick him up from street corners, and try to get him healthy. Sober."

Mom's eyes, now full of tears, meet mine. I nod, my bottom lip trembling with so much might I'm afraid to speak. "Why.. why didn't you tell me? I would've helped you find a new place; I would have flown in and helped you figure it out legally."

I shake my head, the tears abundant now. "I knew you were disappointed in me eloping and when I realized it was a mistake, I just... I didn't want to disappoint you again, and... he needed me. I couldn't turn my back on him like that."

"He was a stranger, Ember. You married a stranger. You could have annulled it and left." Her eyes are searching mine for an answer, for something that makes sense to her, for a reason why a twenty-two-year-old would stay married to a stranger addicted to drugs.

"I told you that you'd see her differently after this. You'd see how truly strong she really is," River says.

"She stayed, and she helped my son. You're right," Ryker says, his voice all smoke and rasp, emotion driving him forward. "She could have left. And if she had, I may have lost my son years ago. But she stayed, having no real reason to stay, and helped him, sacrificing herself along the way." His eyes come to mine, and I swear he's telling me how much he loves me in the intense ways his gaze locks with mine. "Some would say she's an angel because of what she did."

"Sacrificing yourself?" Mom catches on to the part that made me wince. She looks at me, gaze sharp, prodding me for answers. I rub my belly nervously but don't get the chance to come clean. River speaks again.

"He forced himself on her, repeatedly." He drops his head, and Ryker does the same. They carry the shame of Rhett's actions when all I want them to do is let it go. "Does she know about Dr. Longo?" River asks me after he lifts his head.

I shake mine.

"She's been in therapy for a few months now. Actually, I've gone back myself," Ryker says, smoothing a hand through his glossy, coiffed hair. His sex appeal, even mid-conversation about therapy and loss, is off the fucking charts. "When Rhett ran away, River and I sought out therapy. We were advised at the time to undergo grief therapy as if we'd already lost him, in order to cope with the loss of the boy we once knew and the relationship we believed we had."

River crosses the kitchen and rests a hand on his brother's shoulder. Standing hip to hip, I can see all their similarities, even what's not visible. Their matching eyes, big shoulders, and bottomless hearts.

"Now that he's really gone, I've needed a little extra help getting through it."

"You–you're comfortable discussing therapy?" my mom questions, looking surprised.

Ryker shrugs. "It helps. I'm not a doctor; I can't fix myself. Dr. Longo has put me back together and given me peace many times. I have faith he can do it again."

"And are you undergoing grief therapy now?" Mom asks.

He shakes his head, and I love the way River's hand remains on him for comfort. "I'm actually working through what I've learned about him and how he treated Ember." He massages the center of his chest with curled knuckles before finding the bottom of his brandy. "It's been difficult."

I didn't know that. I assumed he was going back to Dr. Longo to work through what happened with Rhett, but I didn't know it was how Rhett hurt me that was hurting him.

And I didn't know that he and River had undergone grief therapy, either.

"I didn't know that," I admit to him, my voice merely a whisper.

He takes my hand again, squeezing. "I didn't want you to worry, baby."

My throat constricts, and my eyes widen.

"Baby?" mom questions, her hands still wrapped around the white porcelain mug, steam wafting off the surface in lazy waves as it cools. "Baby?"

"Mom, I know this is a lot to take in all in the first fifteen minutes of seeing me but..." Boom. Boom. Boom. My heart is beating so loudly I feel like I'm physically vibrating. "Ryker and River and I are... in a relationship."

She snorts once. Her vision pinches as she looks at me, then Ryker, and over at River. She snorts again, and then we sit in a moment of silence wherein the quiet provides the subtext she needs: we aren't joking.

"Three people can't be—" she looks at River, who is stroking his beard calmly, his other hand still on Ryker's shoulder. "You're identical twins, you're blood brothers, you can't—"

Ryker takes her broken questioning in stride. "Pamela, have you heard of the term compersion?"

Mom is too shocked to speak. Ryker hedges on.

"With polyfidelity, we don't feel jealousy. We instead experience *compersion*. That's a better use of energy. It's when you get a deep fulfillment ," he taps his chest, so she knows it's more than sex. "In watching the person you love fall in love with another person." He pats the hand clamped on his shoulder. "I love my brother. And I take great contentment," this time, River taps Ryker's chest "in seeing him love the woman I love."

"And I feel the same," River adds. "And polyfidelity is having the ability and emotional bandwidth to love another person the same way you love your partner. Ember loves my brother. Ember loves me. I love Ember. My brother loves Ember. It's about love and security and having the biggest heart. It isn't about what you think."

"You don't know what I think," mom replies, sipping her hot coffee like it's the brandy the men were drinking.

"I think you're concerned we're sexual deviants. That he and I are in some weird, incestual relationship, but that's not the case," River says, putting it all out there, not letting any fears stay shrouded in darkness. "Our connection is deep, and we're a team. We love together, and we love Ember."

My mom takes another long drink of coffee, her eyes watering from the intensity. She looks at my belly, round with her first grandchild. She looks back up at my lovers. "How old are you both?"

River pats Ryker's shoulder. "He's older by a minute or two, but we're both forty-four."

I can see my mom physically biting into the words "*I'm forty-four,*" but I'm relieved she doesn't say it. Instead, she asks, "how long have you three been... together?"

They let me take the lead on this one, and I'm grateful. "Do you remember three years ago, when I called you crying, telling you I was in a bank as it was robbed?"

Her fingers stroke the chain of her necklace as she nods vehemently. "Of course, I remember. You're my child, and you were trapped with gunmen. I remember!"

"Do you remember anything else I told you about that day?"

"It's the day before you left and then met... Rhett," she recalls slowly, fitting the pieces where she can. Still, when she meets my eyes again, hers are full of questions. We've been feeding her answers, and she looks more confused than ever.

"What else, though? Do you remember?" I want so badly for her to recall it. Because the kismet of the entire last three years is almost too hard to believe.

She finishes her coffee, her hand wobbling as she sets it back down. It's not the sudden burst of caffeine, either. I hate that this is making her shaky. But my mom is smart, and in all the time I spent worrying if she'd understand, I never gave her credit.

She's smart. She's understanding. And she's been a single mother her whole life. She will understand. It may take time, but she *will* understand.

I wait a moment, and then she straightens. "There was a man who kept you company, made you feel safe, helped you keep calm," she recalls, nodding to me. "Right?"

I nod. "That was Ryker."

She blinks incredulously a few times before turning her focus to Ryker for a second, then back to me. "What do you mean?"

"He was there. And then the SWAT team came, and we lost each other in the smoke and haze. And I moved away and met Rhett. But I was drawn to Rhett because he reminded me of Ryker. I didn't know they shared a surname–Ryker and I never exchanged more than first names that day. I just... I saw Rhett and got that flutter that

I'd gotten from Ryker and went with it. After he passed, I flew to Raleigh—I didn't even consider the town being the same as his name; I was so overwhelmed. Anyway, I came here to break the news, and it was Ryker." I swallow, remembering just how shocked I was to see a man that looked like Ryker, and then... Ryker himself.

Her mouth falls open as she blinks at me as if I've just told her I've discovered our lineage ties us to the royal family. River takes the opportunity to move through the kitchen, refilling my mom's mug before refilling his brandy and his brothers. He retrieves a large charcuterie board from the fridge, peeling the foil from the top.

"Get something in your stomach, Pamela. The coffee's strong." He looks at me, brows raised. "You haven't had a snack since what, mid-morning? You need to eat." He hovers his hand above the cold cuts. "Not this, but the rest of it you can have."

Ryker drops a hand to my thigh, our hands no longer joined. "Unless you want something else?" He looks up at Riv. "Do we still have that chicken breast? She really liked that chicken salad you made last week."

River's brows lift as he raises a finger to the air. "I actually do." I watch my mom watching the two men as Ryker stands, joining his brother in the kitchen to assemble the salad.

"I can snack off the board. Mom will hardly eat any of this, and I don't want it to go to waste," I say, plucking a strawberry from the board.

"A single strawberry is not a snack," Ryker chides; the blade of the knife he's using to cut tomatoes shines, and my mom watches it.

River, at his side, thinly slices the chicken breasts he'd grilled a day ago, a smile on his face. "Pamela, your daughter has been having food aversions like crazy. Whenever she even remotely likes something, we prepare extra in hopes that we can keep her on something more than snacks for a few days. Last week I made chicken salad, and she was obsessed." He smiles at me, and I can't help but grin. "She even liked the smell of the dressing," he recalls, "which rarely happens."

"So Riv went to the store and bought a ton of organic romaine and organic chicken breasts, and the next day, she was craving steak," Ryker says with a chuckle, tossing the diced tomatoes in the bowl. He begins shaving fresh asiago as River drops the chicken into the bowl, moving to the sink to wash his hands.

"Luckily, she still likes the chicken salad, though," he says, wringing his hands in the dish towel hanging from the oven. Ryker tosses the rest of the ingredients in, and River lifts the bowl under my nose. "Take a whiff, baby. You want it?"

Holding my hair to my chest so it doesn't drag through the food, I smell, and my stomach rumbles. "Yes, I do." Suddenly, I think I'll die if I don't eat that salad right this second.

Pregnancy is so confusing.

I begin eating after River tosses it, making sure all the romaine is coated in his homemade dressing. Mom clears her throat, her confusion heavy in the air as she peers around at the three of us.

"Do you always cook, or is it just because she's pregnant?"

I don't like the implication that comes with the second part of that sentence, but I understand she's been handed quite a plateful to digest in the last half hour.

"I've always been an excellent cook," River boasts, and it's true. He cooks nearly every single night, and I've never had anything that wasn't delicious. Even that night when he made curry, I thought the smell would ruin me. He convinced me to try it, and I ate two bowls. "My brother is an excellent cook as well, but he doesn't like cooking as much as I do."

Ryker reaches for his drink, bringing it to his mouth but stopping before he sips. "I've grown fond of being fed, it's true, but I don't mind cleaning up."

River pats his shoulder playfully. "He knew he wasn't as good as me, so he became the cleanup guy." He yanks a drawer open and retrieves a pale yellow apron, holding it on display for us to see. "See, this is his dish apron and everything."

River laughs, and Ryker yanks it away from him. "I don't like when the soap gets on my clothes. It never dries right. Then it needs to be washed." He winks at me before putting his focus on my mom. "Tell them I'm right, Pamela. I'm sure you've done your fair share of dishes. Dish soap always leaves those little dark, soapy circles, right?"

I look at my mom. I don't know what she's thinking or feeling, and that unease is worming through me, leaving worry in its wake. But I continue eating my salad, determined to make her see that we're normal, the three of us. She may not be used to it yet, but it's not unlike any other relationship in the sense that we're all here because of love.

She smiles slowly at Ryker, then says, "It's true. I wear

an apron, too." She turns to me, and I'm surprised by her engagement in the conversation. We all know that none of us give a shit about dish soap or aprons, but it's about acceptance and understanding. Partaking in this small conversation is a foot in the door, and her foot is thankfully inside. "Don't you remember I had that apron that said 'Made from Scratch' and had the graphic of a kitty hanging off of it?"

Though I had forgotten, her words jog my memory, and in response, I drop the fork. It clanks loudly against the glass bowl as I bring my hand to mouth, not wanting to show off chewed-up salad as I yelp, "oh my gosh! Yes, I remember now!"

Ryker shoves his back in the drawer and takes a drink. "But we do cook for her, yes. Mostly Riv, as we've discussed, but the truth is Pamela, it's not about food." He lowers the brandy to the counter and shoves his hands in his pockets, rocking on his feet in the most non-threatening way. "We have been and plan to take care of Ember and the baby in all walks of life. Food, finances, dreams, goals, parenting—whatever it is, we have them."

Mom's voice rattles with uncertainty as she asks, "and what does she give in return?"

"Aside from loving us and raising our children?" River asks, looking confused but not frustrated.

"Raising your children?" Mom asks, and I hate that her head must be spinning right now but as nervous as I was to do this, we may as well rip the bandaid clean off. "You plan on having children together after this baby is born?"

Ryker smoothes a hand down his chest, then fiddles with the loose ends of his hair. "Pamela, I loved being a father to Rhett. We had hard times, but I loved him with everything I had. You and I know what that love is like," he says to mom, who nods along. "And I'd like to be a father again, yes. But before that," he reaches out, squeezing River's neck. "River wants to be a father."

He nods with pride. "I do. But don't get confused here, Pamela; the child that is growing in her belly–that is *our* child. We're going to sign that birth certificate and raise it with Ember as ours. In Rhett's honor."

Ryker swipes at his eyes. He doesn't break down often–I still remember the way he and River cried together that first day I came here–but when he does, we let him. We don't try to tell him it will be okay; we don't fill him with false hope. We just hold him and love him until the wave has passed and the sea has slowed.

He gathers himself quickly today, and I'm sure that's because my mom is here.

"You can't marry her, though," my mom responds quickly, and I know now that her reservation is all fear-based. She's concerned for me, and I love her for that; I do. But what she's failing to see is that my relationship is not her burden nor business. I want her to accept, but I'm quickly learning something about myself: it's a definite want, not a must or need.

"I can," Ryker retorts, "or River can. Or we legally bind ourselves in other ways."

She hedges around it but again asks, "so you two... you just love her together?"

That's probably another question that had been floating eerily around her head. Is my daughter involved in some weird incestual relationship? I can't blame her. I even forced myself to ask them that very question, even though I was nearly sure of the answer. But now she knows.

"The intimacy and physicality are with Ember, not one another," River clarifies, his tone far more stoic than I'm used to. But it's an important point to drive home.

Mom studies my eyes before her gaze traverses my chest, down to my belly. When she reaches out and smooths her palm along the rounded bump, my eyes fill. I don't think it's hormones; I think it's that she's on the cusp of accepting this. I feel it with every defining question that cauterizes her burning curiosity.

"Do you know the gender?" she asks, capturing one of my hands with hers. She presses her lips to it in a soothing kiss. "I've missed you so much, Em."

I wipe away another tear as Ryker clears my empty bowl, rinsing it in the sink quickly before popping it into the empty dishwasher. River provides a hanky, and I blot beneath my eyes.

"I've missed you, too," I say, sinking into her familiarity, the scent of her perfume reminding me of the innate safety only found in a parent's soothing tone. "And no, we decided to have it be a surprise."

"I didn't know with you," she says, pushing a lock of hair behind my ear. "And it was the greatest surprise."

"Pamela, would you be interested in going for a drive?" River asks, and I wonder if he and Ryker have loosely planned all of mom's visit or just today. The idea that they'd want her visit to be as memorable and special as possible–knowing she may not accept us–warms my heart.

Warms other things, too.

"Ryker and I would love to show you Raleigh. We'd love

for you to be well-acquainted with where your daughter will be living and where your grandchild will be raised."

"And," Ryker adds with one of his devilish grins. "It's a beautiful town, small but gorgeous, with everything you could need." Another wicked smile that burns my insides, making me feel unreasonably self-conscious as my mother sits by my side. Can she sense the arousal oozing from my pores when I'm around these men? She may be my mother, but she's also a woman. "But I could be biased."

"We can show you the middle school, too. We took Ember there a few weeks ago," River adds.

Mom turns to me, her expression much lighter than I'd anticipated. "Are you thinking of working again?" I can't tell if this makes her happy or if she's just coming around.

I shrug. "I don't know yet. I go back and forth on whether I like distance learning. And after I saw the school here in Raleigh," I drape my stacked palms over my heart, giving a small shimmy at the memory. "So adorable. Has that old book spine, disinfectant, rainy day smell, and everything." I smile at mom. "I realized I missed the smell of schools in real life."

River whistles. "That's... wild. I always hated that smell when I was in school."

Ryker snorts. "It reminded you of detention, that's why."

"Detention," mom teases. She teases River. My heart gallops at her playful tone because it means so much more. "So you were the bad student, and Ryker was the good one, is that it?" She looks between the two of them with a huge smile fixed on her face.

Ryker snatches keys from the counter behind him, tossing them to his brother, who reflectively catches them without looking. "Oh no, we were both hellions. I just blamed Riv. You know, twins and all."

Mom smirks as we stand, Riv and Ryk suddenly behind us to pull out our barstools. "Thank you," mom murmurs softly. River guides her through the hall leading to the garage, and Ryker and I follow closely.

I'm excited to show her Raleigh. But more than that, I'm excited to be with the four people I love the most.

CHAPTER TWENTY

RYKER

"I just... I'm going to call my mom, okay?" Ember says, her voice too wobbly for me to feel good.

"What's going on, Em?" I take a step closer to her and catch my brother's eyes, concern heavy in them. He knows something's up, too.

She twists from my grip, backing toward the stairs. "Nothing; I just want to talk to my mom for a few minutes, okay?" She turns and begins the slow ascent up the stairs, her seven-months pregnant belly keeping her from a quick getaway. She waves a hand behind her, saying, "I'll be down soon, okay? Stop worrying... I'm... fine," she says, a little winded, as she reaches the top of the stairs.

A few beats later, a door opens and closes.

Riv raises a brow. "What did I miss? I went for donuts, and I walked in to Em, seeming... upset." He slides the pink pastry box onto the counter, shrugging out of his winter coat. "Did you push the hospital birth again?"

I pinch the bridge of my nose as I slide an arm into my suit jacket. I've got a meeting with the school board director this afternoon, and I'd like to get into my actual office to review the notes my assistant has put together. But even if I get there now, my mind is here. I won't be able to focus if something is up with Ember.

"I didn't. I didn't do anything. I rubbed her shoulders and brought her herbal tea—"

"The green bag or the blue bag?" my brother asks, eyeing me suspiciously. He still thinks I'm the cause of the mood shift.

"The green; I know she doesn't like the blue anymore," I say defensively because the only bickering in our relationship is this: *me and Riv*. Siblings never stop bickering, even at forty-four.

I glance at my watch. I was going to stop by Dr. Longo's after the meeting this afternoon, and while I was in Oakcreek, grab Ember something sweet from the bakery there, the Wilting Daisy. They're famous for these sugar cookies and Em would love them. And I could use another session. As the birth nears, I miss Rhett unreasonably. More than I ever have, really. He should be here for his child's birth, and there's no amount of happiness I can experience that will backfill the hole inside me, missing my child.

"I think we should eavesdrop," Riv says, biting into a maple bar, icing catching in his dark, ruffled beard. "Then we don't have to guess."

Normally, I'd be against eavesdropping, but I can't do

business with this fucked up belly of nerves. Paired with the extra grief I've been feeling lately, it's too much to balance.

"Fine," I say, buttoning my jacket at the waist. "Let's—"

But then, the upstairs door opens, and Ember's soft voice drifts toward us as she appears at the top of the stairs. "You don't need to come spy on me; I'm off the phone. I'm coming down."

"You heard that?" River asks, shoving the last of the maple bar in his mouth and going in for a second one.

Adjusting my cufflinks, I come to a complete stop as she makes her way to the bottom of the stairwell. Her blonde hair is up in a messy wad, and she's swapped her sweatshirt and yoga pants for a long maxi dress with tiny little straps. Her breasts have been unstoppable in their quest to take over her body, and Riv and I have been loving it. Worshiping what will feed our babies makes us harder than fucking ever. It's new to us and fucking thrilling.

"Why'd you change?" Riv asks around a bite of a chocolate glazed ring.

Pink settles into her cheeks as she slides a lone finger under the strap of her dress, loosening it so it slides down her shoulder. She repeats this seductive movement on the other side, slowly tugging down her dress until her full breasts are bare and on display.

River chokes as he struggles to finish his bite. "I mean, I'm not complaining, but—"

She giggles, and I swallow hard, now just rubbing my cufflink as opposed to actually buttoning it.

"Something happened a few minutes ago, and I got... I don't know. Worried? Excited? Confused? And I had to call my mom and ask her about it. Or talk to her about it? I don't know." She smooths her palms over her breasts, puckered nipples peeking through her thumb and forefinger.

"You can always come to us," I tell her, concern still weighing in my gut. I don't like her turning to someone but us.

"It was pregnancy related." She cocks a brow, her third-trimester saltiness coming through loud and clear. "Have you been pregnant?" She looks at River with the same pointed expression. "Have you?"

We shake our heads. "So then you see why I wanted to talk to my mom."

I nod, and Riv nods.

"When you rubbed my shoulders earlier, I got this... tingly feeling. And I leaned forward to give you more access to my back, but my chest pressed against the counter."

"Are you okay?" I ask, suddenly worried. But then again, she has her tits out. So there's nothing wrong. Women do not deliver bad news with their tits out. "What's up?" I edge closer to her, and so does River.

"I noticed when I was pushed against the counter that... something wet was sliding down my breasts and belly. And I got freaked out and called my mom."

She tips her head forward, and like lost puppies, we follow. She looks at her breasts, and so do we. Massaging herself, she then pinches the hardened tips and–

"Oh my god," River says, voice low and husky.

"What's..." I can't finish the sentence.

I just stare at her full, soft breasts and the tiny stream of white trickling from the darkened tip. My head turns sideways as I watch the cream roll under her breast and sink into the fabric of her dress, bunched beneath.

"My milk came in. But I wasn't sure if that was normal for seven months. I called my mom to ask her. She said most women get their colostrum around now, but only some actually produce milk this early." She takes her eyes off her own breasts, meeting my gaze with hazy eyes. She looks at River with the same wanton, sinful expression. "I think because you two can't leave them alone, the process started earlier."

"No regrets," Riv says in a complete trance. I don't blame him. I lift my head as she continues to knead, more fresh milk bubbling up and then swimming down. The contrast of the pure white as it rolls over her knuckles and down her wrist, settling into the blue silk of her dress, has my cock instantly throbbing.

"Well, what... Pamela said... what, uh," I can't think. I can't speak. I can't do anything but adjust my fat, happy cock and stare at the milk spilling out of her and the way she plays with it, bringing a single drop of it to her lips atop the pad of her finger.

Riv sucks in a sharp breath as the tip of her pink tongue darts out along her finger, collecting the drop. Her lips curl into a rousing smile. "Mmm," she coos.

Riv closes the box of donuts and wags a finger toward the stairs. "Upstairs, now."

"Wait," Em giggles as my brother strokes himself over his jeans before going for his belt buckle. "I didn't tell you the best part."

My mouth pools with saliva, and an anxious tingling sears my lips as I stare at her, cupping her breasts.

"Once the baby is born, some women experience orgasms during let-down." She licks her lips, and I start working on my belt, too. I know I have a meeting in town in a couple of hours and important things to review before then. But... come on. "That's when your body is triggered to release the breastmilk. When your nerves are stimulated, your body releases hormones into your bloodstream, telling your body to push out the milk. It's amazing, really."

"And you think that will be you? Is this something we need to test?" Riv asks, closing the distance between him and Ember, pressing his lips to her bare collarbone. The sound of his mouth on her flesh while my cock is throbbing between my legs does me in.

"Be a good girl and listen to Riv and get upstairs," I command her as I whip my belt free, dropping it on top of Riv's. He stops kissing her to spin her around, earning a light giggle from Ember. He ushers her up, and I follow behind, using one hand to keep my pants up and the other to shoot a text to my secretary. "Reschedule everything for tomorrow except Longo."

Once we're inside River's room, I toss my phone aside and focus on the task at hand.

Ember sits on the foot of the bed, still fascinated with her breasts as she looks down at them, twisting and pinching her nipples. River is very quickly undressing, and I join him, eager as fuck.

"Get in the center of the bed," Riv says, an unspoken "*or else*" present in his searing tone. Ember scoots into the middle of the bed, ditching her dress and panties beforehand. She looks so fucking beautiful as a pregnant woman. We move in on her, climbing onto either side of the mattress in unison. River grips his cock just above the head, opaque moisture beading over the dark slit. "Good girl," he rasps, shaking his cock above her, drops of precum splattering against her belly. "Look how hard you have me, Em," he growls, stroking his length in slow, haphazard movements.

His eyes crawl over her breasts, but I lose focus of everything but her when she palms herself, moaning a little as she leaks. With my cock straining in my hand, I find my place on the bed next to her and waste no time circling around the hard peak of her breast, wetting the area I plan to latch onto.

My dick rubs against her hip and belly as I nestle my hand on her inner thigh, my thumb exploring her wet slit.

"*Ohh goddd*," she draws out the words on a rippling moan, her voice shaking with need.. Her leg collides with mine as she spreads wider, the gentle stroking of my thumb driving her mad. "Everything's tingly," she whispers, her mouth sounding dry.

Finally, I flick her nipple with the tip of my tongue and explore the fruit of a perfect latch. Her skin is soft and sweet, like a ripe peach spreading summer along my tongue. Intuitively I suckle her, drawing her nipple and some of her areola deep onto my tongue. She cries out a jumble of incoherent pleas, begging and panting for more. Of my mouth or my cock, I'm not sure, but I can't help but grind my lower half against hers as I suck, precum now ribboning down my shaft and onto my balls.

Then it hits my tongue.

Warm and sweet, somewhere between sugar and cream, it gushes onto my tongue in abundant streams. The more I suck, the more I'm rewarded with. The first long swallow makes my cock spasm and my balls ache–it tastes so goddamn good. Tasting what she's made to feed our child, I can't help but slide a palm over her belly, a bead of cum burgeoning at the slit of my cock at the soft, warm feel of her.

"Oh my god," she practically screams; she howls and her hand comes to my head as she softly tugs my hair. My eyes, which had fallen closed for a moment as I swallowed a mouthful of her nectar, open and find River.

He's on the other side of Ember now, the pink crown of his cock sliding up over her hip. Precum threads between his cockhead and her thigh, and when I look up at his face, my own cock thrums from what he must be feeling.

Ember is pinching her nipple, River is mesmerized, gazing at her in awe. She kneads her tit, coaxing her milk free, causing it to fall in indulgent drops. His mouth hangs open, salivating, dying for a taste of her. She coats his tongue, and I watch as stray drops of white roll down his nose, others getting lost in his beard. Finally, she giggles before he sucks her breast into his mouth and latches on with a growl.

The mattress dips rhythmically ever so slightly as River's hips grind against Em, and mine do, too. We look at her like horny teenagers, both of us sticky messes on her thighs. She fingers our hair and occasionally, she strokes the top of my shoulder or nudges my cock with her leg. But mostly, she lets us devour her.

Her nipple grows more firm after a few minutes of sucking, and the milk comes faster. I swallow down mouthful after mouthful, moaning against her, worshiping her, silently singing her praises. My cock is a trembling mess as her flow lessens. Drinking her milk feels nurturing and restorative. I feel a strengthening in the bond we all have to each other. I've never wanted to breed her as much as I do now.

I want to sink deep inside, so deep that she gasps a little and needs a minute to adjust to the girth of my fat cock. I want her eyes to water, and then, when she's begging me to rub the base of my dick on her clit, I fuck her hard. Pound into her with unrelenting strokes, like a fucking animal, and blow deep inside of her. So deep inside of her that not a single fucking drop leaks out.

But I don't get the opportunity to suggest River and I go full primal and fuck her breeding style—though that is one of our favorites—because she pushes up to her elbows, our cheeks in each of her palms.

"Please," she begs, and I already know what this is about. I shake my head as my brother adjusts to sitting, holding his cock in one hand, his hair a shaggy mess.

"I'd normally love our wanton goddess demanding a hot mouthful, but not while she's feeding another human," he says to me while he keeps his eyes on her. It's a reminder to stop asking for it, but she hasn't yet.

That's the thing about Ember. She can do anything she wants, and we'd go along for the ride. We're dually fucking whipped. But we'd have it no other way.

"Please," she whimpers, struggling around her belly to reach down. She does, though, with a little grunt and grabs the head of his cock. She twists her palm around it once, then licks her own hand.

His head falls to the side in exasperation, and before I know it, two sets of eyes are on me, seeking approval.

"Think about that," I say, trying to hold true to what we'd agreed on before our cocks were out and hard. "We don't know how much of what you eat gets passed to the baby."

"It won't hurt the baby. I read it in the book," she says, attempting to get out of bed to likely find the book. I push her back.

"Don't," I say as she readjusts her pillow and settles. A lone drop of milk rolls down her breast, and my brother dutifully leans over her and licks her clean. "I believe you."

Her lower lip juts out in an unfairly adorable pout. I stroke my dick, finding it hard and slick, my arousal leaking in thick, slow streams. I ache to unload into her mouth. I throb at the thought of seeing my load on her tongue, my brother stroking to add to it. To put a sea of Raleigh release on her tongue and watch her swallow it with a beautiful smile.

But we said we didn't want to.

"It weirded us out, remember?" I try to remind them, though the way River is back on Em's nipple, sucking at her while his cock drips onto the mattress, I doubt they care.

"Please. And... you first," she says, licking her lips. One of her hands strokes through River's wild hair, and the other reaches out for my cock. She finds it.

I bring myself to her and hover over her, one hand gripping the wall behind her, the other my base. "Please," she says, tracing the crown with the tip of her tongue. "I've been a good girl."

With a groan, I sink into her mouth, my eyes closing against my will. "Goddamn, you are a good girl," I growl, my chest full of pressure. It feels so good I could fucking combust. Explode. I don't know. My hand squeaks against the wall as I grip it harder, my hips roving back and forth as I impale and hollow her warm mouth over and over.

My brother is back on his side at hers, grinding his cock into her thigh with reckless abandon as he licks her nipple. The way she so easily makes us both feel so fucking good–I'll never understand it. She's magic. Everything she fucking does destroys us.

If she only gave him the side of her bare hip tonight, he'd be pleased. That's how bad we have it.

But she wants him as much as she wants me, and as she slows my thrusts with a hand to my groin, she lets me know. Throaty moans ripple around my length, vibrating down my shaft, its after-effects making my balls hot.

"Riv," I husk because his hand is not where it needs to be.

Without looking, he too realizes and drops his palm between her thighs, spreading her with his thumb. She whimpers, and he hisses against her breast as he discovers her wet cunt, stroking her soft and slow, the way she likes with him.

She seals her lips around me so tightly that a familiar feeling zips through my thighs as my gut clenches. Fuck. I'm already going to cum, but how could I not? The taste of her milk still swirls around my tongue, and all I can hear is my cock slipping between her swollen, wet lips as she sucks me.

"Ember," I rasp, clasping my hand to her chin and tugging her back. "Hold your tongue out for me, baby." I wrap my palm around my cock, stroking with a tight grip toward the head. I stop right before my crown and press myself onto her tongue. She moans as the first of my release ribbons across her tongue, hitting the back of her throat. A tiny cough, nothing more, and her mouth is still open. I groan as my cum paints her tongue, marks her lips, and earns me the fucking sexiest little smile I've seen. Even with her mouth open and full of cum, it's goddamn adorable.

Knowing what she wants and how she likes it, she turns to River, who's already on his knees and ready. He grips the wall like me and feeds his cockhead into her mouth. Cum leaks from the corner of her mouth, but I use my finger to push it back inside. The way I can feel his pleasure as his hard cock pulses against my finger makes me so proud of our girl. She takes us so well.

I pull my finger out as he grabs himself, cursing his impending release. "He's gonna need you to open a little wider, baby," I tell Em as my brother's neck strains in thick cords as he tenses. He's cumming; I know that look.

"*Fuuuuck!*" he howls as Em's eyes widen, and she coughs a little. But our good girl keeps it all in her mouth. She tips her head back a little to allow gravity to accommodate the mouthful.

I watch his shaft throb, veins pulsing desperately as he empties himself onto her tongue. When the engorged head of his cock slips free and he's spent, she opens her mouth wide and puts her prize on display.

"Fuck," River pants, still trying to catch his breath. But his eyes are dark and hooded as he fixates on her mouthful. "Goddamn perfect, Em."

I groan my agreement. "Mmm."

Then she closes her mouth and swallows. When she opens again, her bare pink tongue juts out, and goddamn, have I missed watching her do that. It's been too many months.

"Now," she grins. "I'm horny and hungry. But need you to... manage that first," she teases, waving the back of her hand down over her pussy. "Someone eat me, someone feed me." She rubs her belly, and my cock perks up again already.

"What about if we both have a snack, then both get you a snack?" I propose as I smooth my hand along her thigh, spreading her open. I love the way the sunlight drops rays of light along her belly, highlighting the very thing that makes my chest soft and my cock hard.

"God, you look fucking beautiful, Ember," I grasp, sliding two fingers inside her soft center. "You were meant to carry children."

"And have a pussy meant to be bred," Riv adds, his voice smoky and hungry. I drop down between her thighs, sensing how ravenous and impatient he is. I take my turn, sucking her wet clit onto my tongue, making her squeal.

"Ohmygod, Ryk, yes, yes," she moans.

I plunge my fingers inside her again as I stroke my tongue against her clit, loving how she blooms with every pass. She's so swollen, and she tastes so fucking sweet–I don't know what I want more of, her pussy or her milk.

"Yes," she moans, "get mommy off. Make mommy feel good," she purrs, and it's the first time she's ever referred to herself as mommy in the bedroom. My tongue slows as I lift my head enough to peer over her belly. I see Riv twisting her nipple, her breast coated in white streaks of sweet cream.

"Mommy," I growl, "I fucking like that." And holy fuck does my dick like it too.

"Eat," she moans, nudging my jaw with her leg. I sink my face between her legs and bury my tongue inside her, listening to River's rough voice douse her in filth.

"You took a big mouthful of us like a good girl. And then you let us drink you down like a sweet little mommy. So who is cumming on my tongue? Our good girl, or our naughty, sweet, dirty fucking mommy?"

I lick her clit one more time, then press a kiss to her lips, flush from friction and desire. My brother takes my place immediately while I lie next to her, pressing my lips to her neck, smearing the scent of her pussy against her throat.

"You tasted so good," I tell her as I sink my teeth into her shoulder.

"Yes, put your mouth on me," she moans, and I know she means her breast. "Yes, River, yes, yes, ohmygod, Riv," she chants as my brother's shoulders flex and his neck rolls. He feasts on her like it's his death row meal, and the sight of it brings me happiness. I bring my mouth back to her throat, licking and kissing her everywhere as she moans.

She pants unintelligible bargains as she shoves her hands in her hair, breasts heaving. "I'm gonna," she pants, unable to finish the sentence as her eyes roll closed and her head falls back. I look down between her legs and find River hovered over her, the tip of his tongue just barely stroking her pink, blossomed clit.

"I'm cumming; I'm cumming, I'm..." her voice trails off as her thighs tighten around his head. Easily, he spreads her open and presses a few kisses to her throbbing cunt as she swims down from her orgasm.

"I like having a good girl and a dirty little mommy, don't you, brother?"

"Mmm," I grunt, enjoying his dirty mouth as much as Ember does. But he's right—I enjoy all the filthy versions of herself she gives us. And I'm learning very quickly that having a dirty little mommy makes me cum fucking hard.

Sweat collects above her collarbone, and as she sits up, it streams down her chest. Her nipples are pink and sore looking, raw from our ruthless mouths. But she smiles, and my chest goes tight and hot, and I look over to see River wearing the same impish grin as me.

"Now we'll feed you," he says, collecting clothes from the floor. He tosses me items, and I'm not sure whose they are, but it doesn't matter. We dress, and as he smooths her hair back and finger combs the tangles, I step into the ensuite bathroom and run her a warm bath. We both help her up, as standing from laying proves to be a lot of effort with her growing belly. After we help her into the tub, we make our way downstairs to the kitchen.

"I rescheduled the meeting for tomorrow, but I may run into town and grab my shit so I can prepare from home," I tell River. He's privy to the meeting because most of it was his idea. He's in charge of the playground, and I have the business end of the remainder of our plans.

"I'll ride into town with you. I need some more paint for the mobile," River says, pulling his vest on over what I see now is my henley. He zips up and returns his focus to the eggs he's whipping up.

I slide toast into the toaster. "You got any pictures on your phone? I'd love to see."

River is building all the furniture for the nursery. But it's a surprise. The crib is done; the crib that will be in our newly remodeled master is done, and all that's left is the mobile. He rests the spatula along the side of the pan and finds his phone on the kitchen counter. A moment later, I'm staring at the screen, the image of a white and blue looking back at me.

"It's Raleigh-themed." He taps one of the items hanging from the large, painted spokes and zooms in. Up close, I can see it's a yellow duck. But not just any. A smile curves his lips. "It's the mascot from Duckies in town."

I nod, chuckling a little. "I recognize it."

He locks his phone screen. "The rest are like that. Babyfied landmarks of Raleigh."

"I like it," I tell him.

He pushes the eggs around in the pan and looks over at me with concern in his eyes. "Will Ember? I mean, do you think she'd rather have, like, owls or clouds or some shit?"

I shake my head. "No. She'll love it. It's incredibly thoughtful, Riv." I squeeze his shoulder as I butter the now-toasted bread.

In a lower voice, one that can't travel three flights of stairs, he says, "Fuck. How about this morning?"

My hand on him clenches, and he laughs. "We're going to have way too many kids, you know that, right?" I say with a laugh.

Ember is the most breedable, beautiful woman. Seeing her pregnant, witnessing her body change to provide for our flesh and blood—I never want her not pregnant.

He laughs, too, but I don't think either of us is kidding.

CHAPTER TWENTY-ONE

EMBER

I love them.
I love them.
I love them.

"Are you ready?" Riv asks, his voice rattling with excitement. Ryk's hands cover my eyes, his arms heavy on my shoulders from behind.

I love them. I love them *so* much. But my pregnancy patience is razor thin, and having my eyes covered for more than thirty seconds has me about ready to murder Ryker.

"Your big hand is squishing my eyelashes," I groan, batting Ryk's hands away from my face with the impatience of *every woman who is eight months pregnant*. My feet ache, my ankles are more like wobbly, unreliable balloons than *actual* ankles, and my ass is officially in two zip codes. And today, all I wanted was one single sip of coffee, and instead, what I got was my stupid herbal tea made by my stupid hot boyfriends...

Who then rubbed my shoulders and feet until I was so horny I could hardly speak, then one of them nursed me through letdown until I came, while the other fucked me hard through my orgasm.

It's gone straight to the replay bank for later.

But that was ten minutes ago, and my mood has shifted.

Now I'm grouchy and annoyed because *pregnancy*.

"Okay, remember, I can change anything you don't like," Riv says hesitantly. Ryk pulls his hands away, and as I'm on the cusp of a temper tantrum, my impatience turns to emotion.

Again, *pregnancy*.

"*Oh my god.*" My hands come to my face, where I cup them over my nose and mouth, gasping at the sight of a beautiful handmade crib. "Wait," my hands fall away as I gape at River, who has a look of anxious anticipation strung across his handsome face. "Two?" There are *two* perfect cribs, both painted and sanded to replicate the antique white cribs I'd seen in a catalog months back. I'd earmarked the pages, and I guess that was all it took.

"One for our new master suite so we don't have to go between rooms and floors. And one for his room, you know, for when he's in there." He shrugs as Ryker bumps a burly shoulder into his.

"They look fuckin' fantastic, brother."

I'm beaming. I can literally feel myself glowing at the sight. So incredibly thoughtful, not to mention heartfelt and beautiful.

The cribs, too.

Stepping to him, I cup his bearded cheek with my hand, tracing the curve of his full bottom lip with my thumb. "Thank you. They're perfect and beautiful, and I love them so, so much." I seal my words with a kiss and give one to Ryk, too.

"I mean, we could've moved the crib into the nursery once the baby is old enough to sleep alone," I tell him, holding my belly with one hand as I stroke the sleek rail of the freshly lacquered crib with the other.

"Well, the way I see it, if all goes as planned, we'll have another little one in the crib in our room when he's ready to move out," Riv says, his large hand infusing my belly with warmth as he takes space behind me, rubbing me.

I can't help but grin, but I stifle it, feeling playful. Quirking my eyebrow, I ask, "oh really? You want to keep me pregnant, huh?" A tingle moves through my lower half at the thought.

Ryker appears at my side after analyzing the perfect craftsmanship of the cribs. He nips at my neck a little, then brings his mouth to my ear, whispering, "we aren't getting any younger, baby. If we're gonna have more children, we're doing it right away."

My head falls back because his words feel as good as his lips. I want to be their fuck toy, but equally so, I want to mother their babies. I know as challenging as motherhood will be, the difference between misery and happiness is how attentive and helpful my partners are and will be.

"One more thing," River says a little shyly, leaning over the back of one crib to collect another surprise. From the ground, he lifts a large mobile, each item suspended with white string, all invisibly fused to a large beechwood hoop.

The aesthetic of the mobile is so unique and beautiful—much like the men I love.

"I'm making another one for the crib going in our room. One with a motor and music, you know, in case we're a little loud." He winks, and my mind goes places it has no business going right now.

"What's on the ends? Is that a duck? And is that a white rose?" I step closer and bring one of the mobile pieces closer, finding it fleecy and soft.

"They're all staples of Raleigh."

One by one, River explains all six of the token items he babyfied for the mobile, and it warms my heart that this baby will know from the moment it's born exactly how much the three of us love them. There won't be a single question. And it makes me proud to know how much my men value where they came from, and I appreciate how much they love and respect Raleigh. They work so hard every day to keep it a beautiful place to live, a quaint but lively small town with the right amount of charm.

"It's perfect," I say quietly, my eyes filling with more hormonal emotions. "Thank you so much. I love you. I love you both so much," I say, Ryk wrapping his arms around me the moment he spots my tears.

"I'm sorry," I snort as Riv comes up from behind, sandwiching me in the best group hug we can, considering a basketball is jutting out from my belly. "It's the hormones. I know we aren't gushy people. But I just... I love you both so much," I sob, burying my face in Ryker's shoulder. His leather and teakwood scent edges into my brain, and immediately all thoughts of tears are gone.

I push back, though they both keep their hold of me.

"You guys wanna fool around?" I wiggle my brows. Pregnancy hormones are a rollercoaster of insanity.

From behind, I can feel River's response poke into my lower back. He groans, and I reach back, but before I can cup all of him, Ryker stops us.

"Not right now. We need to get up to Oakcreek. We have appointments with Dr. Longo today, remember?"

I groan. I actually enjoy seeing Dr. Longo. The office has a lovely little sixties vibe, with avocado and orange accents, old leather furniture, and vintage vinyl lining his office shelves. He's helped me considerably, and I plan to keep seeing him for as long as I can–though he has mentioned his retirement in a handful of years. Still, my mental plate feels so much more balanced in the last few months, and I know it's because I've learned healthy coping mechanisms and so much more.

"I made you guys some sandwiches for the drive home," Riv says, grabbing his beanie, his messy hair disappearing as he tugs it on.

"Good. Thanks," Ryker says, wrapping his arm along the back of my shoulders. "One of us got hangry on the drive home last week," he remembers aloud, both of us pretending not to know that it was me who turned into a raging mess because I was starving.

"I probably won't be home until after dark; I'm helping Davis with the new siding on the hardware shop," he says against the metallic whoosh of his zipper.

Filtering my fingers through his beard, I find his mouth with mine and lose myself for a brief moment in a hot, sexy kiss. Riv and Ryk kiss so differently, and both of them complement my every need. *His* tongue delves into my mouth, exploring mine with harshness and passion. When I kiss Ryk, his mouth dances with mine, tasting and memorizing me. It's the ultimate dichotomy.

"Text me when you guys are leaving," Riv says to his brother before they share a hug, chest to chest.

Then we head downstairs, Riv getting into his truck as Ryk helps me into his SUV. He shuts the door, and a sharp jolt of energy moves bilaterally across my belly. Reactively, I press my hands to my bump, my heart rate spiking.

Ryker gives me a concerned eye when he slides into the driver's seat. "You ok?"

"Felt like a contraction but probably a Braxton Hicks."

The garage door opens, and light pours over us as Ryk shifts the vehicle into drive.

I certainly hope it's just a false alarm.

CHAPTER TWENTY-TWO

RYKER

I drag the cool blade down, white foam collecting beneath as I do. Another pass, and I drop the razor into the basin, washing the blade free of debris. With my other hand on my chin, I make another careful pass across my jaw, sure not to miss anything.

"Why is watching you shave so fucking sexy?" Ember asks from the bathtub.

River finished the master bedroom remodel last week, just in time, as Ember is now only two weeks away from her due date. The bathroom, which also received a hefty facelift, is now so goddamn big it could be an entire master suite. But, according to Riv, "women want big bathrooms, trust me." He wasn't wrong.

Ember is *obsessed*.

"I don't know, why is it?" I ask, tossing her a wink as I dip the shaver into the gray water again.

She moans a little. "I don't know, but I don't think it's pregnancy hormones either. You are just plain fucking hot." Peeking from the bubbles is her very pregnant belly and her massive breasts.

Breasts that Riv and I have been completely obsessed with for *months*. We cannot keep our mouths off her. You can add years to the man, but he'll always have a teenage boy inside of him that gets hard for a beautiful pair of breasts.

"Oh," she moans a little, but her voice rattles with discomfort this time, and I know this isn't a happy moan. She sucks in a sharp breath through practically gritted teeth. "Another fake contraction."

I wipe the last of the shaving cream from around my ears and the bottom of my nose. "Are you sure? I'm texting Riv."

"Don't," she warns, gripping her sudsy belly with her hands. "It's fine. It's not a real one if I can talk through it."

I roll up my sleeve and plunge my arm into the tub, pulling the plug so she doesn't have to lean that far forward.

"Come on, arms up," I say as I grab her towel off the heated rack nearby. Draping it over my shoulder, I'll never tire of the way her hands feel inside mine as she slides them in. Small, they always grip me so tightly, and I love how she's unafraid to need us.

Slinging the towel over her shoulders, I get her out of the tub and dry her down. She smiles, flirting with me a little by reaching for my cock and licking my neck as I do. I want nothing more than to lie her down and dip my dick into her sweet, wet warmth and feast from her tits as I do.

But Riv is in the yard, working on his raised planter beds. The truth is, I think he's nesting, too. We've had our food and groceries delivered to our home and stocked for us for the last *ten* years, and suddenly we need to source our own vegetables. Anyway, he's consumed. On a mission, and unbelievably, probably nesting hard enough to say no to even the quickest of quickies.

She rises to her toes, catching my bottom lip in a predatory little bite, and my resolve begins to crumble. I'm seconds away from texting Riv when she reaches out, gripping the hot towel rack behind me, hissing through clenched teeth.

"Oh my god," she whines, jerking her hands from the hot rack. "Fuck, I think I–" she can't speak. Her jaw is set in a grimace as she sucks long breaths in through her nose, exhaling shakily.

"Did you burn your hands?" I ask, grabbing her to analyze her palms. They're pink, and a little warm to the touch but likely not really burnt, thank God. "What's the–"

It's at that moment I realize she's not reacting to grabbing the heated towel rack. She's having a contraction that she can't talk through. Draping her arm over my shoulders, I hold her belly and slowly walk her out of the bathroom into the master suite, helping her find a comfortable spot at the foot of the bed.

"We're going in; where's your bag?" I ask, already dialing River. She shakes her head, attempting to argue, but she can't even speak. A sheen of sweat is coating her forehead, her hand pressed to her belly as she rocks back and forth, eyes closed, breathing heavy. "She's in labor," I say as soon as the call connects.

"I'm coming in," Riv says, hanging up immediately.

In the closet, I yank a sundress off the hook and pull it

down over her naked body. Once we get there, she'll be in a hospital gown so at this point, clothes feel like an unimportant necessity. She doesn't complain as I dress her, and that's how I know she must really feel those contractions.

"Where's your bag, Em?" I ask, my pulse starting to race. This is it. This is the moment we've been preparing for and discussing for the last few months.

My eyes warm at the same time a chill moves through me. Rhett's child is about to be born. The last link I have to my baby is about to be brought into the world. Ember raises her head, having made it through the contraction, color slowly reappearing in her expression.

"What's the matter?" she asks, and it is a testament to our love that in the midst of her birthing, she recognizes what I'm feeling.

I don't feed her some bullshit and tell her it's nothing. I follow Dr. Longo's advice and tell her just what I'm feeling. "This baby is Rhett's, and I'm both terrified and excited to see his face again." I smile at her as she runs her palms over her belly. "And I know, boy or girl, I'll see him again today. And I'm just... missing him."

It's difficult to express to Ember how much I miss him. Or at least, it used to be. I explained to Dr. Longo that missing the man that raped her feels cruel, but Dr. Longo explained that to each of us, Rhett was a different person because he was so lost. To me, though, no matter who he was to anyone else, including Ember, he was my son. And through his mistakes and even through his death, I still and will always love him.

Ember understands, and she's been tasked with challenging herself to have empathy when I speak of Rhett's good qualities. And the wonderful thing about her, or one of the many? She forgave Rhett early on. She forgave him to claim her own peace and has been working diligently to find it.

Today will be cathartic in its own right. Challenging and beautiful, but I'm ready for it. Because it will hurt to see his face again, but then we can move forward, which is what life is about.

She nods as River enters the master suite, out of breath, the scent of pine and cool winter morning trailing behind him.

"Fill me in," he says, taking a seat on the long bench adjacent to the bed. It's a bench where we sit to put on shoes and socks. For Ember, she relies on the bench just to get her pants on these days. It's also been the scene of a few Eiffel towers and other things a lot more fun than putting on socks. "The bags are in the closet. You and I are in one bag; Em and the baby are in the other," he says, his breath coming back to him slowly.

"She was having contractions in the tub but could talk through them, but once she stood up and since then, she can no longer speak when they hit." As the words leave my mouth, she doubles over, knees wide to make room for her belly between her thighs.

"No, no, if we go now, I'll be stuck in a hospital room for hours, and they'll stick me with drugs and slow it all down. We have to go—" she ceases speaking as another wave of pain crashes down, engulfing her.

"Yes, we have to go," I say plainly, yanking open the double French doors to our three-person closet, which looks more like an apartment than a fucking closet. Again, River's idea, and again, Ember is beyond pleased.

"No," she grits her teeth, golden strands of hair catching in her perspiration, clinging to her face. "We have to go right when it's time, not this early."

"Sweetheart," Riv says, using a term I don't think I've ever fucking heard him use. He sits next to her, patting her thigh. "We need to go now because you can't talk through the contractions, and you said the book says if you can't talk through them, then it's time."

"I'm not ready yet," she says, "let me have another few hours, and then we'll go, okay?"

Riv looks at her; head tipped sideways. "Ember, be a good girl now. Okay? We need to go. You know we need to go; Ryk knows it, and so do I." He strokes a hand through her hair as Ember's panicked eyes come to mine.

"What if the baby is like Rhett? What if he's born with his disease?" Tears fill her eyes and leak out, streaming down her cheeks. Her words are like a bat to my lungs, rendering me temporarily breathless. "It's a disease, being an addict. What if he's born with it?"

Riv and I lock eyes as she rubs her belly, wincing and groaning through another contraction. They seem to be so close; panic has me unable to sit or hang onto a single thought. But she needs reassurance so I need to shelve my overwhelming urge to get her to the hospital and give her my focus. Kneeling in front of her, I rest my hand on my brother's knee.

"Ember. No matter how this child is born, you have two partners here to help you with whatever comes your way, okay? If he or she is born liking polka music, we'll figure it out. There is no medical condition or disease that this baby can have that would keep us from loving them with our whole hearts. Our entire everything. You hear me?"

Her bottom lip trembles as she glances down to where River has placed his hand over mine in an act of support and solidarity. When her eyes come back to mine, she gives a tiny nod.

"Speak, baby, because I need to know that you're heading into labor knowing what you have."

Riv nods his head, adding, "no matter what, it's the three of us forever, Em. We'll play through any hand we're dealt together."

"You realize that, don't you, Em?" I ask, needing her to speak, to hear her acknowledge she knows our love has no limits and that our relationship is the safety net for anything life throws at her. Right about now, I wish we could all be married.

We'd wanted to wait until the baby was born; that way, Ember could wear whatever white gown she's always dreamed of. After all, when she married my son, she sacrificed a lot without even realizing it, the white dress being the least of the things on that long list.

"I know," she says, River using the edge of his sleeve to wipe her tears.

"Now." I get to my feet and outstretch a hand to her. "We need to get you to the hospital."

She rises, Riv using his hands to give her a little boost as she groans, another contraction likely taking over.

Until a steady rush of warm liquid gushes from her onto our feet. River steps back, pointing.

"Em, holy shit, your water broke," he says, eyes wide,

wagging his finger as amniotic fluid or whatever the fuck a woman's "water" is pools on the hardwood.

"Okay, we need to get her in the truck. Riv, take her down and get her in the back. I'll clean this up and bring the bags; no more waiting."

He nods. "Okay, you heard the man, Em; let's go."

She shakes her head. "There's so much pressure; I'm afraid the baby will fall out if I walk!" Tears coat her cheeks, and Riv looks to me for the answer, clearly growing more and more flustered as the labor progresses.

"Carry her," I tell him before taking her chin and pulling her mouth to mine. I kiss her, then let our foreheads sink together for one last moment. "The baby won't fall out, Em. Okay? But Riv will carry you. And we'll get you there. And then guess what?" I taste her lips one more time, my heart vibrating at the taste of her salty tears. "Then you'll give us our baby. I'm already so fucking proud of you, Em. I love you."

She sniffles. "I love you too." Looping her arms around River's neck, he hoists her up, and they make their way out of the master suite toward the stairs. Quickly, I clean up the mess, grab a fresh towel for the pickup, nab the bags, and head downstairs.

Our baby is coming.

I wish my son was here to father his child, to be the man *I knew* he was beneath his troubles, to know what it feels like to cradle a part of yourself and the woman you love in your arms and plan all the ways you're going to give them the best of life.

But he's not here. Accepting that is still painful but it's true.

River and I are here, and we'll do everything we can to make this and every day after as special as fucking possible.

With River behind the wheel, I slide into the backseat of the truck, wanting to sit with Em on the drive to the hospital. Thank god it's only on the other side of town, but the fifteen minutes it takes is already feeling too long.

Ember's face is white, most of her hair now drenched with sweat. The fatigue of the contractions is clearly setting in. Pulling out of the driveway, I notice she's hardly spoken in the last few minutes.

I rub her leg as River drives, and a block from home, another contraction hits. Riv's green eyes flash in the rearview, finding mine. "Just keep going, stay calm, okay?"

He nods. I knew he'd be a nervous wreck. I suck in a breath, knowing I need to keep it together for all of us. In the bedroom, River may be the more dominant between us, but outside, I take the lead. Business has sharpened my ability to stay calm in the face of chaos.

"Ryk," Em cries out, reaching around her belly between her legs. "Pull the dress up, pull the dress up," she wails, her eyes full of horror. "I need to feel myself, I think... I think..."

Unclipping my belt, I gather the end of the long maxi dress, clutching an excess of fabric in both hands. "Lie back a little," I tell her. "Let me take a look. Just stay calm, okay?"

No matter what's going on, freaking the fuck out is not going to help. Besides, she's probably just feeling the baby move toward the birth canal. The pain is messing with her head, and being on the cusp of giving birth is a frightening place to be. I get it.

"I'm gonna peek, okay? But you're okay. Okay?"

She nods.

"Speak, Em. Tell me you know you're okay."

"I'm okay," she says, voice wobbly, dark strands of wet hair falling across her forehead. "I just, I feel so much pressure."

I nod and then slowly lift the fabric, her knees already open.

"Oh my god," someone says. I blink, and I realize the soft exclamation came from me. In an out-of-body experience, I stare at Ember's opening, completely entranced by what I see.

"He's crowning," I say aloud, to Ember, to River, to myself, I'm not sure. Though panic and anxiety are tearing through me, somehow I cling to my calm.

"But... we aren't there yet," she whimpers, one of her sweaty hands gripping the back of the seat, the other going to her belly as another contraction takes over. I watch in both horror and amazement as the head with dark hair, commingling with blood and amniotic fluid, emerges just a bit more. Ember howls in pain, making the cab of the truck vibrate.

"Oh my god, oh my god," she pants, her eyes full of fear. "I'm gonna have the baby in the truck! We should have left sooner! You're not a doctor!" she shouts, her rapid-fire thoughts bouncing off me.

As much as I know I should probably be freaking the fuck out, the bloody but beautiful sight of life on the cusp of birth is... so calming.

"River, give me the hand sanitizer from the console," I say calmly to my brother as he slows down, a red light ahead.

He flicks open the console and passes the bottle back. I push my sleeves up and douse my hands in the sanitizer, the stringent smell of alcohol burning my nostrils and throat, making me cough.

"Why are you doing that?" Ember asks despite the fact that she *knows* the answer. She doesn't want to believe it, but it's okay; I'll believe it for us all.

"The next time you feel that pressure, roll with it, okay?" I put my hands on her spread knees and squeeze. "Have you pushed yet?"

She sort of shrugs, her eyes still so fucking wide. I know she's scared. And I'm scared, too, and I know Riv is. But we have to focus. As long as we stay calm, we'll be okay. We're almost there. Right?

"Are we close, Riv?" I ask, refusing to let my voice tremble. I peek at the head emerging from her center, and calm washes over me again. My grandson–*my son*–is almost here.

"There's a train," he answers quietly. Peering out the window, I realize... we're only five minutes from the house, meaning there are ten minutes left to get there. I don't know if we have ten minutes. Fuck. I turn my focus back to Ember.

"Listen, Em, when you feel it, just push, okay? We're very close to the hospital; it's going to be fine. I'm here. Riv's here."

"I thought we had, like, *days*. I thought we had so much time. No one in real life really has a baby as quickly as they show in the movies. That's not real!"

"It may not be common, but that's us," I say, with a smile and wink proportionate to the moment. "*Uncommon*."

She braces herself in the cab, saying, "another one. I'm not even pushing! It's just... oh God, Ryk. There's so much pressure. My body is just bearing down on its own." Her nostrils flare as sweat shines under her eyes. "I want to make it there, but I can't *not* push!"

Veins bulge in her temples, striations fill her neck, and her face goes white. "It hurts so fucking bad, Ryk," she cries.

"River, pull over."

As Ember bears down through the pain, I take another look and realize she's on the verge of giving birth. Though I have just one experience with labor and delivery, I know we're moments away. My brother pulls over.

"Come to the back, get in, let her lean back against you, and let her use you to hold onto, okay?" I say to River calmly, knowing that Ember is hanging onto my every syllable and tone.

He nods, yanking off his beanie and tossing it into the driver's seat. I hold Ember's hands, pulling her off the door she'd been leaning against long enough to make room for River to slide behind her. He closes the door, tapping the automatic locks. Ember falls back against his chest, and he immediately gets to work comforting her, pushing sweaty hair off her face, kissing her temples and whispering to her how excited we are for this baby.

It's *exactly* what she needs between contractions. And as she gears up, not even a full minute after the last, I urge her to follow her body's lead.

"Okay, Em, another contraction. Do what feels right," I advise because I have no fucking clue what I'm talking about, but each time she bears down, more and more of that precious life slips out of her, and my instincts tell me to prepare. "Riv, if you can grab my phone out of the bag, call 911 so they can send us an ambulance."

"An ambu, ambu–" she can't even spit out the word as she pinches her eyes closed, another painful contraction fogging her thoughts. "Wh-why?"

"You're going to have our baby, Em. Right here, okay? And you'll be fine, and so will they. But we need a ride to the hospital. Okay?"

She nods. Riv fishes around with his free arm to find the phone and dials instantly. As he fights to be heard over Ember's cries, the message that we need an ambulance is delivered just in time for another contraction.

"I have to push," she says, tears streaking her cheeks. "I have to push. I can't *not* push." She slaps her hands into River's and locks eyes with me for a second before she tucks her chin to her chest, braces her bare foot on the back of the passenger seat, and pushes with all her goddamn might.

Cramped in the backseat, I bend as much as I can to have my body between her spread legs. I slide a hand between her legs as the baby's entire head emerges, the tiniest set of shoulders coming with it. Pink fluid splashes out of her, coating the seat, towel, and her thighs. My eyes fill with tears as the baby's head fills my palms.

His skin is warm and sticky, and a moment after Ember starts pushing again, nearly his entire body has materialized. And my hands are beneath him as she screams for God to help her, and when I'm fully crying to the point I can almost not see, she births him completely, his little feet tangled in the thick, purple cord that falls out of her with him.

One singular, sharp cry pierces through Em's moaning, Riv's cooing, and my tears. For a split second, we all fall silent, and I bring the baby to my chest, tears rolling down my cheeks. I look into his face, and as he opens his dark little eyes, my heart explodes.

I see Rhett, the day he was born, the memory of his squishy little face and his sharp cry cascading behind my eyes. *You would love this feeling if you were here, son,* I think to myself as I stare down into two endless pools of darkness, the baby's little eyes peering up at me. He howls again as I reach for the spare towel to wrap him up before passing him off. As I'm handing him over, I realize my son doesn't have a son.

He has a daughter.

Leaning forward, I pass her to Ember, laying the crying, sticky baby wrapped in a bath towel on her chest. Ember cries as she stares down at her, and I watch as she and River take in this new life together for the first time.

"It's a girl," I rasp, my voice gone despite the fact that Ember is the only one that's been screaming.

"Phoenix," Ember says quietly, cradling our child to her chest with tears coating her cheeks. "Let's call her Phoenix. Nix for short."

"I love it," River says, entranced with the face in Ember's arms. "I see you, Rhett," my brother says softly to the baby, who isn't crying too much. Her eyes are open, and she blinks up at them, her little mouth working. "I see you in there."

River finds my eyes. "I love you, brother."

I nod. "I love you, too, Riv." I cup Ember's knee, unable

to hold her beautiful face in my palm like I'd like since I'm covered in afterbirth. "Em, baby, you did so good. We're so fucking proud of you." I stroke my hand through Phoenix's dark hair. "Look at what you gave us. Look at what you made."

With a smile, Ember slides Phoenix to the side of her chest, lowering her dress to expose her breast. "I think she wants to suckle, she's rooting," Em says, and then I watch as she pinches her breast as if she knows just what to do and slides it into Phoenix's mouth. The baby struggles a little, grunting and crying, but a moment passes then soft suckles fill the cab.

Ember breaks out into tears. "She's perfect."

Outside, an ambulance sounds.

I look at the three people I love the most, and as much as I miss my son, I'm overwhelmed by the love I have right here in this truck.

CHAPTER TWENTY-THREE

EMBER

FOUR MONTHS LATER

I move my fingers along the raspberry-colored flesh circling my areola and smile.

"I have permanent beard and mustache burn," I whisper to River, who is now positioned between my legs, his tongue moving along my pussy in expert strokes. He peers up over my pubic bone, placing a kiss on my clit. I love the way his lips tell a story of a hungry morning; pink, swollen, and shiny.

"I can shave," he offers before dragging his nose between my lips, resuming his mission to feast on me until I orgasm.

"No," I moan, reaching between my legs to stroke his shoulder. "Then I couldn't tell you apart."

A groan comes from my left side, and I look down at Ryker, who isn't finished nursing.

Phoenix is four months old. We learned pretty quickly that nursing is one hundred percent supply and demand. The more hungry mouths I have demanding my milk, the more I make. River and Ryker nurse for functionality–if we're away from home and Nix refuses to eat or fills up, leaving me swollen, full, and uncomfortable, they'll *drain* me. If I have a clogged duct and Nix can't quite clear it, I have Ryk and Riv for that.

This morning isn't functional nursing, though. This morning is *our* time.

After Nix came fast and early, we called my mom to come stay with us. She ended up taking family medical leave so that she could spend six weeks at our house, helping with Nix and getting quality time with her granddaughter. She couldn't get the time until Nix was already two months old, but that worked out perfectly anyway. Before she was fully immunized, River was stressed about anyone being around her who could get her sick. He didn't let Ryk or me leave the house for those two months, either.

It was so sweet.

Mom's nearing the end of her visit, but the last six weeks have been glorious. Every morning, Ryker brings Nix to me, and I feed her. River changes her and takes her to mom, and she does tummy time and reads to her while we... "*sleep in*."

"Mmm," Ryk moans as my hardened, wet nipple slips out of his mouth. "You're extra sweet today." He resumes his latch, using his hand to squeeze my breast. The noise of his swallow makes my clit tingle, and I lose my hand in his luscious dark hair as my orgasm snakes down my spine.

It's not the way River flicks the tip of his tongue over my clit, and it's not how Ryker drinks my breast milk in long, deep swallows, either. The reason I'm cumming, moaning, trembling, and even becoming emotional with every orgasm I have postpartum is simple: the feeling of being worshiped by two men is all-encompassing and so much more fulfilling than just being *fucked* by one.

"Don't cum yet," Riv warns, stealing the pulsing sensation as he lifts his mouth, leaving me right on the edge.

I whimper down at him. "Please."

His grin is dark as he rises to his knees, stroking his swollen pink cock. "Until you're growing my son or daughter, you are not having a single fucking orgasm without my cock; you got that?" He shakes himself over me, precum splattering against my needy flesh.

I nod. "Yes."

"Yes, what?" Riv pulls my legs to his chest, my toes in the air. Ryker licks my nipple, beginning to play and tease as he nears the end of his session.

"Breed me," I hiss, knowing those two words will bring him to his knees. "Fuck your cum into me and give me another baby."

Ryk's sucking intensifies, and they're the only men I've ever met to actually get harder and cum at the idea of that type of long-term commitment. A new life.

He sinks into me with his fat cock as he growls, "*good fucking girl.*"

Ryk's not been left out, but because River is trying to father our next child, Ryk's been taking his turn first, only to pull out or empty himself in my ass. I love when Ryker blows inside my ass, then River fills up my cunt, leaving me sore and full, the warmth dripping from my holes a dirty reminder of how blessed I am.

The promise to make him a baby, to give him a child—it's always the last straw for Riv. Ryk grinds into my hip as Riv picks up his pace, slamming into me with grunts and fervor.

"Fill me up, fuck it into me deep, Riv," I moan loudly, knowing our room is thoroughly soundproof.

"Give it to her, brother," Ryk says, his knuckles grazing my thigh as he begins stroking himself. I watch as he suckles my breast. He peers up at me, mouth full, and suddenly his jerking off isn't good enough.

"Get behind my head, on your knees," I order him.

River, sensing a shift in the shared orgasmic pool, slows his fucking, though I can feel how close he is by his slow strokes and tight jaw. Ryk positions himself behind me on his knees, and I tip my head back to see his chiseled torso above. His cock rests on my forehead, along the bridge of my nose, the throbbing head hovering above my open mouth.

"Hands behind your back," I tell Ryk as the intensity between my thighs increases. With Ryk's hands behind his back, I look back down to River, whose dark eyes are hooded. His hands tighten around my calves as he strokes deeply inside me, growling his need.

"Fuck, Em, I'm fucking close."

Reaching up, I begin stroking Ryker just as River begins to hammer my pussy, fucking me to find his orgasm. Just as his fingers curl into my flesh, making me achy and sore, he stills, a strand of dark hair falling over his eyes.

I twist my hands around Ryker's slick, hard cock, murmuring, "Riv's cumming; right now, I can feel him pulsing. I can feel his cum warming my insides." Then I give

Ryker the final stroke before I just hold him there, the length of his cock hovering over my forehead and the bridge of my nose.

River howls as he floods my cunt with the last of his orgasm, and Ryker's cock flexes right as I open my mouth. Without stroking, I hold him there as he cums into my open mouth in slow, rhythmic ropes. My tongue laps at the tip in between bursts, and when he's finally empty, he sinks back, stealing his cock from me.

I swallow as Riv watches me eat Ryker's release. It's no surprise he stalks over me, resting his body weight on his elbows as he slams his mouth into mine, kissing me with passion and heat. He can taste his brother; I know it because I can still taste Ryker, but the fact they never seem phased by it always does terribly arousing things to me.

"Thank you," I say, reaching between us to stroke his sticky, softening cock. "Thank you for everything." He buries his face in my neck as I tip my head toward the ceiling, Ryker hovering over us. Leaning in, he kisses my cheek before sliding off the bed.

"I should go relieve Pamela or at the very least, make breakfast." He gathers clothes from the floor, dressing quickly. If someone had told me that day on the bank floor that this man would be my everything, that he and his brother would fuck me senseless, nurse on me, and satisfy me in ways I didn't know I needed, I would have laughed.

"Riv, really consider going back to sleep." He feeds a belt through his jeans, feet still bare. "Em, you too. Pamela and I are fine with Nix. There's milk in the fridge if she gets hungry."

River's playground rebuild was so successful the town

begged him for another one across town. He's been putting in extra hours to get it done, and between that and waking up with Phoenix every three nights, he's exhausted. I want him to rest.

When Ryker looks back at us, it warms my heart that he and his brother share a soft smile. Their vulnerability and intimacy have taught me so much about love.

Riv wants to snuggle, and as tired as I am, I'd love to. But my mom is on her last few days, so I slip into the shower and meet mom and Ryk downstairs as Riv catches up on rest.

"Are you sure? It's your last night here," I whine, grabbing my mom by her hand like a child.

She grins, and a wave of pride and honor washes over me. I am so lucky to have her as my mother.

I brought her to this house not too many months back and asked her to accept one of the strangest relationships ever. I worried and fretted over her opinion, and when she left here after that visit, I wasn't sure how she felt.

But she called me after that trip and said something I'll never forget. "You don't have one partner who loves you. You have two. It took me time to understand how you can love more than one person at a time, and I can't say I fully get it. I mean, I don't think I could. But then the way you all were together… It was so real and pure. I arrived unsure, and I left feeling the most comforted any mother could. They love you, Ember, and that's all I've ever wanted for you—unconditional love and safety."

Since she left, Ryker and River have kept in contact with her. River calls her from time to time to check in, help walk her through computer issues, and swap recipes. Ryker sends her articles on investing, her retirement, business, and in recent months, baby pictures. They each have their unique relationship with her, which is exactly what I never knew I always wanted.

She pats Phoenix's bottom, swaying slowly from side to side in the monstrously large nursery River built. "I'm sure. It's your last chance to have a date again for a while until you guys hire some help, so go!"

I check my hair in the mirror hung behind the crib. It's hard to feel sexy in your skin when said skin hangs a bit lower, when every part of your body is softer than its ever been, when purple and pink marks marr your skin, reminding you that you are not the same as you once were. It's hard, but with Ryker and River, it's not impossible.

Because every time I'm in their presence, I feel like the only woman who has ever been in their orbit. Their gazes pin to me when I'm in a room full of people. Their hands are all over me when the three of us steal moments of privacy. Their praise and pride are in my ears nonstop.

My reflection may not show me a version of myself that I adore, but it shows me who they adore, and that gives me the confidence I need.

It gives me everything I need.

I drop a kiss on Nix's head and whisper my goodbyes, leaving her dozing against my mom's chest. Thanking my mom again, I make my way downstairs, where I find Ryker and River waiting.

Each of them in cigarette pants, Ryker's black and

River's the color of wet earth; they both wear fitted white button-downs, tailored to the sleek edges of their physiques. The shirts put on display their strong shoulders and mountainous chests, each of them with a bit of neatly trimmed chest hair peeking out from the open button at the top. Ryker's dark hair is combed back, shining beneath the bright kitchen lights. River's hair is up in a neat bun, his beard trimmed to utter perfection. Their mossy eyes eat me up, and my entire body warms beneath their hungry gazes.

Ryker tells me to spin, and River rubs his palms together like a man on the hunt as I do.

"You look gorgeous, baby," Ryk compliments, catching my hand with his and pulling me into him. We share a sweet kiss, and then I'm twirled into River's arms, adoring the way his muscles constrict around me as he squeezes me tight.

"I second that," he gruffs, his beard setting off a trail of goosebumps along my flesh like wildfire.

I pay them compliments, telling them how impressively handsome they are, and then we drive to dinner. Ryker tells River about a meeting he had today with the school board, talking quietly in the front seats as I relax in the back, letting intermittent moonlight spill over my lap as we drive through a wooded area on our way into town. Just the low rumble of their voices brings me peace, and when I picture Nix sleeping with my mom back at home, I feel so content that my eyes fall closed.

Even with three other people helping out, having a baby is still exhausting. The next time my eyes are open, Riv and Ryk are grinning at me, hands extended, waiting to get me out of the backseat.

"We're here," Ryk says, his voice smokier than normal.

I peer out the back of the SUV, rectangles of orange glowing against the fading sun. We're at the nicest restaurant in town, and it's a place they've taken me to many times.

It's my favorite place, not because it's the nicest but because of the food.

"My first time coming here not pregnant!" I squeal, eager to show the waiters at this place that I can eat a normal-sized meal instead of ordering ten plates and taking two bites off each. Pregnancy cravings had me running up $250 bills for my food alone.

Ryker rests a hand on the back of River's neck, and neither of them moves. Their green eyes are full of depth as they both smile at me, standing still in the private parking lot.

"What's up?" I smooth my hands down my silk dress and double check my nursing pads are in place. I look down, surveying myself. Why are they just standing there?

In unison, without preamble, they both take a knee.

"Marry us," Ryker says, his voice like smoke wrapping around me, fogging my brain.

"We love you," River adds, sounding gravelly and raw.

They each produce a box, and when Ryker opens his, a massive diamond stares back at me. River flips his box open, putting two tungsten carbide bands on display.

"This is your engagement ring," Ryker says before looking at his brother.

"And these are our rings. We'll wear these forever and get you a matching wedding band, that is, if you say yes."

I blink down at the two men waiting for me to say yes as if there is another answer. As if I wouldn't give up my life for theirs. I step forward to Ryker first, cupping his cheek, smoothing my thumb along his velvety lip.

"Rhett gave us the best gift. He gave us each other. He gave us Phoenix. So before I say yes, I want to say to you, the man who gave Rhett life, thank you. Thank you for everything you've given me. And thank you for everything I know you both will continue to give me."

He rises, and River does the same. I grab Riv's hand and press my lips into his bare palm. "I love you so much. I never thought I could love two men this way, but I do. You both complete me."

River's eyes grow wet as he scratches his beard. "I was gonna give a little romantic speech, but..." He grins. "You beat me to it."

We share a laugh, and then before I know it, Ryker is slipping the ring on my finger. Before he lets go, he asks, "Is that a yes?" He leans close, and his cologne makes me dizzy. "Say yes."

I blink and realize I'm crying. I say yes, and I turn to River and say yes to him, too.

―――

Hugs, kisses, and two adjusted crotches later, we're tucked into our private booth, feet commingling beneath the table.

Over dinner, River announces yet another surprise.

"If you want to work at the school, because I know you loved it when we visited—well, they're hiring."

I cock an eyebrow. "What do you mean? Raleigh's small. Did someone retire?" We were just there a few weeks back, and at that time, Ryker expressed his disappointment that they were fully staffed.

He chuckles and casts a knowing glance at his brother. "No one retired. And no one was going to for a while, so... I built another school."

Ryker holds up a hand before I even say a word. "The teachers at the current school are itching to get to the new school. Upgraded everything, and you know, the current middle school is old."

"I love it," I breathe. "I love the smell of vintage school. Book spines and chalk and old bologna."

Ryker chuckles, and I can't help but laugh. "I do," I draw out, "it reminds me of the most beautiful time in your life. When you're a child and all you have to worry about is not being it in Red Rover and remembering your coat at the end of the day. It's so simple and beautiful and perfect and who wouldn't want to exist in a place like that for their job?"

Riv casts a glance at Ryker, looking pleased. "We thought you'd say that. So you take the pick of which classroom at Raleigh Middle that you'd like, and it's yours."

I shake my head. "I don't want you to kick someone out of their space for me. They'll hate me. They'll claim...." I tap my chin, thinking. "Nepotism."

Ryker pats my hand. "You're not my kid, Em. It's not nepotism. You're our wife."

"Well, *will be*," River adds, but it doesn't matter. Hearing those three words... you're our wife... it melts me. Suddenly, I have an appetite for two things and neither of them can be served on a plate.

"Well... I..." I don't know what to say.

"All of them want to go to the new school," Ryker says. "I

met with the school board and the principal this morning. Not only will you get your choice of classroom, but you're going to make a lot of people happy. After all, your husbands are the ones who built the new school and gave Raleigh 100 new jobs."

I cup my hands to my mouth, the large diamond still feeling unusual against my knuckles as it turns. "You guys."

River leans in, and Ryker does the same, and the feeling of their lips skirting the column of my throat drives me mad.

"You deserve to have the job of your dreams after everything you've been through," Ryker whispers, his tongue tracing the lobe of my ear. I shiver hotly as River's hand falls onto my thigh, hiking up my silk dress.

My body grows weak from their words, their admissions, their love. "Fuck dinner," I breathe out, "lets go home and celebrate." I hold out my hand, both admiring my ring with me as they kiss my bare shoulders and throat. "We're getting married."

It occurs to me my mom is at the house, and I'm so happy she's here to celebrate our engagement. "Perfect timing! My mom is leaving this week. Now she can see my ring in person before she goes!"

Ryker and River share a conspiratorial glance. "She... she may already know what it looks like," Riv hedges, shrugging. I look at Ryker.

"We asked her for your hand, and then I sent her the pictures of the rings we were choosing from." He strokes hair from my face. "We wanted her to be part of things, for you but also... for all of us. She's family to us now."

I tip my head back. "I don't want to ugly cry but Jesus."

Riv leans over me to speak to Ryk. "Let's put an order in and pay for them to bring it out to us, and let's go home."

I like that idea, so we order gobs of food and duck out, laughing and smiling and happy.

Happy.

Engaged.

And starving.

CHAPTER TWENTY-FOUR

RYKER

"Can you grab the stroller from the back?" Em asks Riv, kind of doing her eyelash-batting thing she does when she really wants something. Not that we've ever said no.

"You taking a walk?" he asks, finishing the last drink of his water. We've just gone for our run, and Ember's about to go down to the school for her first week before school starts. Boxes of classroom decorations litter the counters, and I've already taken the morning off to help her unload them all. From the high chair, Nix squawks.

Riv slides his fingers through her hair before kissing her cheek. He lifts a piece of pancake to her mouth, and he pulls his fingers away, wincing as she takes a bite. Nix giggles. She loves when he pretends she hurts him.

"Aren't you leaving?" he asks, retying his hair into a messy wad atop his head.

"Not yet," she says, glancing at her watch suspiciously. "But I was hoping to get a few miles in when I get home."

He shrugs and heads to the garage. Once the door slams closed, I turn to her. "We aren't going to be home in time. Plus, you said you'd stop by my office with me after. I have that paperwork to pick up."

She steps close, and the smell of vanilla and toothpaste that I know and love warms me. "I'm pregnant," she whisper-hisses, excitement threaded heavily into her high-pitched tone. "I thought we could tell him right now."

My mind whirrs. Ember is pregnant. With our baby. Phoenix is ours, no fucking doubt, but another baby. My eyes warm, and her excited smile turns soft.

"Aww," she says, rocking to her toes to kiss me.

"I'm just... very happy." My voice is hoarse.

"Me too. And I have a ton of romantic, gushy things to say to you, but," she pauses, glancing at Nix, whose bright eyes twinkle as Em waves a piece of strawberry in front of her. At eight months old, she's really growing into a wild and adorable little personality. She loves laughing. She's always happy. "We need to tell River because I can't hold it in one more second!"

My heart is pounding in my temples and excitement is buzzing through my veins. "How long have you known?"

She lifts Nix from the highchair, resting her along her hip. "Four minutes. But that's four minutes too long!" Nix giggles as Ember bounces on her feet.

I want to cry.

I don't know if it's how excited she is, how much I love what we have, or how excited we all are for the future, but watching Ember smile into Nix's eyes, I feel Rhett. And I feel complete.

The door opens and slams, and Ember's eyes go wide. I wiggle my fingers and outstretch my hands, taking my daughter from her. "Tell him now. I have her."

She wiggles her brows in excitement, pressing a chaste kiss to my cheek. "Okay." Elation vibrates in her voice.

River sets the folded stroller on the ground, then grabs his thermos from the counter. "Alright, well, have fun setting up the classroom. Send me pictures," he says, turning to go. But we don't let him go. Ember grabs his arm.

"Riv, wait." I can hear her nervous swallow. Except, I don't think it's nerves. I think it's... emotion.

She weaves their hands together and squeezes. "I'm pregnant."

A moment passes. I stare at my brother's face, the one that reminds me of myself, and wait. Slowly, his lips curl into a smile, and his gaze lifts from Ember, finding me holding our daughter just a few steps away.

We share a smile because this is what we've wanted. A family, *together*. It's all we've ever wanted, and Ember is giving it to us.

She's giving us everything.

"Really?" he asks, voice husky.

She nods, and when their mouths crash together, my heart expands beneath my ribs. I kiss Nix on the head, savoring her baby scent as I watch the two people I love most share a perfect moment.

Ember swipes her thumb beneath his eye, taking a tear from him. "Thank you," she whispers, earning a questioning look from my brother.

"For what?" he asks. His hands have begun smoothing the length of Ember's arms the way he loves to comfort her.

"Giving us another baby."

Nix stammers, "bay-bay" as River and Ember turn to face her.

"Yes!" Em smiles, reaching for her. "Mommy has a baby in her tummy. Can you say baby, Nixie girl?"

"Ba!" she cries again, her sticky fingers tangling in Em's hair. "Ba! Bay!"

Em brings Nix's nose to hers, wiggling them together. "Close enough," she coos, pressing a kiss into Nix's hairline.

River takes Phoenix from Ember's chest, smoothing his hand up her back in a way that immediately causes her head to fall into his chest. He's the nap king, and even though our hands are nearly identical, somehow, he's got the touch.

"You sure you don't wanna come with us?" Ember asks Riv, but he's still blinking away his emotion as he kisses Phenonix's temple.

He shakes his head. Watching Phoenix curl her tiny hands into Ember's hair, now into my brother's collar–another twinge of contentedness flares beneath my ribs. Maybe there will be a day when I look at the three of them and don't become overwhelmed with emotion. Maybe. But it hasn't happened yet, because this is what we've dreamed of; the day at the bank, I saw this was possible with her–I felt it.

And now we're realizing it.

I will never stop missing Rhett. I will never feel like I did all I could because he's not here, and I am, and that is a cruel and unusual twist in human nature. Because parents should never outlive their children.

Dr. Longo is helping me turn my grief into something more powerful, something that propels me forward as opposed to keeping me stuck knee-deep in my regrets. Regrets hold us back; acceptance moves us forward; that's what he says. And I'm working on it.

I feel luckier than most parents that have lost a child. In our grief group–because River and I have started going to a monthly grief support group–so many parents share the same crushing sentiment– "if I could just see my child one more time."

We have Phoenix. We get to see Rhett every single day, and that is a blessing that keeps me moving some days. Because we love Ember, we love our lives now, but there are days when the grief knows no depths and has more pull and power over me than I can battle. On those days, I look at Nix, and somehow, I surface.

We're all on a journey, and it won't be without hiccups, but we're beyond surviving. More than a year after his death, we're learning how to thrive. And now, we're expanding that thriving love.

"Nah, Nix and I are going to go into town to the hardware store and get some bolts for the swing." He wipes his eye with the back of his hand, still battling his excitement. "Aren't we, baby girl?"

Her fingers stroke his shirt, but she doesn't respond because, as always, in his arms, she's a goner. Ember grabs the wrap from the counter and begins wrapping the two of them up. A moment later, a sleepy Nix is strapped to my brother, and Ember is ready to go.

"We are definitely celebrating tonight," Ember whispers to River, on her toes, pressing a kiss into his beard. "Daddy."

He groans. "Speaking of that, don't forget your pump." He wags a finger at me knowingly. "Don't let her get too busy to use it, too. No more clogged ducts. Remember how bad that hurt?" His fatherly gaze travels to Ember, where he raises his brows in warning. "Em, promise me you'll use it."

She whines a little because we know she hates using it. A few weeks ago, we were out buying school supplies. She'd gotten so excited about setting up her new classroom at the old school that shopping for school supplies turned into looking for classroom decor, and before we knew it, we'd been out three hours. Nix had been asleep, and when she woke and nursed, Em was still so full, but hell-bent on waiting until we got home.

It took a solid day and a half of valiant efforts on our part to get that duct unclogged, but thankfully we did. "Remember, that duct took almost two days to clear, Em," I remind her, grabbing the black Nylon bag from the counter, the one with the pump inside.

Ember loves the connection that comes with sharing her milk with us. The closeness, she's said, brings her more comfort than she's ever felt. She explained it as an emotional closeness but also, something about it makes her feel bonded to us in ways she's never experienced. Sharing something so private and intimate, something so special and fleeting—it bonds us in ways that can't be seen. It brings us together as a throuple in ways that can't be obtained through sex or conversation.

While we couldn't have articulated the experience as well as Ember, neither River nor I disagreed with her when she laid out exactly how she felt about it.

It may have started in the bedroom with excitement and

pure arousal—I still remember my first taste. I never knew it would be something that got me aroused and brought intimacy. In truth, I didn't think that anything that brought so much intimacy could ever be arousing. But it's both, and it's so fucking powerful. We've even discussed keeping her supply up after we're done having children.

"I know," she complains, taking the bag from me. "And for the millionth time I told you guys, I really thought it would be okay."

River drops a hand to her belly, fanning his fingers over it. "You're really pregnant."

She nods. "I really am."

He shakes his head as I pour coffee into my tumbler. "Goddamn." Then, a low whistle. "Fuck, I love you," he says, taking her cheek to pull her into a kiss. Crossing the room, we share a light hug as Nix sleeps between us. "Love you, too, brother."

One more glance at my watch, and I know we've got to go. Ember is getting her keys to the building today, but the principal is showing up to hand them off and let us in. She's been worrying about her first impression all week.

After I load the boxes into the SUV, Ember checks her hair and makeup, I slide into my suit jacket, and we head into town.

"Starting the school year pregnant means you'll be on maternity leave by the end of the term," I say as we drive through town, the trees in Raleigh slowly withering away as our summer creeps into early fall.

She nods. "Yep. And I'm already poking around with the other teachers I've met to see who would make a good sub."

We've already discussed Ember's working and how we'll

take care of the kids while she's at school. River is bent on watching the kids as much as he can and bringing them with him to the job sites as much as possible. He says he'll vet and hire a nanny to come with him, but he wants them around one of us at all times.

Working in an office with meetings and board rooms really doesn't allow me to have a playpen in the corner, but considering how diverse River's work is around town, he can make that dream a reality. Our kids will never be saddled with just a nanny, never spend a day where they never see their parents. We'll all work, despite the fact that none of us have to, and we'll teach our children that working hard and spending time with your family is the real wealth and affords you the most happiness.

"You'll choose the right one; I'm sure," I tell her, reaching for her leg. She brings her thighs together, trapping my hand.

"Wanna do something fun for Riv tonight?" She wiggles her brows, and suddenly, I want my hand back. Because we're just a few minutes from the school, and I'm not sure feeling her soft legs and hearing her naughty plans is a good idea. I need to walk out of this vehicle, after all.

"I do," I say, stealing my hand back. "But I don't know if we should discuss this now. I'm already hard."

I don't have to look at her to know she's surveying my crotch. "Don't even think about it," I laugh as she reaches across, attempting to grab me. I catch her by the wrist as I bring the SUV to a stop in the school parking lot. "Save all that energy for Riv. I'll do whatever you want. Just tell me, and we'll make it happen."

Her eyes sparkle, and I know whatever she has in store

for a celebration will be fucking wicked and beautiful.

"You'll do whatever I want, huh?"

I smile. I've known that I belong to her ever since I caught her checking the time at the bank. "Whatever you want." And I mean it.

The thing about trust and loyalty is that when they're real, they're unwavering.

I am loyal to my brother and Ember. I trust them. That trust and loyalty are reciprocated. Our bond is unwavering. It took years to find a woman who could show us that devotion, who we knew had a strong enough constitution to handle a relationship like ours, who could be open and vulnerable and also strong enough to love two men at once.

The way she slipped so easily into that role didn't surprise me. Watching her shower my brother with love and affection fills me with that same love and affection as if I were in his shoes. And it's not a twin thing. It's the compersion of our polyfidelity. It's channeling what could be jealousy and anger into deep satisfaction and adoration.

Leaning back against the chair, I settle in, gripping the arms with anticipation.

River is on the edge of the bed, completely naked, knees spread. Between his legs, Ember sits on her haunches, smoothing her hands up and down his thighs.

"Tell me, what do you want right now?" The way she asks so softly makes bumps rise along my skin.

His hair is down, messy, yet somehow rakish all the same. I notice the slight tremble in his hand as he presses it softly to Ember's cheek. Sliding his thumb between her lips, her mouth opens at his urging.

With the answer, Ember lowers her lips to him, sucking his crown into her mouth. His spine softens, and his shoulders slope as his body sinks into the sensation. A moment later, she slowly pulls away, a string of saliva trailing between her mouth and his cock.

"Say it," she says softly, using the tip of her tongue to tease him, tracing his length and tasting his balls. Leaning back onto his palms, watching him survey her between his legs makes my pulse pick up.

Kneeling nude before him, taking him deep into her throat, the mutual groans of desire filling the room have me reaching between my legs.

Finding myself in the same state as my brother, I grip the base of my cock, stroking up slowly just once. He lets her suck him again, her hands kneading and tugging his full sac as she does. Once she pops off him with swollen lips and flushed cheeks, he gives her what she wants.

"Be a good girl and make me cum, Ember."

We found a woman who gives us everything... and enjoys praise? Fuck. I stroke myself again, knowing my time holding back is limited. Cumming from enjoying the orgasm of someone you love isn't for everyone, but the way it's a whole-body experience does things to me that I don't even get when the three of us are together.

She whimpers along his length until her lips are flush with his groin. River is rougher than I am, but today, he tenderly strokes her hair as she bobs on his cock. He watches, head tipped to the side, and even whispers words of encouragement.

"You look so beautiful taking it all like that."

"God, Em, you're a fucking sight."

"What a good girl you are for us."

Up and down, she bobs, and up and down I stroke, the pulsing in my lower half mounting into an undeniable tension.

Both hands fall on her head as he nears his peak, his eyes tightening with strain, his voice merely a whisper of smoke. "Em, fuck," he says, sounding breathless, looking like a man on the edge. I squeeze the head of my cock, holding back as long as I can, knowing both of my partners well enough to know how they'll want this to end.

As sweat glistens on his chest, and Ember's spit drips from River's balls, pooling on the floor, I get to my feet.

With one hand on the mattress holding him steady, my brother summons me with a wave of his hand. Rising, I finally get to see things from his perspective.

Ember on the floor, mouth open, a smile lifting the corner of her eyes, the wide pink pad of her tongue ready to receive.

"Ready?" he asks me without eye contact or ceremony, and I grunt my response.

Heart beating, veins buzzing, I keep my gaze locked on her tongue as white streaks dance across, painting her in the thing she loves so much.

We stroke in unrehearsed unison, our fists sliding forward to our crowns as we cum in long, demanding waves. Like a good girl, she uses her fingers to push in the ambitious ropes, all while keeping her mouth open for us to fill.

The last pearly bead drips from his head, and I shake my

cock once, making sure she gets everything. With a wink, she retracts her tongue, closes her mouth, and swallows.

When she gets to her feet, she's already smiling. "That felt like a reward for me, not you," she laughs, quickly glancing at the baby monitor. Nix snoozes soundly, allowing Ember to bring her focus back to us.

"No, that was perfect. Thank you." His hair curtains his face as he leans in to take a kiss from her lips. It's longer than I expected, and I can hear their tongues working, giving me a second wave of arousal.

When he releases her, he starts to redress, and she brings her mouth to mine. "And thank you for a great day in the classroom," she says, smiling against my lips until we're locked in a hot, greedy kiss. We've been together all day, but it's never enough.

"Now," she says, peeling herself off me to gather her clothes. "Let's get dressed and Facetime my mom with the good news."

"Yes!" Riv says, scooping Em up, only half dressed, making her squeal. Her feet dangle a foot off the floor as he spins her around, her sweats on but chest bare. "Grandma times two," he says playfully, still spinning Ember as she twists in his arms.

"Stop!" she giggles. "Unless you want me to spray milk everywhere!"

He laughs heartily, the sound of their mutual laughter filling voids in me that I cannot fill. They're putting me back together, and there will always be a piece of me that can't be filled because of my son. But this helps.

River dips down in front of her, sealing his mouth around Ember's nipple before she can tug her tank top down. His groan and growl tell me he's taken a mouthful of sweet, creamy milk before pulling away, allowing her to get dressed.

She swats him away playfully, and I follow behind them out the door, feeling more sated than I ever have. River turns to catch my gaze as we're walking down the hall.

"She's sweet tonight, like nectar." He winks, and we continue downstairs so we can call Pamela and let her know our good news.

But all that's on my mind as we dial Ember's mom is getting my own taste of Ember's sweet nectar.

Last year I was broken by the news she brought me. And now I realize I wouldn't be here without that news. I wouldn't have this beautiful dynamic and this fulfilling relationship.

Fate can be cruel, but it can also be kind. And I'm proof of both.

CHAPTER TWENTY-FIVE

EMBER

Almost four months later.

"Inside voices," I say, bringing a finger to my lips and tapping it there to set the tone. Only six-year-olds don't really care if you are trying to make your calm parenting bleed over to the classroom. Right now their biggest concern is finding the class hamster, which means a lot of squealing.

"And," I say, fearing for Chuckie's life. "Let's return to our table so our feet aren't scaring him away."

Holding my large belly, I bend down and survey the little library area tucked into the corner of the classroom. As suspected, Chuck is there, going to town on the corner of a paperback that has probably been under the shelf for a decade.

Rising, I brace my hands on my lower back and contemplate my options. If the kids know he's found, he will definitely get caught and potentially squished to death in an effort to procure his safety. Glancing at the wall clock; I see the bell is due to ring any minute. Rather than alert the kids, I decide to see if I can rope Ms. Harris, the teacher next door, to help me catch Chuck.

The bell sounds, and after reminding the kids to get their lunch bags, not to leave their coats, and to make sure to tuck in their chairs—I'm finally alone. Picking up the handset on my desk phone, I dial the room next door.

"Hi, Mrs. Raleigh," she says cheerfully. "Are the little mouth breathers wearing you out?"

Laughing, I tell her the truth. "No, but I am getting pretty tired. I didn't work during my first pregnancy, not on my feet like this. I'm so tired. And I can't see them, but I'm pretty sure my feet are houses at this point."

Ms. Harris laughs. "I remember that feeling all too well." A pause. "Can I help you with anything? Did they change the copier code again?"

"Actually, I don't know about the copier code, but Chuck is loose and I could use help. I'm a little too top-heavy to crouch down and grab him, but he's under the bookshelf."

She laughs again. "Sure. I'll be right over."

As promised, Heather Harris appears in my doorway, her dark hair in a stylish knot at the base of her skull. She's wearing a nice pair of black slacks and a bright red top with a stylish knot in the side. Her smile is warm and playful when she says, "the hamster catcher has arrived."

After two failed attempts, Heather lies flat on the ground, her beautiful blouse pressed against the old linoleum floor.

"I will buy you a new blouse if you ruin it by catching this damn hamster," I tell her.

"Ha!" she cheers, pushing herself off the floor with one hand. In the other hand? Chuck, clutching a shred of a 1990 chapter book between his little claws.

"Thank you! I spotted him earlier, but I was afraid the kids would trample him trying to catch him."

She passes him to me, then wipes her hand on her thigh. "Oh, I'm sure they would have. Six-year-olds can't control their excitement. I totally get why you called me."

I rub my stomach after placing Chuck in his cage, making sure the lock is actually latched. "In a few months, I'll be back to seeing my feet and catching hamsters but... not yet."

Heather smiles before opening her mouth as if she were on the cusp of adding to the playful discourse, but she stops herself. Her eyes fall to my chest, where they linger awkwardly for a moment. Trailing her gaze, I look down to see a large wet spot forming on my top, right over my nipple. I tug the neckline away, peering down my top. Fishing a hand around, I replace the nursing pad that slipped free and reach for my sweater draped over the back of my chair.

"Disposable nursing pads never stay in place," I tell her, clarifying. I wrap the sweater around my torso so no one spots my leak on my way out.

Still, having told her it's just a breast milk leak, she stares at me like I'm an alien.

"How old is Nix?" she asks, still looking a little puzzled.

"Almost one year," I say, dreaming of a few weeks from now when we can throw an insanely ridiculous party for her. One she won't even remember, I realize, but still. I have an entire Pinterest board I've brought to life dedicated to the celebration. Just thinking about it excites me.

"You're... still nursing?" There's no judgment in her tone, but the question is strange.

"Yeah," I reply, chewing my bottom lip as I debate on whether or not I tell her the truth. "I am nursing Nix still, but... My husbands like my milk, too."

She swallows, her gaze holding mine. "Can I ask you something?"

I nod, ready to field one of the usual questions: do you all sleep in one big bed? Do River and Ryker cross "swords"? The things people ask you, thinking they're entitled to knowing the inner workings of your life simply because you're different from them is absolutely crazy.

But Heather is a co-worker, so I keep my smile on as she falls into a chair in front of my desk. I sit, too.

"How did you get used to it?" she worries, her hands together in her lap, but her eyes never leave mine.

"Get used to what?" I rub my belly, feeling the little one inside me hiccup. I love that feeling. The feeling of life breathing and growing inside me. I find myself smiling as I repeat. "Get used to what?"

Finally, her gaze goes to my stomach as she watches my hands smooth over it. "A throuple."

When I get her attention again, her eyes shine, and I know that my response is going to tip her internal scale one way or another, so I choose my words carefully.

"I fell in love twice at the same time, and it just so happened that those two men fell in love with me, too. And I got lucky because they wanted to love the same woman, have a family with the same woman, and wanted me."

She nods, hanging on every word.

"But you can't share if you don't fully love both equally. When you're tempted to be jealous, you have to work hard to channel that energy into love.. Or else... it will never work."

"And Ryker, you met him first, right?"

I nod, not wanting to remember the day in the bank. We're so far beyond it that going back to it sometimes feels somber.

"So... he doesn't mind you and River being together? I mean, well, that is if you and River are together alone," she says, her words coming quickly, nerves jumbling her.

I laugh so she knows I won't be offended by her questions. "No. He doesn't. Because he trusts me, and he trusts his brother. Polyamory doesn't work if you aren't trusting and loyal."

She nods and then seems to get lost in her head, so I throw her a lifeline.

"You and Marley thinking of adding a third?" I ask, almost feeling silly for the suggestion because Heather and her partner Marley have always come off as so conservative. Yet, when I first referenced Ryker and River as both being my husbands, she didn't have an outlandish reaction. Maybe she already knew; it is a small town. Or maybe... "Hey, Heather, you know you're safe to talk about anything with me, okay?"

My words seem to help her relax, and she falls back against the chair. "We are. I mean, we already did."

My eyebrows shoot up. "Really?" I can't help but be

excited knowing that someone else is living their best life, despite the judgment that often comes from others. Here in Raleigh, we're now loved. But it took River and Ryker a long time to earn that and I reap the benefit of the struggles they overcame.

"Yes, but… it's admittedly been a little rocky." She volleys her head. "We're in month two, and I feel like all of us are either arguing or fucking, and there's no in-between."

I laugh. "Well, we don't really argue, but I will say that Ryker and River are really open about their beliefs in polyamory and polyfidelity. If you, Marley, and… your third… ever want to come have dinner, please, do."

"That would be great," she says, exhaling with relief. "I mean, I know we can do it. I just think we jumped into it before knowing how hard it would be."

I think of River's dark eyes watching me from the chair in our room as I rode Ryker last night. With how big I've gotten in the last month, I'm the most comfortable on top, so they've been taking turns with me. There's never an ounce of jealousy.

"Let's set up a dinner." With a deep breath, I get on my feet and tuck in my desk chair, grabbing my bag from my desk. We walk to our cars, swapping phones to exchange numbers. Before she gets into her car, she stops me.

"Did you… you said Ryker and River enjoy your milk?" she whispers the word milk like it's naughty.

"They do." I don't make her ask, but I can tell she wants to know but isn't sure what to say. "I mean, I'm still nursing Nix, but they have their fun, too. Honestly, Heather, I've never done anything with anyone that was so intimate and bonding. And yeah, it feels a little kinky, too," I say with a wink, being completely honest. "It's not for everyone, but while we're having babies, we're enjoying it."

She smiles. "I really admire how open you are about everything. It's so... refreshing."

I slide into my seat, leaving my car door open. "Well, life is really, stupidly short. I don't want to spend it pretending. And if someone hates us for loving a certain way, they aren't meant to hold space in our lives."

"It's that simple," she says, and I don't know if she's asking or telling.

"On paper, it's that simple. In real life, it takes work. But if you don't work for what you believe, what's the point, you know?"

She buckles her belt. "I know." Locking her phone, she smiles. "I will be calling you to set something up, okay?"

I nod. And a few minutes later, I'm headed home. Ryker calls, and I use my Bluetooth to answer.

"Hey baby, how was your day?" he asks, the sound of Phoenix and River laughing in the background. My heart swells, and blood rushes to the sensitive spot between my legs. Hearing my guys and our girl together is a spike of adrenaline after a long day of herding first-graders.

"Good, and hey, guess what?" my voice rattles with excitement. To think we could help another throuple figure out how to make things work is truly exciting to me.

"What's that?"

"Heather Harris and her partner have a third, now. But they're struggling to figure out the ins and outs of it all. I told her they could come have dinner, and we'd all talk."

Because I'm on speakerphone, from the background I hear River's booming voice. "She's comfortable talking about it?" He asks because we all know, these discussions can be hard.

"Yeah, I think she really wants it to work." I flick my blinker on before waving at another teacher in the car adjacent to me at the stop light. The way the entire town feels like a friend is something I didn't know I wanted, and now I don't think I could live without it. I guess it's lucky I love this place, considering I now bear the same name as it does.

"Did you tell her the only truly hard part is legally marrying?" Ryker asks. Ice clinks against glass, and I know he's having his post-work drink. I love tasting Brandy on their lips. It's the only way I get to taste booze these days.

"Not yet," I say, "but I will."

It's true; being in a three-person relationship means one person won't have their name on the marriage license. And while to some, that could leave issues hanging in the air, for us, it was easy.

I didn't marry either of them.

We all wear rings; we consider all of us in a union. Legally, however, I changed my name to Ember Raleigh, and then Ryker and River added my name to the house deed and everything else.

Ryker is the father of Phoenix, legally, and River will legally be the father of the baby I'm growing. Though in truth, who signs what doesn't matter after this. They're all ours, we're one, and that's that.

Ryker likes to keep me on the line the whole drive, but once I'm home, I'm met at the backdoor by the most beautiful sight.

Two barrel-chested men, comfortable in sweats and t-shirts, our beautiful daughter between them. She stands, a tiny arm wrapped around each of their legs, wobbly as ever. River's fingertips stroke through his beard as Ryker sifts his hand through his shiny hair. The three of them, casually waiting for me, makes my chest ache.

    The best ache.

    The ache that comes with limitless, unbridled love.

EPILOGUE

RIVER

"T*here* it is." My brother's groan rattles the walls. "There's the back of your throat," he rasps, collecting Ember's hair in his fist so he can see her better as she bobs on his dick.

I hold her hips from behind, watching her suck him down as I move in slow strokes inside of her. We like to cum at the same time, me and Ryk, so I'm pacing myself as Em deepthroats him.

We've been in this position plenty of times, and like it always is–it never fucking gets old. Each time I sink into her, tight little pussy even after three kids, it feels like the ultimate high.

"You're gonna swallow my cum while Riv fucks his into you, isn't that right?"

I used to have a filthy mouth, or so I'd been told. But as time has gone on, my brother's dirty tongue has come out to play. He narrates the moment, his observations driving me fucking wild.

"He's gonna *breed* that cunt, Ember, you watch. He's gonna fuck his cum deep inside you, so deep not even a drop slides out. And as he's filling you up, I'm gonna paint the back of your throat. So be a good girl, and *get ready*."

My hips jerk and my balls tighten, and I know if he keeps this up, we won't be cumming at the same time at all.

With a slurp, Ember begins bobbing on his cock. She moans, and the noise doesn't help my cause, so I pull out.

Approaching the edge, I topple over at the sight of my glistening, veiny cock resting on her velvety smooth ass, paired with my brother's final warning– "*suck it deep, Em. Here it comes.*"

His eyes close, his neck strains as his head falls back. Dropping his hands to her shoulders, he barely grips her as his hips stop. His bare belly flexes, tightening as his orgasm barrels through him.

Re-entering her, I fuck her harder, loving the sound of her swallowing his release as I pump mine into her, one hot thrust at a time.

She moans around his length, and I swear I cum harder at how she sounds with a mouthful of cock and cum–it's fucking hot. Still fucking her, now slowly, as the last of my orgasm rattles my spine and curls my toes, I watch my brother pull his cock from her mouth, bend down and take her mouth in a searing kiss.

Their mouths stay together, tongues clashing as he grabs under her arms and helps her off her hands, resting just on her knees. Still buried inside her, she rests her back against my chest. Turning her head, I find her mouth and take it, giving her a short but passionate kiss. With her hands now resting on Ryker's shoulders, she wiggles forward, and my softening cock slips out of her, a stream of cum sliding down her bare thigh.

I run my hand along her skin, coaxing my cum back into her dripping cunt where it belongs.

She turns, and though I can only see her profile, I know she's speaking to me when she says, "thank you."

I smack her ass, leaving my palm on her to soothe the ache. "Thank you for making me cum like a fucking water hose," I growl. "That was so fucking good."

Ryker barks out a laugh, smoothing Ember's hair down. I love her sex hair, and he always tries to fix it for her. Maybe one of the only places we differ when it comes to Ember. I like her looking like we just fucked her, and he likes her looking like we're about to fuck her.

"Thank you," he says, kissing her. She repeats the words back to him.

After sharing a sexual exchange of any kind, it's important to us that we express our gratitude. That each partner in this relationship understands and accepts the vulnerability of true, raw, uninhibited sex. To be able to say whatever we feel, to touch and explore each other in a space so safe that nothing is off the table or goes misunderstood–it's powerful. Expressing gratitude for creating that safety is important to us.

We may have the type of relationship where we must profess our love every time we part, and we may not be typical, but we have our own rules that work to keep us harmonious, to keep us building on our bond, to make our love grow over the years as opposed to crack or shrink.

Ryker and I head to the bathroom, where we each nab a towel and run it beneath warm water. Ember knows to wait in bed for us. She knows part of our process when we fuck this way is cleaning her up, looking after her. It completes some emotional circle for us; without this step, we both feel off.

Returning to the bedroom, we find her on her back, still completely nude, full breasts in her palms. "Please," she whimpers. "Ridge is sleeping, and I really hate the pump." She sticks out her bottom lip in a pout that makes my cock hard again, already.

When I was twenty, I thought of myself nearing fifty and envisioned a beer gut with sex once a month. I never envisioned getting harder than I did back then, but then again, I didn't know that life could be limitless as long as you had courage.

Slowly, I drag the towel down her pussy, collecting the stray cum. She wiggles her lower half into the mattress, tempting me to fuck her or eat her, but when I look up to see my brother's already wiped the saliva from her chin and neck and is kneading one of Em's breasts. Milk bubbles up, then curls around her breast for only a moment before Ryk catches it with his tongue. An errant lap becomes a deep pull, and I kneel between her legs, still cleaning her up, watching her stare with pride and adoration at my brother, whose eyes are closed.

She strokes her lithe fingers through his hair, whispering something down to him. I can't hear the words, but the sentiment gives me chills. I squeeze her foot, and she looks up at me.

Without a word, she tips her head to the side, offering

me up the spot next to her.

I toss the towel aside and lie down. She moves her breast to my mouth, and before I can have a taste, she grabs my chin. "Guess what?" she asks, eyes hazy.

I shake my head. "I don't know, what?"

She strokes her thumb through my beard, and my cock thickens in response. "You know how you were saying you wanted Ridge to be a big brother?"

My mouth nearing her nipple, I jerk back at her words. "What?"

My brother's bleary eyes peer at me over Ember's bare breast, his chin resting on her nipple. "I took her today for the official test. She wanted to surprise you."

I look at her, anxious to hear her say it again. "You're pregnant?" The way my heart thuds when she says those words. This is the fourth time hearing them, and fuck me if it isn't the best this time.

Nix was a surprise to us all, and the day she told us she was pregnant, I'm not sure we celebrated how we should have, considering the bleak circumstances.

The news of Ruby, our second daughter, surprised me. I'd wanted it and we'd wanted it, but I wasn't completely aware of how hard getting pregnant can be. Ember had made us keep our hopes low, and she'd mentioned how it took some people a year to get pregnant.

It only took her two months, which is why Ruby's announcement came by surprise. A fucking great surprise.

With Ridge, she'd told me first, and we decided how we'd break the news to Ryk. Though we didn't know which of us truly fathered the baby, as we fucked freely after Ruby, I'm glad she told me first. It was so fucking fun surprising him. Ember wanted to make Ruby wear a onesie that said 'big sister' on it, but because the time we found out was near Rhett's birthday, I told her we should tell him then.

Nix and Ruby look so much like him. Like us. He's always sober and reflective on Rhett's birthday, as am I but not to the extent that Ryk is. And rightfully so. But I thought news of a new life could change the tide a little. At least that year. And it did.

Now, hearing the words that another soul to shape and love, guide and teach is on the way? Fuck. It never ceases to be amazing.

This child isn't biologically mine; it is ours. It wouldn't matter if neither Ryker nor I were the biological father, either. We're a family, and love is what binds a family. Blood can link us, but love is what keeps us afloat.

"If it's a boy, Eli. If it's a girl, Everleigh."

She blinks at me, and my heart swells at the fact that I could get lost in her beauty. Drown in her warmth. Dissolve into her untapped kindness. A smile curls my lips just thinking about how fucking perfect she is for us.

"What?" Her lips quirk as she questions my grin.

"Just thinking how goddamn glad I am that there are bank robbers out there."

My brother tips his head back in raucous laughter. Ember giggles.

"Don't you think that if that hadn't happened, we would have found each other somehow?" she asks, stroking her hands through our hair. "I think us being together is fate."

I look across at my brother, then at Ember. What we have does feel a lot like fate.

And I'll never take that for granted.

REVIEWS

I hoped you enjoyed Ryker, River, and Ember. If you enjoyed this and want something similar in a smaller form, check out my standalone novella, Cherry Pie, also available in Kindle Unlimited.

Thank you for taking a chance on me and thank you for reading my book.

Your feedback and opinion matter to me! If you have a minute, you Amazon review is greatly appreciated!

Thank you again for spending your down time on my book. It means so much to me!

XO

Daisy

PATREON

I write erotic novellas over on my Patreon. So if you like my writing style but want something shorter in length, I release a chapter every week.

Also, you'll get access to commissioned NSFW art featuring your favorite heroes and heroines from my books, Men of Paradise and Wrench Kings included!

You'll get access to everything in my one and only tier. Quarterly merch coming soon!

Come on, hold my hand.

Patreon.com/DaisyJane

(Content ages 18+)

ALSO BY DAISY JANE

Series:

Wrench Kings (3 Books)

The Wild One / a reverse age gap romance / MF / Book 1

The Brazen One / a grumpy/sunshine romance / MF / Book 2

The Only One / a femdom romance / MF / Book 3

Men of Paradise (3 Books)

Where Violets Bloom / a stalker romance / MF / Book 1

Stray / a femdom romance / MF / Book 2

With Force / a CNC romance / MF / Book 3

Oakcreek (2 Books So Far)

I'll Do Anything / a bully femdom romance / MF / Book1

After the Storm / an alpha MM romance / MM / Book 2

The Millionaire and His Maid (3 Books)

His Young Maid / an age gap boss/employee romance / MF / Book 1

Maid for Marriage / an age gap romance / MF / Book 2

Maid a Mama / a surprise pregnancy romance / MF / Book 3

The Taboo Duet

Unexpected / an age gap Daddy figure romance / Book 1

Consumed / a Daddy kink romance / Book 2

Standalones:

The Other Brother / dual POV / MF

The Corner House / single POV / MFMM, MFM, MFM with an HEA

My Best Friend's Dad / age gap instalove novel / MF

Waiting for Coach / age gap novel / student teacher / MF

Hot Girl Summer / a taboo step sibling romance / MF

Pleasing the Pastor / an age gap virgin romance / MF

Release / a taboo MMF, MM, MF romance

Raleigh Two / a taboo MFM romance / MFM

Novellas:

Cherry Pie / very taboo why choose / MFMM

ACKNOWLEDGMENTS

Thank you to everyone on my team for the continual love, support, cheerleading, tear-drying, virtual hand-holding, and so much more. Randi, Jes, Kris, Marissa, Aspen, Ashlee, Morgan, Allie, Brittney & Shelby, your loyalty and support means so much. You ladies have been there through thick and thin, and I'm so lucky to have you all.

Laura. I almost don't want to tell the world about you, and what a superb reader and developmental editor you are — I don't want to share you! Thank you for all of your hard work and insight. You are an absolute gem, and working with you has been nothing but enriching and fulfilling. Thank you!

My High Sodium Intake girls. Separate, we're obviously amazing. But together? Unstoppable. THANK YOU for the support, love, friendship and more. I don't know what I did to earn you both, but I'll never let go now.

To my readers. Thank you for reading, thank you for reviewing, thank you for the thoughtful messages, social media engagement, and sharing my work with others. Your support is everything.

To my husband. For everything.

Printed in Great Britain
by Amazon

27529324R00169